MENDING HEARTS AT THE CORNISH COUNTRY HOSPITAL

JO BARTLETT

Boldwood

First published in Great Britain in 2025 by Boldwood Books Ltd.

Cover Design by Lizzie Gardiner

Cover Images: Adobe Stock

A CIP catalogue record for this book is available from the British Library.

Paperback ISBN 978-1-80483-970-6

Large Print ISBN 978-1-80483-971-3

Hardback ISBN 978-1-80483-973-7

Trade Paperback ISBN 978-1-80635-227-2

Ebook ISBN 978-1-80483-968-3

Kindle ISBN 978-1-80483-969-0

Audio CD ISBN 978-1-80483-977-5

MP3 CD ISBN 978-1-80483-976-8

Digital audio download ISBN 978-1-80483-972-0

This book is printed on certified sustainable paper. Boldwood Books is dedicated to putting sustainability at the heart of our business. For more information please visit https://www.boldwoodbooks.com/about-us/sustainability/

Boldwood Books Ltd, 23 Bowerdean Street, London, SW6 3TN

www.boldwoodbooks.com

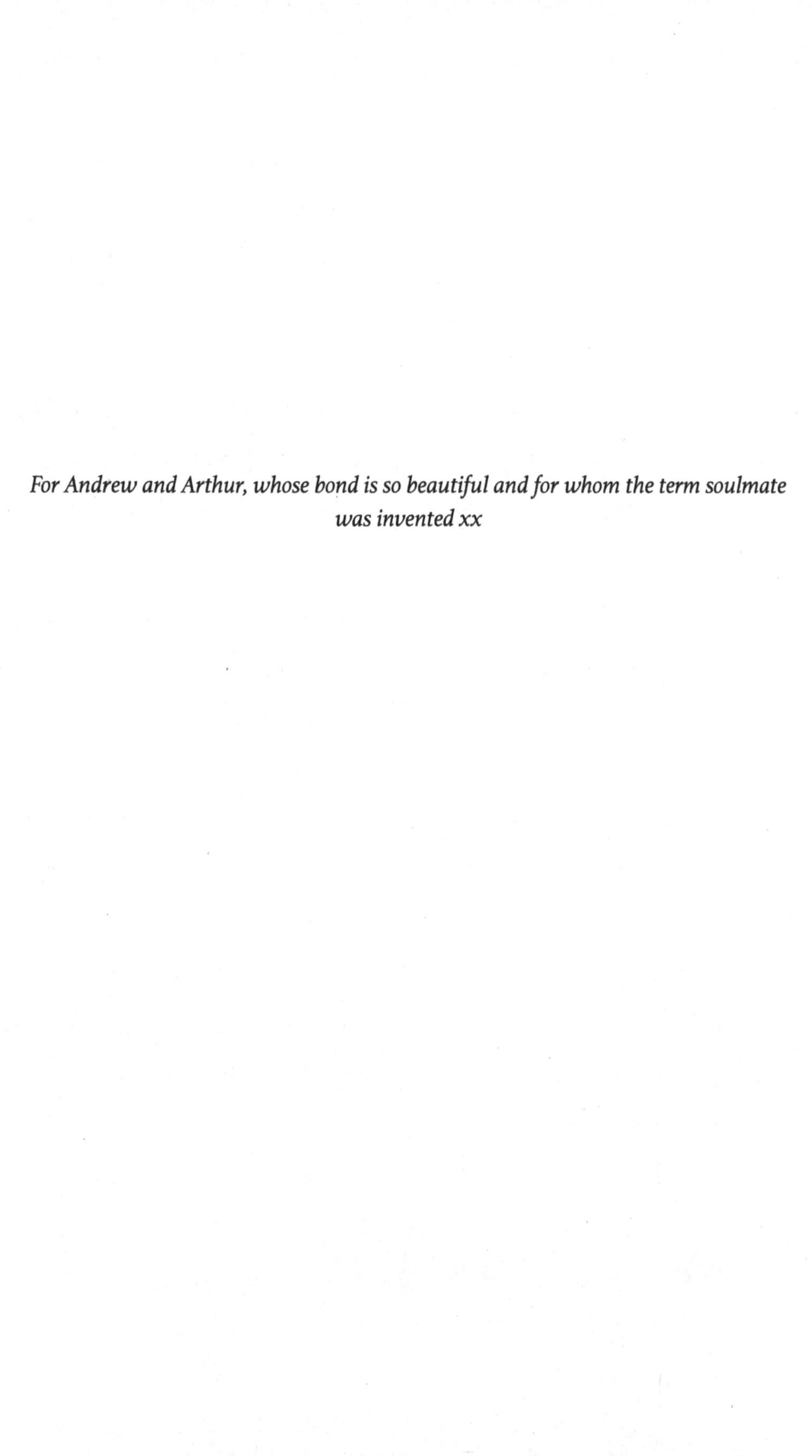

For Andrew and Arthur, whose bond is so beautiful and for whom the term soulmate was invented xx

1

Eden could have recited the episode of *Paddington Bear* her son was watching word for word. She could have done the same thing with every episode of the series on Netflix, because she'd listened to each of them at least two hundred times since the show had become Teddie's obsession, his comfort blanket in a world that felt unpredictable and scary. It was funny when she thought back to all the plans she'd had for motherhood when she'd been pregnant. She was going to be one of those craft-loving mothers, who sat side by side with their child doing finger painting and colouring in, or making elaborate Picasso-esque portraits from artfully arranged pasta shapes. Screen time would be strictly limited and she absolutely would not, no way ever, allow a child to become so obsessed by a TV show that she sometimes suspected he loved it more than he loved her. But then she'd never expected to have a beautiful little boy, with a smile that could light up any room, who also happened to be autistic.

Teddie didn't play the way other children did; he wasn't interested in any of the mountain of toys he got for his birthday or Christmas. His favourite thing in the world was standing by the widescreen TV in his grandparents' lounge, just as he was doing right now, his arms shooting up in excitement and a wordless shout of delight bouncing off the walls, as Paddington embarked on another adventure. Teddie's stimming was his way of expressing himself, because he didn't have the words. Eden's mother called it 'Teddie's dancing', and most of the time the action was joyful enough for a casual observer to believe that's what it was. He might be non-verbal at four years old, but he'd learned his own way of communicating and getting the adults who knew him best to understand what he wanted.

Before Teddie was born, it had been Eden's mother and Teddie's father who had caused her the most worry. Now she was back living with her parents, her worries about her mother weren't so pronounced. Karen was trying really hard to be a different person to the one Eden had grown up with. It wasn't easy to undo the impact of her mother's past behaviour, and she wasn't sure she'd ever fully trust in Karen the way most people trusted their parents, but they'd made a lot of progress, especially since she'd come home. As for Teddie's father, she had no idea where he was and she didn't want to know, but he continued to haunt her thoughts and every time the phone rang she was still terrified it might be him, or about him. Jesse's behaviour had ended up controlling almost every aspect of her life, but the level of manipulation he'd applied had meant she'd barely even realised it was happening at first. He'd played the victim so expertly and made her believe she was doing something awful every time she tried to exert her independence or even have an opinion of her own. It had affected her ability to trust in anyone or anything in the end, even her own judgement, and she might never have made the break away if it hadn't been for Teddie. Her son had given her the strength to walk out and not look back. She couldn't allow Jesse to take up space in her head any more, and the concerns she might once have had about him paled into insignificance against the worries she now had about their son. Although currently her biggest concern was how she was going to drag Teddie's attention away from the TV before they both ended up being very late.

'Come on then bubs, it's time to go.' Eden knew the only chance she had of getting his attention was to switch off the TV. Within seconds of pressing the standby button on the remote and setting it down on the table, Teddie picked it up again and handed it to her, his bright blue eyes so expectant she almost gave in. They couldn't be late, though, not today. St Piran's hospital, where Eden worked in the A&E department, was undergoing an inspection by the Care Quality Commission and the last thing she wanted was to let any of her colleagues down by being late for a shift. Again.

'I'm sorry Teddie, but we've really got to get going today, I promise you can watch some more *Paddington* later.' Eden always spoke to Teddie as if he understood every word she was saying, but one of the hardest parts of his diagnosis was having no idea whether or not he did. She didn't know whether the promise she'd just made her son gave him any comfort, or whether the action of turning off the television had left him fearful that he might never see his beloved cartoon bear again. The second hardest part of his diagnosis was that there was no way of knowing whether Teddie would ever speak. She longed to hear him call her mummy, but more than that she wanted him to be able to tell her he was okay, or even that he wasn't. She hoped with all her heart that it would happen one day, but in the meantime she'd continue to be his voice, and to fight for all the things he needed, even if that felt like scaling Everest in concrete-filled wellingtons.

Scooping up her son, Eden headed towards the front door, picking up both of their rucksacks on the way, feeling like one of the sherpas she might have met on Mount Everest. Teddie almost certainly wouldn't be willing to walk all the way to nursery, despite the fact it was less than two hundred metres from their front door. He might start off okay, but after anything between four and forty steps, Teddie would suddenly go completely limp, like the bones in his legs had turned to jelly and she'd have to carry him. The only time he didn't do that was when he was 'making a break for freedom', as Eden's mother called it. Teddie could suddenly decide to run with no warning and absolutely no sense of danger, which meant of the two options, Eden preferred to carry him.

Despite the fact that there were only around seven things Teddie was prepared to eat, he was surprisingly heavy and if they'd been going any further, she'd have put him in the buggy designed for children with special needs, which she'd purchased when he'd outgrown his pushchair. Thankfully they were only going across the road to Little Sunbeams, the on-site nursery that had opened at St Piran's hospital the year before. When Teddie had started there, Eden hadn't held out much hope of him settling in, especially after his previous nursery had suggested he reduced his session times to just an hour a day because of the demands he placed on staff time. How Eden was supposed to balance that with a job in A&E was anyone's guess.

Much to her surprise, Teddie seemed to be far happier at Little Sunbeams, but even there he only did three half-day sessions a week. Thankfully Eden's parents were able to help her out the rest of the time. She had a part-time contract for twenty-two hours a week, but the shifts were split between days that could start as early as 7 a.m., or as late as 3 p.m., as well as overnights, which no nursery could accommodate, so her parents' support was invaluable. Eden was also trying hard to save for her and Teddie to get a place of their own, so she picked up extra night shifts whenever she could. Buying a place in Port Kara was going to be far from cheap and the messy end to her relationship with Teddie's father had meant walking away from their joint savings, just to escape. All she'd had was the little bit of money she'd managed to squirrel away. It was yet one more reason she was thankful that she'd had her parents' place to return to.

'Come on bubs, at least try to cling on a bit to make it easier for Mummy.' Eden issued the instruction as she shut the front door behind them. Her parents had gone out early to get a round of golf in at The Dunes, a course on the other side of Port Tremellien, with stunning views of the sea and what her father described as the best bacon sandwiches in Cornwall. Today her shift was starting at 9 a.m., and whenever Eden was able to take Teddie to nursery herself, her parents would book themselves an early tee-time, sneak in a quick nine holes and finish the morning with a late breakfast, before heading back to pick up Teddie. It was one of the only occasions when her mother seemed to relax; the rest of the time she was looking up her latest obsession on the internet and getting involved in whatever groups or activities that threw up. Still, if she was going to be addicted to anything, there were worse things than the internet, the whole family could attest to that.

Dashing across the road, Eden was thankful she could see the building where Little Sunbeams was situated. It was close enough for her to believe she could get there, despite the rucksacks that insisted on slipping off both her shoulders, and Teddie doing his very best impression of a human paving slab. He might not be willing to cling on right now, koala-bear-style, in the way she wanted him to, but there was no doubting he'd give her a hug if she asked for one. In all the challenges of his diagnosis and the uncertainty of what that meant, one thing Eden had always been grateful for was the fact that he was so affectionate. Teddie could give the tightest, most passionate hugs, which had the power to make the whole world right, if you were on the very short list of people he deemed deserving of one.

Sometimes the fierceness of his affection got the better of Teddie, and he'd sink his teeth into Eden's shoulder because he didn't have the words to tell her how big his feelings were. It hurt, a lot, but she'd realised a long time ago that when it came to Teddie, she had to take the rough with the smooth, and she wouldn't have traded those hugs for anything, even if they occasionally came at a cost. In the groups she belonged to for parents of autistic children, it had soon become clear that not all of the children were able to demonstrate affection, and it would have broken Eden's heart if Teddie had been one of them. All the hard days, the battles for the support he needed, and the looks from people who didn't understand his behaviour, faded to nothing when he put his little arms around her neck and squeezed her tight. It would have been so much harder without that.

Drop off at the nursery always went the same way. Eden would take Teddie over to 'his' corner of the nursery. It was an area that had been specially created for him; it was cordoned off with half-height wooden panels, almost like an indoor Wendy house, without the roof. It had sensory toys, with light, texture and sound to engage Teddie, and most of all it afforded him space away from the demands of other children, which were often too much for him. Shannon, who managed the nursery, and who was on Teddie's very short list of those who deserved his hugs, was someone else Eden was incredibly grateful for. She'd understood Teddie's needs from day one and she didn't view him as some kind of burden, like the staff at his first nursery had, and Eden loved her for it.

'How did he sleep last night?' It was the same question Shannon always asked and until recently the answer had often been the same too. Terribly. For the past two months there'd been some more variety in Eden's response. Teddie's paediatrician had prescribed melatonin, because of the difficultly he had with sleeping, like many children with autism. It had been a game changer for all of them. It didn't mean that every night was a good one, but sometimes he slept as much as ten hours without disturbance. The first time he'd had a good night, Eden had woken up with a start, sitting bolt upright in her bed, gripped with fear about why he hadn't woken. Teddie had been fine, but it had taken some getting used to, and there were still nights when neither of them got anywhere near as much sleep as they needed.

'Pretty good and he managed some toast and peanut butter this morning.' Eden smiled. 'But if there are any issues today, please can you call Mum, rather than me? She said she's willing to risk getting banned from the golf club by taking a call on the course and I'm not going to be able to get away from work, not when we've got the inspection.'

'Of course, but there won't be anything we can't handle, will there, Teddie?' Shannon brushed a hand over the blond curls that were so like his father's and such a stark contrast to Eden's straight, dark brown hair, although he had the same sky-blue eyes as his mother. Even as Shannon ruffled Teddie's hair, he didn't look at her. He'd just started responding to his name, but it was still pretty hit-and-miss, and it required a lot of tenacity just to get him to react.

'Thank you.' Eden's shoulders relaxed a little bit. It had been a few weeks since Teddie had experienced one of his meltdowns, when no amount of comforting could take the edge off his heightened emotions. There was nothing that could be done other than to let the feelings play out, but that wasn't fair on the other children. So, when it happened, either Eden or her parents would collect Teddie and take him home. She really hoped today wouldn't be one of those days. She looked over at him now, as he tipped one of the sensory toys upside down, watching bubbles of colour drip slowly in the opposite direction, mesmerising him. 'I'm just going to slip away, while he's not watching.'

Eden almost whispered the last words, knowing Shannon would understand why she wasn't saying goodbye to her son. If she slipped away, she'd be out of sight and out of mind, but if she made a big fuss of leaving it might cause him unnecessary distress.

'See you later. He'll be fine, don't worry.' It was the same assurance Shannon gave her each time, and Eden knew it was true, but that didn't stop her worrying every spare moment she got during her working day, about whether Teddie really was okay without her. The upside of a job as demanding as hers, was that she barely had any of those spare moments when she was on shift and it was just one more thing Eden was thankful for.

* * *

The emergency department was busy as usual, and Eden glanced quickly at the patients waiting to be seen. They were a mixture of ages, from the elderly to very young children, one of whom was sobbing loudly, his face buried against his mother's chest as she tried to soothe him, looking as if she might be on the verge of tears herself. Two rows in front of them was someone Eden recognised. Ali was such a permanent fixture of the emergency department that he should have had his own chair, and she didn't need years of training to guess the reason for his visit.

Hurrying through to her locker, despite the fact she was early for once, Eden dropped off her rucksack and took a deep breath to ready herself for the shift ahead, and to try and put aside her worries about Teddie for long enough to focus on her job. He'd be fine, deep down she knew that, but having sole responsibility for worrying about him almost from the moment he was born had changed Eden. Her parents worried about him too of course, and they'd shouldered a lot of responsibility for his care since she'd come home, but when push came to shove it was down to Eden to make sure her son was okay. She hadn't planned to be a mother, hadn't felt ready, but from the moment he'd come along he'd become the reason for everything she did. Despite the reality, at work it was easier to be the carefree version of herself she'd been before she met Jesse and her world had been upended in a way that had left her fearful about whether she'd even survive the experience. It was why she'd had to take Teddie and run while they had the chance.

Jesse had taken away her freedom bit by bit. It had started by him guilt tripping her every time she did something that didn't involve him. He became paranoid and threatened to hurt himself if she didn't do what he wanted, saying he couldn't cope without her there, playing on her sympathy for the trauma he'd experienced as a child. It had meant she hadn't ended the relationship when she knew she should. Then the behaviour had escalated, and he'd lied to her so much she was no longer sure if any of their relationship had been based on truth. He'd told her he couldn't have children, due to treatment for childhood cancer, and then she'd fallen pregnant with Teddie. It had added a whole new layer of control and guilt tripping. Did she really want to be the one who came between Teddie and his father, when both she and Jesse had been put through so much by their own parents? It was only when she could see Jesse's behaviour negatively impacting on Teddie, and his complete inability to put his son's needs before his own, that she realised staying with him would do Teddie far more harm than good.

In the years with Jesse it hadn't felt like she'd had a life of her own and even now it sometimes felt as if her only identity was as Teddie's mother. She didn't resent that, because it was the most important part of her life, but work provided the respite that Eden had to admit she needed. When she was nursing, she didn't have to be the mother fighting to find her son a place in a school that could meet his needs, and being told there weren't enough spaces to go around. It seemed insane for the local authority to want to put him in a class with children who'd be learning phonics and writing their names, before Teddie could even say 'Mama', and she wasn't prepared to accept it. Going along with it wouldn't be fair, not to Teddie, the other children, or the teachers. She'd fight tooth and nail to get specialist schooling for her son if she had to, and advocating for Teddie brought out the tigress in her. On shift she was another version of herself altogether, the Eden who liked nothing better than a laugh with her colleagues, hearing about the minutiae of their lives and offering up her advice when she was asked for it as though she knew how to make the best kind of decisions. The truth was that most of the decisions she'd made in the past had been because she thought they were right for other people, rather than for herself. It was partly a legacy of the issues she'd had with her mother when she was growing up, but her tendency to put other people's needs before her own had rocketed to a whole new level during her relationship with Jesse. He'd robbed her of the ability to fight for what she believed in, because it was easier to go along with what he wanted. Becoming a shell of who she was had robbed her of her confidence too, but all of that was changing. Now she did what she thought was best for Teddie and for herself, because Eden had finally come to realise that if she didn't look after herself, she wouldn't be able to look after him either.

'Any sign of the inspectors yet?' Eden lowered her voice as she approached Meg and Zahir, two of the A&E doctors, who were huddled together by one of the computers like students cramming for their final exams.

'One of the inspectors is interviewing Eve.' Zahir pulled a face. 'It's her first day back and she's been dragged straight in for the third degree.'

'Poor thing.' Eden hadn't even met Eve yet. She was another doctor on the team, but she'd taken extended leave for personal reasons before Eden had even started at the hospital. As Eden had quickly discovered, St Piran's could be a hotbed of gossip and usually someone would have had an idea why Eve needed personal leave, but no one seemed to know much about Eve at all and, according to the other nurses, she'd kept herself pretty much to herself since joining the team. Meg had been brought in on an agency contract to cover Eve's leave period, but now she was being kept on permanently too, following some other staffing changes. Meg was probably the person Eden was closest to in the department, they'd started at the same time and they had a similar sense of humour. Although if Eden was honest, she didn't know that much about Meg either, not beyond the superficial. Meg would probably have said the same about her, and Eden was glad that her new friend seemed happy to keep things surface level. They could have a chat and go for lunch together, but Meg wasn't constantly suggesting drinks or drawing on Eden's time outside of work. Meg didn't ask Eden probing personal questions either, and Eden returned the favour. Despite that, she knew her friend had been nervous about meeting the person whose job she'd been covering, although from the sound of things she still hadn't had the chance to put a face to a name.

Eden looked over her shoulder to check who was listening before continuing the conversation, as if expecting one of the inspectors to jump out from behind a cubicle curtain. 'It seems a bit unfair when Eve's been off for so long.'

'Apparently they wanted to speak to her about how Human Resources and the department management handled her request for leave and her return to work.' Zahir, who was acting clinical lead, looked pensive. 'She's either in there telling them I've been empathetic and supportive, or that I'm a total arsehole; either way my ears are burning.'

'I wouldn't say you were a total arsehole. You do have some redeeming qualities, I just can't remember what any of them are right now. So I might need to do some revision before the inspectors call me in.' Aidan, one of the most senior nurses on the team, grinned. He could get away with taking the mickey out of Zahir because everyone knew his jokes were intended to lighten the mood, and everybody loved Aidan.

'Whoever invented keeping in touch days has a hell of a lot to answer for.' Zahir smiled despite his words. Aidan was currently on paternity leave, after the arrival of his baby daughter, Ellis. He and his husband, Jase, had finally been able to fulfil their dream of becoming parents with the help of a surrogate. He was taking six months' leave, and Jase would be doing the same once Aidan returned to work. Now that he was in the second half of his leave, Aidan was doing weekly keeping in touch days and Eden always looked forward to him being on shift.

'I think if you bought some end-of-shift doughnuts from *Americana* we might be able to remember some of those redeeming qualities, don't you?' Eden raised her eyebrows, enjoying the fact that she was starting to feel relaxed enough with her colleagues to join in with the jokes. It had been a long time since she'd felt this settled, and when the only reason she had for looking over her shoulder was hospital inspectors, rather than an obsessive boyfriend.

'At this rate you'll be getting some of those broken biscuits I reckon they scrape off the factory floor to sell in those multipacks.' Zahir attempted a stern look, but didn't quite pull it off.

'To make it up to you, I'll take a look at Ali when it's his turn for treatment.' Eden didn't miss the look of surprise that crossed Zahir's face. Treating Ali was definitely seen as drawing the short straw, and she'd heard some of her colleagues conspiring to assign the task to agency nurses more than once. Despite knowing the examination would be far from pleasant, she never minded seeing Ali. He needed help and that's what she'd gone into nursing for. No one had promised her it would all be sticking plasters and lollipops for cute kids, and it definitely wasn't. But there were lots of people like Ali who needed rescuing, often from themselves, and Eden had always been drawn to the people who needed rescuing. It was in her blood.

'Are you sure? I'm pretty certain you've been the one to deal with Ali the last three times he's been in.' Meg wrinkled her nose. 'I've only been in the cubicle once when he took his shoes off and it's not an experience I'm keen to repeat.'

'I wouldn't mind if he didn't keep getting infections on purpose, just to try and get more medication.' Zahir shook his head.

'I think you have to be pretty desperate to do that though, don't you? So I never think of him as a time-waster, just someone with a mental health condition who doesn't seem able to get the help he needs.' Eden had been called a soft touch more times than she could remember, but she always tried to see the reasons behind a difficult patient's behaviour. Although she had to be careful sometimes to balance that tendency with following hospital procedures. If there was such a thing as trying too hard to fix a patient's problems, she'd paid the price for that on a personal basis, but she didn't want to become one of those jaded nurses, the type she'd worked with in the past, who saw every patient as an inconvenience. She'd rather do too much than too little.

'I agree with you, and he's so young to have got himself into such a state. It's really sad.' Aidan sighed. 'I knew the first shift I worked with you that you'd be an asset to the department, Eden, and as usual I was right. And I'm not even saying that because you're willing to deal with Ali's toxic toes.'

'I'm not sure that's an official medical term, is it?' Meg laughed, knowing full well it wasn't.

'I don't think there's a medical term that would do them justice.' Aidan grimaced. 'But whatever we call them, Eden will deserve more than a doughnut at the end of the shift. How about we all go for a drink after work?'

'Sounds good to me.' Zahir clearly didn't need much persuading.

'Yeah, maybe. I just um... I'll let you know nearer the end of the shift if that's okay.' Meg looked as if she was desperately trying to think of an excuse, but wasn't able to come up with one in time. Eden knew that feeling only too well and she could tell that Aidan was about to put her on the spot.

'What about you, Eden? Seeing as the drink is in honour of you being so selfless.'

'I can't think of any reason why not.' She gave him a half-hearted smile, and what she'd said was completely true. She couldn't think of any excuse that wouldn't reveal far more about her personal life than she wanted her colleagues to know. They already knew she had a little boy, but they didn't know why she was still fearful of leaving her mother in charge of Teddie when her father wasn't around too, despite her mother having been sober for years now. Tonight was her father's metal detecting club meeting, and he'd be heading out an hour before she got home. Even those sixty minutes worried her, but she knew it would break her mother's heart if she realised just how much panic that induced for Eden. She could justify the tiny risk that arose from leaving her mother in charge for that long while she was working, but she couldn't justify leaving her alone with Teddie for any longer, just so that she could go out for a drink, especially when it had been alcohol that had almost ripped their family apart forever. She had the rest of the shift to come up with a reason, but for now she'd just have to go along with the idea.

'Brilliant, it's about time you and Meg came on an A&E night out. The only time I've seen you outside of work was at Wendy and Gary's wedding, and I desperately need an evening out that doesn't involve me and Jase talking about the colour and frequency of our daughter's bowel movements!' Aidan winked. 'Hopefully Eve will be able to make it too. That's got to be the best reintroduction to work that I can think of. I'll put a message on the WhatsApp group and see who else fancies it.'

'Great.' Eden's smile was more genuine this time and she really hoped Aidan would get to enjoy the night out he deserved, even if she wasn't a part of it. 'Right, my shift is officially starting in five minutes and I better get on with seeing some patients, or the inspectors are going to have a field day.'

She was more than ready to lose herself in the working day ahead. Whatever it threw at her, she knew it would be a respite from the worries of her own life and she couldn't wait to start.

* * *

All of the patients who came into A&E were triaged by a member of staff, according to how urgent their conditions were deemed to be. As a result, Ali ended up being the fourth patient Eden saw.

'I'm so glad it's you.' When Ali smiled, it took about twenty years off him. Most of the time he looked as though he had the weight of the world on his shoulders, but his whole face transformed when he smiled, and the ravages of his lifestyle almost disappeared. He was thirty-two, but looked two decades older. He'd had a problem with drugs and alcohol since his early teens and had told Eden about his experiences of bouncing from foster family to foster family, before ending up in a residential home. Both of his parents had been addicts and it broke Eden's heart that his future seemed to have been predetermined almost from day one. Not least because that could have been her fate too, if her father hadn't made sure he met the basic needs of his children, when Eden had been almost certain they were going to lose her mother to alcohol. Her father might have buried his head in the sand about his wife's addiction, hoping it would somehow magically go away, but at least he'd been there, solid and reliable, even if he was in denial about just how troubled Eden's mother was. Ali hadn't had the same privilege. He'd had no one but himself to rely on, and it was no surprise he'd repeated the behaviour he'd witnessed every day growing up. His life felt like a reflection of the one Eden could have had and, whenever she was confronted by something like that, it brought out a desperate desire in her to save the person whose life could so easily have been hers.

'It's always lovely to see you too.' She smiled at Ali and he gave her a quizzical look in return.

'I think you might be the only person who ever says that to me. Especially in this place.'

'I'm sorry, Ali.' Eden laid a hand on his arm. His clothes were clearly in need of a wash and he smelled of damp, like an empty room in a long-abandoned house and she had a horrible feeling he was every bit as lonely. 'Where are you staying now?'

'I'm sofa-surfing.' She'd have known he was lying, even without the shifty look in his eyes.

'Are you sleeping rough?' Eden's chest ached at the thought. Ali didn't deserve this, no one did.

'There's an old caravan on one of the farms out towards Port Tremellien. It must have been for seasonal farm workers, but there's a row of mobile homes for them now and the caravan seems to have been left to rot away. It's mostly dry, and it's warmer than it would be if I was sleeping outside. I just have to be really careful not to be seen, so I can't come and go unless it's dark.' Ali made it sound like a minor inconvenience, and Eden's heart broke a little bit more, because he probably saw it that way, too. He was grateful to have the use of a grotty caravan that sounded as though it was falling apart, but even then he couldn't call it home. He wasn't doing anybody any harm, or using a resource anyone else wanted, but he'd be thrown out if he was discovered, she knew that as well as he did.

'I wish you'd let me put you in touch with someone who might be able to find you a more permanent solution.' Eden knew of a local homelessness charity, called Domusamare, which her mother, Karen, had recently started fund raising for, but Ali was already shaking his head.

'I can't be hemmed in like that, in a hostel. It reminds me too much of the residential home.' He shuddered at the memory. 'I'd rather take my chances and have my freedom. I'm doing okay.'

'But you're not, are you?' Eden's tone was gentle. 'Otherwise you wouldn't be here.'

'It's just my foot.' Ali shrugged, but the shifty expression was back. 'The wound seems to have flared up again.'

'Have you been looking after it?' It was a pointless question, because she already knew the answer.

'I've been doing my best.' It was a lie. Despite how difficult it was for Ali to take care of himself properly, he wouldn't even have tried. He'd had problems with his feet for years, according to his notes. Just before Eden had started at the hospital, he'd sustained an injury that had led to an infection, and the view of her colleagues was that he was deliberately neglecting the injury in order to access pain-killing medication. It was something to top up the methadone he was already prescribed, alongside whatever other drugs he could get his hands on, no doubt. She didn't blame him, like others might, she understood the impact of having a parent with an addiction only too well.

'You don't have to lie to me.' There was still no edge to Eden's voice; she wanted to help him and he needed some tough love, but experience had taught her that there was a fine line between that and completely alienating someone who felt as though no one was on their side. She hadn't always trodden that line effectively, but she wanted to get it right with Ali. 'I know you're struggling, and that you feel like it's worth suffering physical pain in order to try and numb the emotional kind, but any medication we can offer you isn't going to alleviate those feelings for long and you could end up losing your foot altogether if this carries on. We need to find another solution, Ali.'

'I don't think there is one and even temporary relief from what's in here makes it worth the risk.' Ali pointed towards his head, and Eden's heart broke for him all over again, as she touched his arm for a second time.

'Let's see what we're dealing with then.' She blinked several times in quick succession to stop herself from crying. Tears were pointless; they wouldn't help Ali. She had to find some other way of doing that, but right now he had a physical injury that was far easier to find a solution to. She just had to try and persuade him to take it. The trouble was, she knew from personal experience just how difficult that might be.

2

Drew never tired of the journey to work. If he lived anywhere else, he might have missed the Scottish scenery even more than he did, but if anywhere could rival the beauty of the place he'd left behind it was Cornwall. His house was on the road between Port Kara and Port Agnes, not quite in either village, although his postal address put him in Port Agnes. It meant his nearest neighbours were far enough away for them to have to make the effort to see one another, which thankfully they never did. It wasn't that he didn't like people, he did, but he was choosy about who he spent his time with. Drew wasn't the sort of person who could become fast friends with just anyone. He'd always valued quantity over quality, and he had a handful of good friends he'd met over the years, from university to previous jobs, but they were spread all over the country and he didn't get to see them very often. It didn't bother him as much as he suspected it should. His job could be all-consuming, but sometimes he did feel as though there was something missing, he just wasn't sure what it was. Maybe it was family, but he hadn't had that for a long time, so he should be used to it by now.

The journey to the hospital always helped him to get into the right headspace for work. Usually he walked or cycled, but there were days when he drove. The winding country road between home and hospital gave snapshots of spectacular views of the sea and soaring cliffs on one side, and countryside on the other. There were high banks in places, typical of the Cornish landscape, which sometimes obscured the view, but even glimpses of such wonderful scenery were enough to make him look forward to the journey.

The first thing Drew did when he got to work was to visit the hospital shop. Today was no different and he placed the two newspapers he'd just bought inside his messenger bag, putting the wine gums into a side pocket. He made the same purchase every time, and on the days he wasn't working at the hospital, he'd buy the same papers and a packet of wine gums from a little shop almost a mile away from his house. It was part of his day, a sense of routine, that got it off on the right footing. Whatever else the day might bring, he knew those papers were there, folded the way he liked them, always side by side, never one inside the other. At any point in the day, no matter how difficult it had been, he could stop for a moment and take a wine gum from the packet, knowing exactly how it would taste and how the texture of the familiar sweet would feel in his mouth. It was strange how something so simple could be comforting, but he needed that one certainty in a job like his.

'Did you do anything nice at the weekend?' Gwen, who ran the hospital shop, asked just as he'd been about to turn and leave. He'd already thanked her for serving him, and wished her a nice day, so he hadn't been expecting any follow-up small talk.

'I was working, so I wouldn't say nice exactly, but it was interesting.'

'Was it for the hospital or the coroner's office?' Gwen was the sort of person who had a way of finding things out. Drew didn't usually share the details of his life with anyone. He preferred to keep himself to himself, and he wasn't in the habit of telling everyone he met that he split his time between working for St Piran's as a hospital pathologist, and as a Home Office-registered forensic pathologist supporting the work of the police and the coroner's office. It meant he was in the position of being able to undertake postmortems following suspicious deaths, including where a crime may have been committed, as well as working within the hospital pathology team. Occasionally, as Gwen had discovered during one of their conversations, he could also be called out to the scene of a crime. Most pathologists specialised in one field or the other, but not Drew. There were personal reasons why both fields were important to him, and the extra study it took to qualify for each specialism hadn't felt like a barrier to him, it was a bonus. Studying made him happy. He liked the sense of being grounded and completely certain of the information set out in front of him. Facts made him feel safe and, unlike people, textbooks seldom lied, at least not on purpose.

'I was working with the police.' Drew's tone was matter of fact. Cases where there might have been a murder hadn't always been easy for him to face, but it was a skill he'd developed over the years. He'd needed to get to that point if he was going to be able to help the deceased person, when the only way left of helping them was to discover the truth. If he thought too much about the person behind the body, he might unravel, and there were almost always people relying on him to discover what had really happened to their lost loved one. The saddest cases were those where there was no one other than the police or the coroner waiting for the outcome, no family or friends who cared about the cause of death. Drew always cared enough to do his best work; after all, he'd been the one waiting on news like that in the past. But he couldn't think about who that person had been before, or he'd lose his objectivity.

'I bet it was that body washed up on Polzeath beach.' Gwen didn't wait for him to answer, which was just as well as he'd had no intention of doing so. 'It's so sad. It said in the paper that he was only thirty-two. That's so young.'

'I can't talk about the case I was working on, but you're right, thirty-two is young for someone to lose their life.' Drew shrugged. It was a statement of fact, rather than something that particularly touched him. The man whose body had been washed up on the beach was five years younger than him, but all that mattered to Drew was that he'd been able to establish the cause of death, which along with some CCTV evidence the police had obtained, meant the coroner would almost certainly conclude it was an accidental drowning, due in no small part to the man's intoxication. Drew hoped the outcome would give the family closure and some comfort too. Achieving that was the part of the job he would have described as enjoyable, but it wasn't the kind of occupation that sat comfortably with a word like that.

Instead, Drew changed the subject, asking the kind of question he knew he was meant to ask, even if he had no idea what he was supposed to do with the answer. 'How about you? How was your weekend?'

'We had a dance competition in Padstow and came third.' Gwen smiled, and Drew tried to work out what her expression meant. Was she pleased to have been beaten by two other competitors? She seemed to be, so he returned her smile and nodded.

'That was a good result, I take it.'

'There were twenty other pairs in the contest, so, yes, we were thrilled.' That was one of the things he liked about Gwen, she was upfront and happy to spell things out for him when he was struggling with the nuances of the conversation, without taking any kind of offence.

'Congratulations.'

'Thank you, although rumour has it that the female half of the pair who came second has been heating up more than casseroles for one of the judges since his wife died eighteen months ago. So we should probably have come second.' Gwen frowned for a moment and then broke into a broad smile. 'Still, good luck to them; whatever kind of dumplings she's serving up to him, I hope they're having fun together. They deserve it after both losing their other halves to bloody cancer.'

'I'm sure they do.' Drew was desperately trying to think of a way to end the conversation without seeming rude. It wasn't that he wasn't pleased for Gwen, or even the rival dancer and the judge she was seeing, despite the fact he had no idea who they were. Drew just had no idea how to prolong the conversation, or even if it was appropriate to do so. It was a tightrope he seemed to be permanently balanced on, and he still got it wrong far more often than he wanted to. It was another reason he liked his job; it was the perfect excuse to break off from conversations when he had no idea how else to finish them.

The funny thing was it was only small talk he struggled with; the important conversations didn't faze him nearly so much. He could present complex reports at court cases and respond to whatever questions were thrown at him. With his closest friends he could get into deep and meaningful conversations about all kinds of topics, but the social niceties of casual conversation with strangers or acquaintances felt so much harder. 'I'd better get going, I've got a tissue collection first thing, for a patient who died this morning. His family want to try and take something positive from his death, so they've given permission for us to take samples for research.'

'I wish more people understood what you did, Drew. I bet there's a lot more to it than anyone thinks.' Gwen leant forward conspiratorially and gestured towards the poster on the noticeboard behind her. 'Although if you're up for going to the Friends of St Piran's murder mystery evening, just promise you'll be on my team and I'll keep you in wine gums for a month. Third place in the dance competition might be okay, but I'd kill for a win at the Friends of St Piran's murder mystery night!' She was still laughing when he replied.

'I'll think about it, I promise.' It was the second time Gwen had mentioned the murder mystery evening and Drew had absolutely no intention of attending, but something else he'd learned over the years was that outright refusals, with no feasible excuse, could be considered rude. He didn't want to go, but he needed to come up with a believable reason so that it wouldn't hurt Gwen's feelings, because he really didn't want to do that either.

'I'll see you tomorrow, Drew. Same time, same place, same order.'

'I'm such a bore, aren't I?' Drew stiffened, it wouldn't be the first time someone had used that word to describe him, but Gwen was shaking her head.

'Not at all. Everything feels right with the world once I've seen you and taken your order. I like having things in life I can rely on.' Gwen smiled again and he wished he could believe her, but he'd been told he was boring and weird plenty of times before – as well as other names he preferred not to think about. The worst had been the people who said one thing to his face and another entirely behind his back. That was another reason he liked his job, the dead never passed comment about the kind of person they thought he was. He respected them, regardless of their background, their past, or how they'd come to find themselves on his table. And they returned the compliment, by always being honest. After all, the dead couldn't lie.

* * *

Drew spent most of his work time at the hospital. Even when he was working with the coroner's office and the police, postmortems often took place in the hospital mortuary, but he worked elsewhere when the need arose. His responsibilities for St Piran's included lab work, undertaking analyses of samples to diagnose illnesses and direct treatment, but the majority of Drew's time was spent performing postmortems ordered by doctors after in-hospital deaths, with the permission of the family. The purpose was to find out more about how their loved one had died, providing the answers they needed and contributing to medical research into a range of diseases. It was the desire to understand more about the progress of cancer, and how it affected the body, that had first made him want to become a pathologist. Drew was an only child, but he shouldn't have been. His elder sister, Flora, had died of a glioblastoma at the age of eleven, when Drew had been just eight years old.

Flora's death had cast a long shadow, not just over Drew's childhood, but the entire family. He missed her even now; she'd understood him in a way that no one else had ever seemed to do, before or since. He wanted to be able to contribute to a greater comprehension of not just the illness that had killed her, but every illness that took someone away from the people they loved. The desire to contribute to the field of forensics had come later; the result of his mother's death, a second family tragedy he still wasn't sure had ever really been resolved, even more than a decade after it had happened.

Hospital pathologists split their time over a range of pathology services, but the breadth of Drew's training and expertise made him the natural choice to undertake postmortems, answering questions that couldn't be answered in any other way. When he'd joined St Piran's, he'd been told he'd be expected to develop a specialism which complemented those of others within his team. Despite all the pathologists on the team being given the option to carry out hospital postmortems and some of the non-suspicious deaths referred by the coroner's office, Drew's unique range of skills and experience meant that undertaking postmortems had naturally come to take up more of his time and they'd fast become his specialism. The diversity of his role meant that no two days were ever the same, which might seem an odd choice for someone who valued order and certainty as much as he did, but he couldn't imagine ever wanting to do anything else.

'We're going to be busy today.' Saskia, his assistant, pulled a face as he came into the mortuary. 'One of the consultants from the emergency department has asked if we can review a patient who died in the early hours of this morning. He was on ACE inhibitors, and they suspect it's a stroke that took him, but despite him being on treatment for high blood pressure some of the family seem very shocked by his death. His blood pressure was raised, but only just enough to have the lowest level of medication prescribed. They want to rule out any adverse reaction to the medication, and make sure there was nothing else at play. It would be really interesting if we didn't find any of the ACE inhibitors in his system, but found something else instead...'

Sometimes Saskia had far too much imagination, but that was no bad thing in their line of work. She'd be well suited to forensics, and occasionally he worried that she might move on from the hospital. He relied on Saskia and he could trust her, but most of all they were used to one another. She didn't try to engage him in chatter about their personal lives, probably because she'd worked out that he didn't really have one, and that he found it hard to know what to say in response to any updates she might give on hers. It wasn't that he didn't care, or even that he wasn't interested, he just didn't know what to say in response. They'd quickly come to understand one another and form a good working relationship, despite the lack of small talk. Saskia's official title was anatomical pathology technologist, but Drew preferred to think of her as invaluable. She did so much of the preparatory work that made his job easier and a lot of the liaison with other staff and departments.

'We're also waiting on a decision from the coroner's office about a potentially unexplained death in Port Tremellien.' Drew didn't miss the rise of Saskia's eyebrows as he spoke; his words had already piqued her interest. 'She was brought in overnight and they're reviewing her medical records, but it looks likely we'll have to add her to the list too.'

'I would say we might need coffee, but I know you better than that, and I've got no doubt you have a packet of wine gums ready to help you through the day.' Saskia smiled and Drew shrugged in response. He couldn't help wondering what Saskia made of him. They rubbed along well together, and she always seemed as happy to work alongside him as he was to have her assisting. They both had the option to work with other people, but Saskia never chose to do so. She didn't look the way someone would expect a mortuary assistant to look; he knew the stereotypes better than anyone, and Saskia didn't fit any of them. She was young and pretty, and clearly cared a lot about her appearance. It wasn't that Drew didn't care about the way he looked, but no one could have accused him of following the latest fashions. He didn't care about clothes, but he dressed in the kind of classical way that would have been impossible to assign to any particular trend. The things he wore were well made and expensive, but he only ever updated his wardrobe when things needed replacing.

'You know me, I'm easily pleased.' Drew's voice gave away the hint of a Scottish accent, but a private education had softened it to a point where his roots weren't obvious. That was something else he was glad about. It resulted in far fewer questions about how his life had taken him from one end of the UK to the other. He didn't want to get into the story with complete strangers; he didn't want to get into the story with anyone.

'Listen, I'm not knocking your addiction to wine gums.' Saskia's smile was broad and genuine. 'If a few more people were addicted to them instead of other substances, we wouldn't be nearly so busy.'

'That's true.' Drew nodded, his thoughts turning to the postmortem he'd performed over the weekend. The man's addictions had cost him his life, the state of his liver confirming that drink had been a problem for him for a very long time. Somewhere along the line the man had become reliant on alcohol, needing it to get through the day, and addiction was something Drew had witnessed at close quarters. There was nothing he could do directly to help a deceased person by the time he was examining them, but he hoped the work he did might eventually contribute to finding solutions for all kinds of diseases, including addiction. It was a thought that allowed him to continue keeping his own demons at bay.

3

Eden's next shift at the hospital was an early one. She'd started at seven in the morning and was due to finish at 4 p.m., so her parents had taken Teddie to nursery. His Thursday sessions ran between 1-5 p.m., and it meant she'd be finished in time to pick him up, even if her working day overran a bit, as it so often did. He'd settled well at Little Sunbeams, but his face still lit up whenever she or one of her parents picked him up. It was a smile that said he was happy to see them, even if he didn't have the words. She looked forward to seeing that smile every time she had the opportunity to collect him, and after the day she'd had, she needed to see it more than ever.

Eden had been on her feet all day, and the waiting room in the emergency department had got busier and busier as the shift progressed. It was a recipe for frayed nerves and when a fight had eventually broken out between two of the patients it had been no surprise, except that they'd been a married couple in their sixties. The two of them had come in after an accident in the garden, when they'd tried to take down the branch of an old tree. Eden had triaged both of them and although their injuries weren't serious, nothing more than a few cuts and bruises, it had been clear from the start that the husband was blaming his wife for what had happened.

'Silly cow. I told her to keep the rope taut, but she got distracted like she always does.' Michael's assessment of his wife had been less than flattering, and Eden got the impression that it wasn't the first time he'd spoken about her like that. She'd tried to smooth the waters, although a big part of her had wanted to tell him that he ought to have a bit more respect for the woman he was supposed to love.

'You'd be amazed by how often accidents like this happen. DIY injuries keep us in business.'

'She needs to learn to listen.' There was a curl of his lip that made Eden really uneasy, and she'd decided that the assessment of his wife should be more than physical.

'Are you in pain?' Eden had looked at Isabel when she asked the question, and the older woman had nodded. 'Whereabouts is the pain?'

'In my bum, and I've been married to him for forty years.' Isabel had tried to smile, but it went all wobbly. 'Other than that, it's on my right-hand side; the end of the branch hit me like a whip, but I don't think anything's broken.'

After examining Isabel, Eden suspected she was right, but what she was most concerned about was whether Isabel's spirit might be broken. The feisty comment about Michael had given her hope, but then she'd started parroting what she must have heard him say on the way in to the hospital.

'It was my fault, I should have held the rope tighter, but when he cut through the branch I couldn't seem to hold on. I should have tried harder, I shouldn't be so weak.'

'I don't think many people could hold on to branch like that, and I doubt very much it's the technique a tree surgeon would use.' Eden had softened her tone after that, not wanting Isabel to think she was berating her too. 'Was it your idea or your husband's to take that approach?'

'It was Michael's. Everything we do is his idea.' Isabel's response had made Eden's heart sink, but it was enough to tell her that it might not just be her physical injuries they needed to focus on. Eden had recognised herself in Isabel's words; the same lack of autonomy over her actions because her partner dictated everything. Jesse had controlled their whole lives and she'd had a horrible feeling that Isabel was a victim of some form of coercion, but getting her to admit it could be next to impossible.

'Do you get any say in things?' Eden had been in this situation often enough to know that sometimes the best approach was to tread carefully, not just on a professional basis but in her own life too. Back when she'd been with Jesse, if anyone tried to suggest he was controlling her, she'd shut them down. Part of the reason had been because she didn't want to admit she was being manipulated, but she'd been terrified of the consequences too. She was scared that Jesse might follow through on the threats he'd made about hurting himself, but there was something else that frightened her. After so long together, she'd had no idea who she was without Jesse any more and whether she even had the ability to make her own decisions. It had felt as if he'd stripped away the old Eden bit by bit and she'd almost become robotic, operating only on his command. In the end, her love for Teddie had been what had made her realise the old Eden was still in there somewhere. She'd had no way of knowing whether Isabel felt the same, but pushing the other woman too hard would almost certainly have made her clam up altogether. For a moment, Isabel had held her gaze and, she'd thought her patient was going to confide in her, but then the other woman shrugged.

'It's fine, he knows best about these things.' Isabel's expression hadn't matched her words, and Eden had decided not to let it drop that easily.

'If you feel like you're being pushed into things you wouldn't choose to do, or that you don't have the right to say no, then it really isn't fine.'

'It's not that bad, I'm exaggerating.' Isabel's face had looked like a mask, and Eden had a horrible feeling she spent most of her life wearing that same mask. It was something else she'd recognised only too well, after years of pretending to be okay when all she'd really wanted was to find a way to escape.

'There are organisations that could help and I could give you some information.'

'No!' Isabel's response had left no room for misinterpretation, as she cut Eden off. In the end, all Eden could do was record her concerns on Isabel's notes. When she was seen by another member of the team, there would be a second opportunity for Isabel to open up, although Eden suspected she never would. The last thing she'd expected was for Isabel to suddenly find her voice and a whole lot more, as she and Michael waited to be seen. Eden had heard him continuing to make comments to his wife about how stupid she was, when she'd called other patients in to be triaged. Despite the busyness of the waiting room, the space around Michael and Isabel was an indicator of how uncomfortable his behaviour was making other people feel, too.

Eden had just decided she needed to speak to someone else on the team, despite what Isabel had said to her about not needing help, when the older woman had suddenly got to her feet and swung her handbag like a baseball bat before launching it at her husband's head and shouting at him at the top of her voice to 'shut the eff up'. He'd reacted instantly, by grabbing hold of her hair. Eden had shot forward to try and separate them, but one of the porters and a couple of other patients got there first. The couple were separated and Isabel was taken to another part of the department, while Michael shouted that he wanted the police called and that he was going to have her arrested.

Eden hadn't been able to see Isabel again, because there'd been other patients who needed triaging, but Esther, the head of the nursing team, had come to find her afterwards, for a debrief. She'd told Eden that Isabel's sister was coming to the hospital to pick her up, and that her sister had been urging her to leave Michael for years, after four decades of coercive control. He'd never actually hit her, which was why she tried to convince herself that his behaviour wasn't that bad, but all those years of belittling and controlling her, and lashing out with insults and demands had ground her down. In the end, it was the fact that it had driven her to physically lash out at him, that had made her want to take action. Isabel had told Esther she was frightened of what she might do next otherwise and had asked her to pass her thanks on to Eden, because she'd shown her that there were still people who cared. It was something she'd almost stopped believing after so much abuse from Michael. They couldn't be sure whether Isabel would stick with her intention to finally leave him, but at least she was safe for now.

It was days like this that reminded Eden how much better off she was on her own. It had taken her far too long to break away from Jesse. He'd been able to manipulate her into believing that he couldn't live without her, and that she'd be responsible for what happened to him if she left. The first time she'd tried to go, he'd rung his sister, Sadie, telling her he couldn't go on without Eden. Sadie had arrived begging Eden not to leave, and to hold on just long enough for him to get stronger. Jesse and his sister had lost their parents by the time they were both in secondary school, as a result of addiction and suicide, and they were all each other had. Eden had understood that bond only too well, because of what she and her brother had been through together growing up; their mother's addiction had blighted their lives too, if not to the same extent. Sadie had been the only constant in Jesse's life, and somehow she'd managed to break the family curse, in a way that he hadn't. She desperately wanted to save her brother from the fate their parents had faced, and when she'd stood in front of Eden, pleading for her not to risk Jesse's life by leaving, Eden had realised that by agreeing to stay there was a chance she might never be able to leave. She was effectively handing down her own prison sentence, but in that moment, she hadn't been able to see any other way forward.

The thought of what it might mean for her own life had terrified Eden, but not as much as what she might be responsible for if she left. Looking back now it was easy to see she'd been manipulated and that it had never been her responsibility to save Jesse, because the only one who could ever really do that was him. Back then she'd been so deeply entrenched in his problems and the trauma of his past that she couldn't see what was going on. She'd had her father holding their family together and keeping a roof over their heads. Even though her mother's drinking had taken a huge toll on all of them, it couldn't compare to what Jesse and Sadie had experienced. They hadn't had any stable parental influence and it was almost as if Eden had survivor's guilt, because she'd always had one parent to rely on, at least to an extent. Her mental health hadn't spiralled in the way Jesse's had, so she *had* to stay and try to save him from himself, despite how much she longed to leave. It wouldn't have made any sense to an outsider looking in, but he'd been so skilled at twisting her reality that she'd forgotten she had a choice.

The reasons she'd stayed with Jesse for so long were very different to those she suspected had kept Isabel with Michael, but just like her patient, Eden hadn't been able to see a way out either. Now she was free of Jesse, she had no intention of getting involved with anyone again. And it wasn't just herself she needed to protect; Teddie was her number one priority and she couldn't imagine letting anyone into her little boy's life. She'd seen how some people reacted to Teddie's stimming, and how little understanding there was of ASD. The last time she'd picked him up from nursery, she'd had a row with a man in the car park, who'd taken exception to Teddie reaching out and brushing a hand along the side of his car. It was part of the sensory stimulation Teddie enjoyed, and he often reached out and touched everything from hedgerows to fence panels. The only time he willingly walked any kind of distance was when he had the opportunity to trail his hand against a surface.

The reaction of people like the man in the car park was part of the reason why she'd turned down an invitation to go out for drinks with Dean, one of the paramedics. She'd never been the sort of person to want to date casually and she couldn't imagine it leading anywhere, not with Teddie to consider. There were so many aspects of his behaviour that people judged and felt they had the right to comment on. If she got into a relationship with someone, there was a good chance that person would think they had the right to intervene, which could cause Teddie distress. She couldn't risk bringing anyone into her son's life who didn't understand him, something his own father hadn't even done. It might mean she was going to be on her own for a very long time, possibly even forever, but her relationship with Jesse meant she was fine with that, because she didn't want to risk making that kind of mistake again either.

'How was he today?' Eden asked his key worker, when she arrived at nursery to pick him up. As she scooped Teddie into her arms, he gave her one of his famous smiles and her spirits immediately lifted, thoughts of her difficult shift with Michael and Isabel already beginning to fade.

'He was a little bit emotional after his grandma dropped him off, but he soon settled down. He's been doing more parallel play recently, which is a really positive development in preparation for when he starts school.' Shannon had a great way of drawing out the positives, but Eden hated even thinking about Teddie having to make the transition to somewhere new.

'That's great, thanks for today.' She smiled at Shannon, as Teddie tightened his grip on her. It was his way of saying he was glad she was there. The strength of his embrace was another sensory reaction, but those hugs were Eden's favourite thing in the world.

Teddie was getting really heavy and, as they crossed the car park, Eden decided to see whether today was a walking day or not. Putting him down, she kept a tight hold of one hand and he immediately reached out with the other to trail his fingers along the door of a car that was within touching distance.

'Come on, bubs.' She tried to pull him away by tugging gently on his hand, not wanting a repeat of what had happened the last time. The thought of someone shouting at Teddie made her frightened of what *she* might be capable of. But he was resisting her attempts to pull him away and, when she looked up, she realised it was already too late. There was a man watching them, his keys in his hand and his expression unreadable.

'It's okay, he's not doing anything to your car.' Eden's tone was sharp, but she couldn't help going on the defensive, as she waited for him to shout that she shouldn't be letting Teddie touch his precious car, just like the other man had done. Except this time it was different, the expression of the man holding his keys relaxed into a smile and it transformed his whole face. He suddenly looked warm and friendly, instead of austere and foreboding. He had warm brown eyes that crinkled in the corners, and reddish-brown hair that looked as if he spent a lot of time running his hands through it.

'Don't worry about it, I just didn't want to startle him by pressing the unlock button on my keyring, so I was just waiting until he'd finished.' The man had a gentle tone, with the hint of an accent that she thought might be Scottish, but she couldn't be sure. 'My only concern is how dirty his hands might get. I'm not exactly one of those people who washes their car every Sunday afternoon.'

'Thank God for that, or you'd probably be a lot more uptight about things.' Eden returned his smile, just as Teddie decided to join in the conversation in his own inimitable way.

'Gay! Gay! Gay!' He shouted his favourite sound, which had no link to the word it sounded so much like. The speech therapist had suggested that Teddie might be trying to form the word 'okay', but it was certainly effective in getting people's attention, and Eden just hoped it had never inadvertently caused anyone upset.

'Sorry, he isn't directing that at you.'

'It wouldn't bother me if he was.' The man was still smiling, but heat rushed up Eden's neck.

'I know, I wasn't suggesting that there was anything wrong with being called gay, it's just that...' She was tying herself up in knots, with no idea how to finish the sentence. The man standing in front of her probably had her pegged as both homophobic *and* a terrible parent. She knew for certain she wasn't the former, and she hoped with every fibre of her being that she wasn't the latter either, but it was a question she asked herself every single day.

'I know you weren't.' He really had the kindest eyes, and some of the tension eased from Eden's shoulders. 'I work at the hospital too, I think I've seen you at the shop. Oh God, now I'm panicking about saying the wrong thing, and wondering if I've just made myself sound like a stalker. I promise I'm not.'

She laughed. 'I'm glad I'm not the only one incapable of holding a normal conversation. Shall we start again? I'm Eden, I work in A&E, and so, yes, you'll definitely have seen me at the hospital shop. Caffeine and chocolate are the only things that get me through a shift some days.'

'I'm Drew. Drew Redford. I work in pathology and Gwen knows my order without me having to say a word, because it's always the same. The shop seems to be the heart of the hospital, especially with her running it.'

'Now you come to mention it, I think I have seen you before.' Eden tried not to stare too much. There was definitely something familiar about him, a feeling that she already knew him somehow, but she was certain she didn't. Maybe it was just that she'd seen him around, or maybe he looked like a celebrity she couldn't quite put her finger on yet. Either way she felt weirdly at ease with this complete stranger, something that didn't happen very often, especially not since she'd been back home.

'I've got one of those faces. I tend to blend into the background.' Drew was selling himself short. He was a good-looking man and once upon a time, before Jesse had come into her life, Eden might even have been forward enough to suggest they meet for coffee one day. There were four bistro-style tables outside the shop, which had made it a bit of a hub for staff meet ups, and it was the only place in the hospital where you could get a decent coffee-shop-style latte. But she wouldn't be suggesting that. What Jesse had put her through put paid to any interest she might once have had in Drew, no matter how nice he seemed. Instead she just smiled again.

'Sorry, I really will try to prise my son away from your car in a minute. Teddie just likes sensory things, and running his hand along the side of cars in particular seems to be his latest obsession.'

'I hope you don't mind me asking.' Drew looked suddenly uncomfortable, and then he shook his head. 'No, sorry, it doesn't matter.'

'Were you going to ask if Teddie has autism?'

'Yes, but I know it's none of my business. It's just that I have ASD, well I was diagnosed with Asperger's Syndrome originally, but now they call it high-functioning autism. They're all just labels, though, aren't they? It's just that I recognised some of the sensory things I used to do as a kid.'

'You've got ASD?' Eden furrowed her brow as Drew nodded. The hardest thing about Teddie's diagnosis was not knowing how it would affect his development. ASD was such a broad spectrum, and she'd already come to terms with the fact that her little boy might be what was called a 'forever baby', a child who would never be able to live independently. But because he didn't have any intellectual disabilities, there was a chance that he might eventually learn to speak and hit all of the milestones that a neurotypical child would already have met, which meant he might one day have a job and be able to live on his own. There was no way of knowing what he'd be like in a year's time, or five, or ten, but the thing that scared her most was the idea that she might one day no longer be around to protect him. She didn't know any adults with autism, at least she hadn't until she met Drew. It would be good to talk to someone who had some insight into ASD, even if it turned out Drew and Teddie were on opposite ends of the spectrum. There were support groups, but her shifts made it hard to commit to attending them on a regular basis, and the meet ups she'd gone to had only made her more fearful. Comparing Teddie to other children with autism had strengthened her concerns for his future, rather than calming them. But that direct comparison wouldn't be there with Drew. It was time to be brave.

'I don't suppose you...' She hesitated, thoughts of Jesse suddenly filling her head and she was struck by how easy it had been to get herself into a situation she couldn't get out of. Just the memory of how easily Jesse had taken over her life made her wary. He'd taken away her ability to trust her own instincts and the belief that anyone would want to spend time with her without some kind of hidden agenda. But this was for Teddie, and she wasn't going to let his father take this away from her too. 'I don't suppose you'd ever fancy meeting up for a coffee, would you? I don't know any adults with ASD, and I'd love to hear what support worked best for you when you were growing up, and what you wished your parents had done to help that maybe they didn't. I'm on my own with Teddie, so it's all on me to get things right for him.'

For a moment he didn't respond and she was worried that she'd said something to overstep the mark. She had no idea of Drew's family background, he might have been raised in care for all she knew, and here she was – a perfect stranger – asking him deeply personal questions. It had been a stupid idea, and she was about to offer a profuse apology when he nodded.

'I'd like that.' He handed her a card with his name, contact details and job title on it.

'This says you're a forensic pathologist; I thought you worked at the hospital.' Suddenly she had a vision of him in a hazmat suit, standing by a white tent in an area cordoned off from the public.

'I do, but part of the role involves carrying out postmortems for the coroner's office, and I'm also registered to work alongside the police on suspicious deaths. Sometimes that's at the hospital, and sometimes it's elsewhere, but I'm here most of the time. Definitely often enough to meet up for coffee.'

'That's great, I'll send you a text.' Eden didn't want to suggest a date for meeting right then and there, which Drew might have felt beholden to agree to. If she sent him a text later, it would be easier for him to tell her he'd changed his mind, or to make some other excuse about why they couldn't meet, and she wanted to give him that option if that's what he wanted to do. She had no reason to believe that was the case, but she'd spent years living with a man who'd told so many lies that even he didn't seem to recognise the truth any more, which made it hard to take anything on face value.

'Okay then.' Drew nodded, as Eden lifted her son into her arms. It was the only way to prise him off the car. 'Bye, Teddie.'

The little boy didn't respond, but Eden held up his hand to wave goodbye, something else she didn't normally do.

'See you soon.' Eden's words were about as casual as they came, because she knew there was a chance that Drew would change his mind and she didn't want to build up her hopes. She'd been let down enough times in the past to learn that keeping her expectations of people on the low side was the best way to avoid getting hurt. As she and Teddie continued the short walk back home, she found herself considering the possibility that Drew might turn out to be a disappointment too. He'd seemed to understand her son so well, something few people were able to do, and she just hoped she hadn't read him wrong.

4

'Eddie, guess what, I've got an interview for a job at St Piran's. I might be coming home!' Eden's brother, Felix, was the only person in the world who called her Eddie, and she loved that he had a name for her that was theirs alone. It was part of a bond they'd developed during childhood, when they'd needed each other far more than children should have to. Things had changed now though, and their parents were different people to the ones who'd raised Eden and Felix, but the mistakes they'd made in parenting had created a bond between their children that nothing – not even five thousand miles – could diminish. Felix had been living in California and working in a hospital in San Francisco for the past eight years as an occupational therapist. He'd been talking about coming home ever since Teddie had arrived, but it was only now, four years later, that he was starting to apply for jobs.

Felix had made trips home as frequently as possible since the birth of his nephew and before that Eden had been out to visit him. It had been Felix who'd finally made her see that she couldn't stay with Jesse, and that doing so was going to hurt Teddie in the long run. If anyone else had said that to her she'd have got angry and defensive, told them that she knew what was best for her son, and that they didn't understand how much Jesse needed her too, or the threats he'd made to end his own life if she left him. But coming from Felix it had been different. She knew there was no other agenda with him except having hers and Teddie's best interests at heart. There was none of the baggage with Felix that there was with her parents, which meant she trusted him more than anyone else on earth. Now he might actually be coming home, not just to the UK, but to Port Kara and working in the same hospital as her.

'That's brilliant. When's the interview?'

'The day after tomorrow.'

'Are they doing it over Zoom or something?'

'No. I'm at Gatwick. I landed at Heathrow three hours ago and got the train here. Now I'm killing time in a coffee shop before I fly to Newquay.' Felix made it sound as if he'd popped around the corner for a coffee, rather than flown halfway around the world and then circumnavigated London, with another flight still to come.

'Why didn't you tell me, I'd have picked you up from Heathrow.'

'That's exactly why I didn't tell you.' Felix sighed. 'You, little sister, are too giving and too kind, you always have been. So I wanted to make sure it was a fait accompli before I told you what I was doing.'

'Do Mum and Dad know?' Eden loved her brother, not least for the way he always found a way of considering her, but she wished he'd let her do this for him, and she was cross at the idea that her parents might have known and not told her.

'I was going to tell Dad, but I knew he wouldn't have been able to stop himself from telling Mum, and I didn't want a big OTT scene with her at the airport. You know what she's like, she'd have been there with a big placard saying "welcome home Felix", like we're in a show about family reunions.' Felix laughed, and he wasn't wrong. Their mother was prone to over-the-top displays of her love for her children. It wasn't that Eden doubted the sincerity of her actions, it was just that it couldn't undo everything that had gone before. It couldn't take away the knot of anxiety that had taken root inside Eden when she was just a child, or her desire to fix the broken people she came across, just like she'd been desperate to fix her own mother, long before she should have had any kind of responsibility. It had impacted on Felix too. The fall out of their mother's years of alcoholism and their father's diminishing of what had gone on, had undoubtedly been one of the drivers for him wanting to move abroad. Eden was convinced it was also the reason why Felix had never had a serious relationship. At least not one he'd thought serious enough to share with her. Now he was coming home and maybe he could start over again too, do things differently this time, just like Eden was. There was no more fixing broken souls for her, but maybe for Felix the difference would be in opening himself up to the possibility of a proper relationship.

'Yes, Mum probably would have done exactly that, and she'd have wanted to post a video of it online too.' That was another habit their mother had developed. It was as if documenting special moments with her family were the proof that she was no longer the person she had been. In a way Eden could understand that, but she wished her mother didn't need other people's validation quite as much as she did. It was as if one addiction had been replaced by a series of others, but at least none of them were as dangerous to her health. 'I'm coming to pick you up from Newquay, I don't care what you say.'

'I can live with that, Eddie.' Felix paused for just a second. 'That's if Dad's around to keep an eye on my amazing nephew.'

Eden smiled down the phone, even though her brother couldn't see her. He was putting Teddie first and he understood why, even after all this time, she couldn't quite bring herself to trust her mother entirely. It was just one more thing she loved Felix for, but he didn't have to worry on this occasion. 'I'll bring Teddie with me. He's not at nursery today and I'm not on shift again until the day of your interview.'

'You don't have to drag him out. I'll get the train.'

'No way. It's only half an hour's drive and he'll be watching *Paddington* all the way. He'll love it, and for some reason he never seems to forget who you are, even if it's been six months since we've seen you.' Teddie had a bond with his uncle that Eden couldn't have begun to explain, and he was one of the handful of people who were on the receiving end of his powerful hugs. 'What time does your flight land?'

'I should clear baggage reclaim by 4 p.m.'

'We can't wait to see you.' Eden was smiling again, and she hoped Felix could hear it in her voice, but just in case he was in any doubt she wanted him to know how happy she was that he might be coming home for good. 'I can't believe you might be getting at job at St Piran's. That would be brilliant, so for God's sake don't do anything stupid to blow the interview.'

'Well thanks for the pep talk, that eases the nerves right off!' Felix started laughing again. Eden had been joking about the interview, but she realised a part of her meant every word. She really wanted Felix to get that job, not just for himself but for her and Teddie too, because she had a nagging feeling that very soon she was going to need her brother around more than ever.

* * *

When Eden met Felix in the arrivals area, she put Teddie in his buggy, rather than risking whether he was willing to walk. She didn't want to have to carry him all the way from the car and his habit of running off, on the days he was prepared to walk, seemed to have got worse lately. The last thing she wanted was for him to break free and try to make a run for it in the airport.

'Well aren't you two the best homecoming sight I could possibly hope to see.' Felix's smile was broad and bright as he greeted them. He had an even tan that emphasised the white of his smile, and the same dark hair and blue eyes as his sister. He was a good six inches taller than her at well over six feet, and he looked as if the outdoor life in California suited him. He hadn't lost the soft undertone of his Cornish accent, though. It had never been pronounced, but there was still a hint of it there and Eden was glad. She'd been pleased for Felix when he'd followed his dream to live and work abroad, but deep down she'd always hoped he'd come home and the fact that he still sounded like a local made it easier to believe he might stay.

'I can't believe you're here!' Eden hugged her brother. She didn't want to pin all her hopes on him getting the job at St Piran's, but she couldn't seem to help it. Home would feel more like home to her if Felix was back. When Eden had returned to Port Kara after she'd finally left Jesse, it had been because it was the only place she could go. She didn't have enough money to buy somewhere for her and Teddie, and she knew she'd need support if she was going to work and take care of her son. When she'd suggested to her parents that she rent somewhere nearby, they wouldn't hear of it. She'd told them she was saving to buy a place and they'd soon realised that for years Jesse had been draining her of all her financial and emotional resources. When she'd still wavered about moving back in, her mother had played the card she often did these days.

'Please say you'll move back in with us, love.' Karen's tone had been almost pleading. 'You wouldn't just be doing it to help you get through a tough patch, you'd be doing it for me too. Giving me a chance to make up for all of the ways I let you down before. Please. I need this even more than you do.'

That had sealed the deal. She hadn't felt pressured by her mother, because she'd known how hard her mum was trying to make up for the past and she wanted to give them the chance to repair their relationship as much as her mother did. Karen was determined to be a completely different kind of grandparent to the mother she'd been, in the grip of her addiction. But Eden had known – no matter how well things went between them – that it could never completely undo the years of turmoil that her mother's alcoholism had caused, because of how much it had shaped both her and Felix. Her brother was the only person she completely trusted, especially after what had happened with Jesse, and despite her mother's best attempts, she still had her guard up with everyone else.

Her parents were much better company than they'd been when she was growing up, and she enjoyed spending time with them, but it was almost like getting to know two brand new people she'd never lived with before. All the good memories she had of growing up in that house involved Felix, and his absence had made it feel far less like home. She wanted to build a new life in Port Kara for her and Teddie, and she was making new friends since starting work at the hospital, having spent years with Jesse's behaviour isolating her and preventing her from forming friendships. Growing up it had been difficult to have that too, because she could never invite her friends back to her place when her mother's behaviour was so unpredictable. She was in touch with a few people from before she'd moved away, and there was scope to build those friendships up again, but she still wanted Felix back in their home town too. He was the one person she'd been able to rely upon her whole life, and she wanted Teddie to have his uncle around.

'Oh believe it, I'm back, and the first thing I want is one of Ted's cuddles. It's been far too long.' Felix let go of Eden and moved to crouch down by his nephew's buggy. 'Hello, beautiful boy.'

'You can get him out, if you don't mind carrying him back to the car. His two modes are human paving slab, or the next Usain Bolt.'

'So we've got an Olympic champion in the making, have we?' Felix unbuckled the straps on the buggy and lifted Teddie out. Eden held her breath, wondering if her son would remember his uncle this time, but she needn't have worried, Teddie reached up and pressed the palm of his hand against Felix's nose, pushing it in and out as though he was pressing a buzzer. It was just one more of his sensory-seeking habits, but it was also the ultimate sign of acceptance on Teddie's part, and Eden couldn't help smiling.

'This is new.' Felix laughed. 'I'm just glad you still think I'm worthy of your attention, Teddie, and I promise not to be such a rubbish uncle from now on.

I'm here for it all, helping out with nursery runs, looking after you when Mummy is at work. I've just got to make sure I get that job.'

'You will.' Eden took hold of the handles of the buggy as they headed in the direction of the car park, suddenly almost as certain he'd get the job as she was that she wanted him to. When he'd been away, she'd done her best to push down how much she missed him and how much she wished he was around. Now that there was a very real chance of him coming back, all of those feelings had come rushing to the surface and the emotion caught her off guard for a moment, forcing her to swallow against the threatened tears that seemed to come out of nowhere. Thankfully Felix didn't seem to notice; the last thing he needed was extra pressure on him, and they were soon chatting as if no time had passed since he'd last been home.

By the time they'd reached the car park, they'd talked about just what their mother's reaction to him coming home might be. Felix had made Eden promise not to tell her in advance, because Karen would have refused to wait at home and the airport reunion he'd been dreading would be brought to life. He'd told Eden that he'd booked an Airbnb so he could prepare for his interview and then work out a plan if he got offered a job. He wasn't sure how long he was staying yet, but he'd rented the holiday let for the six weeks he'd said he was taking off work, so that he'd have enough time to get things sorted and find somewhere permanent to live if the interview was successful. Their parents' end-of-terrace cottage had three bedrooms, so every room was already allocated with Eden and Teddie living back there, which meant it wouldn't have been practical for him to stay for that length of time. Although as they approached the car park pay point, Felix made it clear he wouldn't have been staying, even if there had been room.

'I love Mum, but I don't think I could ever live under the same roof as her again. I don't know how you're doing it.' Felix grimaced.

'I haven't really had a lot of choice.' Eden matched his expression. 'Although it isn't too bad most of the time. I just wish Mum didn't try so hard. She keeps doing research and showing me all these crackpot theories that the internet tells her will "cure" Teddie's autism. She still doesn't seem to understand that it's a difference in the way his brain works, not an illness.' Eden swallowed against another emotion, but this time it was anger. She knew her mum meant well, but that didn't stop the rage that bubbled up inside her whenever these so-called 'cures' were bandied around. It broke her heart that her mother focused all her energy on the belief that Teddie needed to be changed, rather than understood, and altering that mindset was a battle she knew her little boy would have to fight his whole life.

'Oh I bet, she's sent me a few of them too.' Felix shook his head. 'She even asked me to look into some ridiculous theory about heavy metals in food causing autism, as if you just need to stop feeding Teddie the aluminum foil you wrap his sandwiches in, and give him the sandwiches instead. Honestly Eddie, don't you realise where you're going wrong!'

Felix grinned and she nudged him gently with her elbow, because he was still holding Teddie. 'Never mind that. I think we might have a bigger problem than Mum's wild theories. It seems you, dear brother, have been Americanised after all. Round these parts it's pronounced ally-min-yum foil not a-loo-min-um. So you can cut that out!'

'Oh, well, if you want me to talk like a proper local.' Felix had suddenly adopted a far more pronounced West Country accent. One that was sadly quite rare in large parts of Cornwall. 'I shall do so dreckly; I don't want anyone mistaking me for a grockle.'

'That would never do.' Eden poked her tongue out at him. She'd missed their silly exchanges so much. Reaching into her bag, she pulled out her purse, but as he went to swipe it away from her, it fell to the floor.

'Sorry, but don't think for one minute I'm going to let you pay for the parking.' Handing Teddie to her, Felix reached down and picked up the purse, and a white business card that had slid out as it fell. 'Who exactly is Drew Redford and why are you consulting a forensic pathologist? Is it so you can plan the perfect crime, for when you finally crack and murder Mum?'

'Now that's an idea, but no. You remember. I told you about him, he's the guy I met in the car park, who has ASD. I suggested we could meet for a coffee, because I just wanted to talk to someone who has grown up with autism, to get a bit more insight into how I might be able to help Teddie.'

'And have you arranged to meet up?' Her brother gave her a look which proved he knew her far too well.

'No.'

'And why is that?'

'I don't know, I've been busy and—' She couldn't finish the sentence without admitting that a big part of her didn't want to contact Drew because she didn't want him to turn out to be a disappointment. Or, worse still, that he might become one of those rare people Teddie was able to form a bond with, but who then disappeared out of his life as quickly as he'd arrived in it. Eden had guarded her own heart ever since Jesse had let her down as badly as he had, and she guarded Teddie's heart even more ferociously. Letting someone new into their lives was always a risk because it made them vulnerable to getting hurt again. Even the idea of making a new friend felt far riskier than it should have done. Eden had carried that load largely by herself for his whole life and, despite how exhausting that was, at least it was within her control. As for having a personal life of her own again one day... that was an even greater risk and one she definitely wasn't willing to take.

'And you're full of crap.' Felix grinned again, having got the measure of her excuses straight away, but he wasn't done yet. 'The reason you haven't called is because you're worried you might like him and you never want to allow yourself to like anyone again after what happened with Jesse.'

'Why are you so annoying?' The flush on Eden's cheeks would have given her away, even if she'd tried to deny it. So she may as well be honest with herself as well as with her brother. There'd been a flash of attraction towards Drew, but she pushed it out of her head as soon as the idea had occurred to her. She didn't want to meet up with Drew because she had any interest in forming a romantic relationship, no matter how attracted to him she was. She was interested in Drew because he seemed to understand Teddie on a deeper level than most people. The last thing she wanted in her life were any more complications and she needed to remind Felix of exactly why that would be such a bad idea. 'I don't want to get involved with anyone else, especially not anyone else who needs "fixing". I've been there, done that, and got the scars to prove it.'

'What makes you think Drew needs fixing?' Felix widened his eyes. 'Please don't tell me Mum's brainwashing is getting to you, and you are starting to buy into the idea that ASD needs fixing?'

'No, of course not.' Eden's flush deepened, despite her words, because her brother had got it spot on again and she was mortified that he was right. She was guilty of making the assumption that because Drew had autism that it somehow meant he'd have problems that would become her responsibility to fix, if they were to get into some kind of relationship. She hated herself for thinking that way, and for the arrogance of believing that a successful man in his thirties might somehow need her, a woman whose life was far from figured out. Never mind the fact that a relationship was the furthest thing from her mind, or the wild assumption that he'd have any interest in her even if she did want that. She was getting way too far ahead of herself and overthinking everything, just like she always did. It was yet another legacy of her life with Jesse and her inability to just trust her own instincts, because he'd done his best time and time again to convince her that they were wrong.

Eden sighed. 'I want to meet him for Teddie's sake; I'm not trying to find myself a boyfriend. That's all I meant.'

'I think the lady doth protest too much.' Felix grinned as she stuck out her tongue. 'Okay, so you don't want another relationship. Fair enough. But there's no harm in making a new friend is there? Especially one who understands ASD so well.'

'No, there's definitely no harm in that.' Eden knew her brother was right, but it didn't explain why she was suddenly far more aware of her heart beating in her chest, as if she'd had far too much caffeine.

'Well if that's the case, then arrange to meet him. It might just be coffee, but it could become a great friendship, or maybe something even more amazing. But you'll never know unless you reach out to Drew. Don't let Jesse take your present or your future from you, he's already taken far too much of your past.' Felix fixed her with a serious look for a moment, and she eventually nodded.

'Okay, I'll set it up.' Slipping the card back into her purse, she told herself she would keep the promise. But there was no rush, and for now Eden's biggest concern was how over the top their mother's reaction was going to be to the news that Felix was home. Possibly for good.

* * *

Their father's mouth literally fell open at the sight of his son walking into the house, carrying Teddie in his arms. With Eden just behind.

'Oh my God, Felix, what the bloody hell...' Dave Grainger clamped a hand over his mouth, and look towards his daughter. 'Sorry love, I know you don't want Teddie's first word to be a sweary one, but this is a bit of a shock.'

Eden didn't want to tell her father that she no longer cared if Teddie's first word was bloody, or even something worse, she just wanted him to speak. Six months ago, when she'd moved in with her parents, and Teddie was five months away from his fourth birthday, she'd still hoped his first word might come before that milestone. All new mothers ached to hear the word Mama, but that ache had intensified over the last four years to the extent that it was almost a physical pain. She wanted to hear him say it so badly, but she wanted to hear him say something – anything at all – even more. It could be the key that unlocked a path of communication between them. Eden would do whatever it took to be her son's voice, but she still wanted him to have his own and to know that the things she was fighting for on his behalf were the things he really needed.

'I hope it's the good kind of shock, Dad?' Felix embraced their father with Teddie wedged between them, the little boy not seeming to mind.

'Of course it is, but why on earth didn't you let us know you were coming?' Their father stepped back as Felix released him, rubbing his eyes, as if he couldn't quite believe what he was seeing. 'We could have rolled out the welcome mat, your mum would have cooked your favourite dinner and I could have made some cake pops and turned it into a proper celebration.'

Eden couldn't look in her brother's direction, otherwise she'd have laughed. Their father had 'perfected' his recipe for cake pops in time for Felix's tenth birthday, and he'd proudly unveiled them on the day, to the bemusement of his son and all of the other ten-year-old boys. Felix had wanted a laser tag party, but their mother had forgotten to book it and she'd gone on a bender when the oversight was discovered, ranting about how she was useless and everyone hated her, and attempting to numb the pain with red wine and vodka. Instead, Felix's party had taken place at home, a damp squib of an affair, where rain had even stopped play in the garden. It wouldn't have been hard for the cake pops to be a highlight of the event, but Eden wasn't sure she could find the words to do justice to just how dry they'd tasted. Unfortunately, their father hadn't seemed to realise and it had become his way of marking every special occasion since then. Neither Felix nor Eden had ever been able to swallow one of their father's cake pops without the aid of water. Lots of it.

'I didn't want you go to a load of trouble, that's why I've rented an Airbnb for while I'm here. I didn't want Mum trying to rearrange the rooms or make up a bed for me downstairs. Where is Mum, by the way?' Felix craned his neck to look towards the back room. Teddie had slid out of his grasp and was dropping a ball into an empty box over and over again, clearly enjoying the sound it made as it bounced around inside each time.

'She's at her book club. She should be home any minute.' Eden's father glanced at his watch, at the precise moment she heard the sound of her mother's keys in the lock. Karen had managed to find a tee-total book group, because watching the other group members sharing opinions about the latest Richard Osman novel over a glass of merlot, could so easily have been the path to ruin for her.

'Here she is, she's going to be thrilled to see you, son.' Dave clapped a hand on Felix's shoulder, and Eden finally exchanged a glance with her brother. Just like her, he was probably wondering whether their mother would react the way her husband expected her to, or whether she might be upset, at least at first, that Felix had kept it quiet.

'Felix!' Karen shrieked his name as she spotted her son, hugging him tightly and launching a flurry of the same questions his father had already asked him. By the time he'd answered them all, she'd pulled away and her mouth was slightly downturned at the corners. 'I can't believe you're staying in a holiday rental. Haven't you seen any of that stuff online about what goes on in those places?'

'Should I even ask?' Felix widened his eyes, but there was probably nothing their mother could come out with that would shock either of them all that much.

'You've got no idea when you book these places who they belong to and what they get up to. Some of them have been used as brothels and I've even read about ones that have satanic artefacts lying around that could cause you long-term problems. Aren't you worried about what might have been going on there?'

'Funnily enough, no.' Felix rolled his eyes, and Eden had to dig her fingers into the palm of her hands to stop herself from telling their mother she was being ridiculous. Karen had an addictive personality, so it had been almost inevitable that when she finally managed to stop drinking, something else would take its place. She'd started quite a few different hobbies and she went all in on every single one of them, but there was one obsession that overrode everything else. Karen spent hours on internet forums and conspiracies sites, getting sucked down a rabbit hole of outlandish ideas and opinions, which

Eden's mother mistook for fact. After all, they had to be real if someone had written them down and published them on the internet.

'You can try to make light of it, but don't tell me you've never stepped inside a building that has a bad atmosphere, and heard your inner voice telling you to get the hell out of there. What if this place is like that?'

'Oh yeah, I know the feeling.' Felix looked as if he might be experiencing it right now. 'But none of the five-star reviews for the apartment I'm renting mentioned anything about satanic pentangles being scrawled on the wall. It'll be fine, Mum, I promise.'

His voice softened towards the end and he put an arm around her shoulders. 'We'll have the best of both worlds this way. I'll get to see lots of you while I'm here, but you won't have to rearrange the whole house to try and make room for me. I can even have all of you over to dinner at mine too. That's if the holiday let passes your satanic ritual inspection, of course.'

'You shouldn't joke about that kind of thing, Felix.' Karen laughed despite her words, and Eden forced herself to smile too. She understood why her brother hadn't mentioned his upcoming interview to their parents, he probably didn't want to build up their hopes, as well as hers, if it ended up coming to nothing. But she couldn't shake the feeling that he was hedging his bets and keeping his options open about going back to San Francisco permanently, even if he was offered the job. He'd seemed really keen, but now she wondered if there was something he wasn't telling her either. Maybe it was because Jesse had spent their entire relationship saying one thing and doing another. Although if she couldn't trust her brother, she couldn't trust anyone and she had to stop letting her imagination run away with her, otherwise she could end up as paranoid as their mother.

5

Drew and Saskia had spent all morning in full PPE undertaking a postmortem ordered by the coroner's office, on a patient who'd been very close to death when he was discovered by walkers on Bodmin Moor, less than twenty miles away from the hospital. By the time the man had reached the emergency department, he'd gone into cardiac arrest and, despite attempts to save him, had sadly died. There was every indication that he'd fallen and that the shock of his injuries and exposure to a violent storm overnight had ultimately caused his death, but it was Drew and Saskia's job to keep an open mind and undertake the postmortem as if it wasn't already a foregone conclusion. If Drew ever reached the stage where he thought he had all the answers before he even started, it would be time to leave the job.

In a place as beautiful as the Cornish Atlantic coast, it seemed hard to believe that tragedies occurred. Of course accidents happened everywhere, and the stunningly rugged coastline and beautiful moorland within easy reach of the area each held their own risks, despite their appeal, especially if people chose to ignore the basic principles they needed to follow to safeguard themselves. Just like the man who'd gone into the sea for a swim, drunk and alone as night was falling, the moorland walker had taken foolhardy risks. He wasn't wearing the right kind of clothing for a walk on the moor, and he hadn't had a phone with him when he was found. He hadn't been wearing a coat either. He was ill-prepared, but that didn't make it any less of a tragedy. In Drew's experience, many people, especially men below the age of forty, carried around a feeling of invincibility. He'd never had that; perhaps it was because of his neurodiversity, or maybe it was because of Flora's death and the way it had affected Drew and everyone else around him. Either way, that sense of surety had alluded him, and he wasn't sorry. Not when he saw what it cost so many others.

Despite the sometimes foolish behaviour, Drew never blamed the people whose death became a part of his working day. Anyone could make a mistake, and even if their actions had been reckless to the point where the outcome had become almost inevitable, Drew didn't judge. He hadn't walked a mile in any of their shoes and he didn't like the idea of judging people on that basis. It would have made him far too much like his father, and that was one thing he definitely didn't want to be. Drew's father had spent his professional life judging other people, in his role as a high court judge, but his personal life had been far from beyond reproach. He was a cold and manipulative man whose affairs and cruelty towards Drew's mother had driven her to the edge more than once. No one who'd encountered him on a professional basis knew the real him, and he was a skilled actor even with some of his inner circle, playing the bereaved father after Flora's death to an Oscar-worthy level. Yet he'd failed to be there for his broken-hearted wife, or the son left bereft by the death of his sister. All he really cared about was his career and the things that inflated his already sizeable ego, including the string of much younger women fooled into believing his public persona. So no, Drew didn't want to be like his father, not the least little bit.

'I'm going to go to the shop after I've cleaned up.' Drew made the announcement as Saskia began the scrub down process, once Connor Deakin's postmortem was complete. They'd been able to confirm that his cause of death was as suspected. Evidence of both drugs and alcohol had been found at the scene, although the toxicology report that would confirm the extent of the role they had played in his death would take several weeks to be finalised. Taking drugs and drinking definitely wouldn't have helped the way Connor's body had responded to the exposure overnight, and the compound fracture to his left leg had also caused internal bleeding. It was no less of a tragic loss of life, but at least his family didn't have to contend with the fact that someone else had been involved in his death.

'What's the matter, did you forget your wine gums this morning?' Saskia turned to look at him, her eyes widening in response to Drew's announcement.

'No, I think it might just be a two packets kind of day.'

'I didn't know they existed.' By now she was looking at him as if he'd suddenly sprouted two heads. He should probably have been offended that something as simple as him deciding to make a second trip to the hospital shop in one day seemed so extraordinary, but he was a creature of habit and he could hardly blame his assistant for being shocked. The truth was he didn't want her questioning him further, because he didn't like lying; in fact, he hated it. The first pack of wine gums were still untouched and the reason he wanted to go to the shop had nothing to do with wanting to buy more of them. He wanted to go there because the early shift in the emergency department would be finishing soon and he'd seen some of the A&E staff at the shop, grabbing a coffee after work. He couldn't be sure Eden would be there, but there was a chance she would.

Drew couldn't have explained why he wanted to see Eden, even if he'd been up front with Saskia about his reason for going to the shop. Eden hadn't got in touch with him to arrange to meet up and, even if she had, it would only have been for them to talk about her son. He couldn't rationalise his reason for wanting to see her, because it wasn't rational. He wanted to see Eden because he was attracted to her, and he didn't want to be. Relationships were complicated, and in Drew's experience, far more painful than they were worth. Yet here he was, lying to his assistant about where he was going, with the sole intention of hoping to see Eden.

'Double wine gum days definitely exist and today is one of them.' Drew shrugged. 'Can I get you something? You've worked really hard today. You always work really hard, and I'm sorry if I don't tell you enough, but I'm very grateful.'

He meant every word, but as Saskia looked at him again, tilting her head to one side as she did, he suddenly realised she might think he had an ulterior motive for the compliment he'd just paid her. He was fifteen years older than Saskia, and any kind of romantic connection was the last thing on his mind when he thought of her. Although the nuances of social interaction could be as treacherous for Drew as open moorland could be to a drunk man who'd left his jacket and phone behind in the pub. He wanted to tell her that he absolutely didn't mean anything by the compliment, except to express his gratitude for her help, but the last thing he wanted was to make things worse. He'd done that far too often in the past.

'Thanks, Drew.' Behind the clear screen of the face shield she was wearing, her expression relaxed into a smile and the tension left his shoulders. Saskia knew him well enough now and there'd been no misinterpretation of what he meant. Thank God. 'I appreciate working for a boss like you too. You're always giving me the opportunity to learn and you treat me like an equal, even though you've got enough certificates to wallpaper this whole mortuary.'

'Not quite.' Sometimes Drew just couldn't help being literal, but he needed to get out of here before he said something else awkward. 'So can I get you anything?'

'I'll have a Snickers bar if they've got one and a can of Coke. My boyfriend thinks I'm a total weirdo, but I'm always ravenous after a postmortem. Maybe it's just my body reminding me that I'm alive.'

'Could be, but there's nothing wrong with being a weirdo. The world needs us.' Drew knew there was a good chance that Saskia had deliberately reminded him she had a boyfriend, but he was trying not to overthink it. His head was already full of how to handle imagined conversations with Eden if he did bump into her, he didn't need anything else to worry about.

* * *

The first half of Eden's shift had been just as she'd expected it to be. She was in A&E paediatrics and had looked after patients with the kind of fairly routine childhood injuries and infections they often dealt with. There'd also been a ten-year-old boy who for some reason had decided to see if he could charge down his classroom door using his shoulder and had ended up with a broken collarbone instead. It wasn't until towards the end of her shift that Bea, an eight-year-old girl, was brought in by her very worried parents, who'd been keeping her off school for the past week with flu, but she seemed to be getting worse.

'I can't understand why she isn't getting any better. We've all had the flu, but she's getting more and more listless.' The little girl's mother, who'd already introduced herself as Sara, had clutched her daughter's hand tightly as she spoke. Bea had hardly even seemed to respond.

'Can you tell me a bit about her other symptoms?' It had been easy to see how terrified Bea's parents were and Eden had done her best to be as reassuring as possible. Over the years, she'd discovered that time spent on trying to stop the parents from panicking always paid off and it was the best way to ensure she got the information she needed. A parent frozen with panic wasn't what Bea needed right now.

'She's just so tired, and Bea's normally a proper little live wire, isn't she, Tom?' Sara had looked at her husband who'd nodded, his eyes never leaving his daughter's face. 'She doesn't want any food, only water. She's had abdominal pains, and an upset stomach and vomiting, even though she's barely eating. She's lost so much weight just in the last week, it feels like she's fading away. She seems completely out of it today too, like she barely knows we're here. It's terrifying.'

Bea still hadn't responded, despite the obvious fear in her mother's voice and Eden had been grateful for that in a way. The last thing she'd wanted was for the little girl to be frightened, too. Early in her career, Eden had decided to specialise in emergency medicine, and she'd worked across both the adult and children's areas of A&E, as most of the nurses on the team did. It had become more challenging working with paediatric emergencies since she'd had Teddie, because the cases she dealt with felt closer to home, and the losses hit her even harder than before. Although thankfully they were few and far between. Despite how difficult those cases were, Eden had decided she'd rather be on the inside trying to cut that number even further, than on the outside just hoping and wishing for miracles.

'Okay sweetheart, the first thing we need to do is run some blood tests to see if we can get to the bottom of what's making you feel so poorly.' Eden spoke directly to Bea rather than to her mum and dad, to see if she responded any differently to a nurse than she did to her parents. She'd been about to explain to Sara and Tom that the team would also monitor their daughter's vital signs and ensure she got some IV fluids to replace the electrolytes she'd lost since becoming ill, but as Eden leant in closer to the little girl, she caught a distinctive fruity smell, almost like pear drops. Given her other symptoms, it was very likely to be a sign of diabetic ketoacidosis, caused by high levels of ketones and blood sugar, as a result of the body burning fat for energy, instead of glucose. It was caused by insufficient insulin and it was life threatening.

With the situation suddenly so much more urgent, Eden had immediately sought support from her colleagues. Unlike the nursing team, most of the doctors in A&E were either specialists in adult emergency medicine or paediatrics. Sometimes staffing levels meant that adult emergency doctors had to support the work of the paediatrics team for more routine cases, but more complex ones were always referred to specialist paediatricians. Eve Bellingham was a hospital manager's dream, because she was qualified and experienced in emergency medicine and the sub-speciality of paediatric emergency medicine, which meant she could work more broadly across both teams. Thankfully, Eve had been on shift too and was available to lead on Bea's treatment.

Eden's hunch had quickly been proven correct and treatment had commenced as soon as the little girl's condition was confirmed. Bea had been given fluids, as well as insulin and potassium to stabilise her condition. She'd been given a life-changing diagnosis of type 1 diabetes, but she was going to be okay and that was all that was important in the end. There'd be a lot for Bea and her parents to learn and get to grips with in the weeks and months to come, but it was days like today that made Eden even more glad she'd chosen the career she had. Something that hit home all the more when Eden had gone to say goodbye to the family, just before the end of her shift.

'We've got to get her that puppy we've been talking about.' Bea's mother was speaking in urgent tones to her father, and neither of them had noticed Eden at first. 'I promised her if she got better that I'd get her one, and she is going to get better, Tom. So I can't break that promise.'

'She can have anything she wants.' Tom had smiled at his wife and then, turning slightly, he'd finally caught sight of Eden. 'Because she is going to be okay thanks to this brilliant nurse.'

'It was a team effort, but a lot of it's down to Bea too; she may be small, but she's a tough cookie.' Eden had looked at the little girl, who was still resting, but who she could already picture beaming when she heard the news that she'd be getting a puppy.

'She is.' Sara was stroking her daughter's hair as she spoke. 'But please don't underplay what you did, it was amazing. You saved her life by knowing what questions to ask and getting her the help she needed. Losing her would have killed me and Tom too, and it would have ruined the lives of everyone who loves her. That's huge and I know not everyone appreciates the work you do, but I promise you we'll never forget it.'

'Thank you.' Eden had accepted the hugs that both Sara and Tom had offered her in turn. It felt good to have made so much of a difference, but despite what they said it really was a team effort.

It had been a long shift and Eden was completely exhausted by the end of it, but when Eve had suggested they go for a coffee afterwards, with Meg and Isla, one of the other A&E nurses, she'd realised she wanted to go, despite the temptation to just head back home and flop down on the sofa. Her parents had picked Teddie up from nursery at lunch time to take him swimming at the pool in Port Tremellien, and she had no reason to rush back. Her mother was trying hard to be the perfect grandmother and having her father there reassured her that Teddie was in safe hands. Given how infrequently the chance arose, she didn't want to miss the opportunity to spend some time with the others outside of work.

Eve had been a bit standoffish since coming back from leave, and although Eden was friendly with Meg she never felt as though she'd got far below the surface. This felt like too good an opportunity to get to know her colleagues a bit better, and to keep trying to build up the friendships that had been missing from her life for so long. Felix had said he'd come and find her after his interview, so she'd sent him a quick text to let him know she'd be sitting at one of the tables outside the hospital shop for the next half an hour or so, and after that he could find her at home.

'I'll get the drinks.' Eden made the offer before any of the others could get ahead of her.

'We should be buying for you.' Eve smiled. 'If you hadn't realised so quickly what was wrong with Bea, things could have got far worse.'

'It was just a lucky hunch.' She tried to brush it off, but Eve was having none of it.

'No it wasn't, it was down to skill, experience, and excellent instincts. I wish every nurse I've been involved with had those same qualities.' An unreadable expression flitted across Eve's face. For a moment Eden wondered about her choice of words; she hadn't said 'nurses she'd worked with', she'd said 'involved with'. But Eden was probably just reading too much into something that meant nothing at all.

'Either way, it's my round. You sit down with Meg and Isla, and I'll grab the drinks.' Eden grinned at the expression on Eve's face. 'It's okay, I'll let you pay when we go somewhere really expensive, like that new wine bar by the harbour in Port Agnes.'

'I'll hold you to that.' Eve was smiling now, and Eden felt a surge of hope that this new life of hers might really be everything she'd desperately hoped it would. There was nothing and no one stopping her from building new friendships any more, not now that Jesse was out of her life, and moments like this felt as if they could be the start of something.

Eden walked into the hospital shop, but she couldn't see anyone at the counter. There was a stockroom behind it and, although there was a bell to ring for service, she waited there for a moment, not wanting to feel as though she was hassling any of the volunteers for service. Whoever was on duty, was probably trying to get a stock take done too, so she stood there and waited, hoping someone might suddenly emerge. Less than a minute later Gwen appeared, muttering something about having found some more wine gums out the back. It wasn't until she looked up that she spotted Eden and suddenly stopped dead, putting a hand to her chest, as if seeing her was a total shock.

'Sorry, Gwen, did I make you jump?'

'No, well, yes, I suppose you did a bit, but luckily not enough to make me wet myself.' Gwen laughed. 'At least I hope not, although at my age it's a close-run thing.'

Eden laughed along with her. It hadn't taken her long to realise that Gwen was more than capable of living up to her reputation of not only being the font of all knowledge about St Piran's, but someone who wasn't afraid to tell it how it was. Gwen might also use humour that was pretty close to the edge of what some would deem acceptable, but Eden loved her, everybody did.

'I didn't want to ring the bell and disturb you if you were busy out the back, but it sounds like you were expecting someone else to be here?'

'When I went in to check whether we had more wine gums in stock, Drew Redford was standing where you are now, but it looks as if he's disappeared in a puff of smoke.' Gwen craned her neck forward towards the half-windowed wall of the shop that looked out on to the bistro tables, and the hospital entrance beyond them on one side, and the corridor that led off to all departments on the other. 'He's definitely done a vanishing act. I'll have to rope him in to help me and my husband out with our magic act.'

'You've got a magic act?' Eden shouldn't have been surprised when Gwen nodded.

'Yes, Barry the Magic Man and the Great Gwendini.'

'Sounds brilliant, I'll have to come along and see that for myself one day.

Although if I don't get the coffees in for that lot soon.' Eden gestured towards her colleagues sitting around one of the bistro tables. 'I won't need magic to make me disappear.'

As she gave Gwen their order and waited for the drinks to be made, Eden tried not to wonder whether the reason for Drew's sudden disappearance had anything to do with her. It couldn't be that though, she was just overthinking it again and making the assumption that she was on Drew's mind, when he probably hadn't given her a second thought.

Once she took the drinks out to the others the conversation flowed easily. Eve opened up a bit and told them about some of the work she'd done when she'd been at St James's hospital in Leeds. Although when Meg had asked her what had made her come back to Cornwall, her answer had been the same vague explanation about family issues that she'd given when she'd gone on extended leave just before Eden had joined the team. Meg had been the one directing questions at Eve, and Eden had found herself wondering if that was Meg's way of avoiding having to say too much about her own situation. Although the truth was, Eden hadn't told them much detail about why she'd come back to Cornwall either. She'd mentioned the break up with Teddie's father, but not how toxic things had been for years before then. Or how she'd ended up getting involved with a man like Jesse, because of a childhood that had made her want to rescue every lame duck who crossed her path. She didn't want to dump all of that on them. In any case, this was Eden's chance to reinvent herself, and it had taken her a long time to finally realise that the only people she needed to save were herself and Teddie.

Thankfully Isla's contribution to the conversation was light-hearted and fun, regaling them all with updates on Aidan and Jase's experiences as new dads. She had first-hand insight because her boyfriend, Reuben, was Aidan and Jase's nephew. Isla also updated them on the latest about the relationship between Amy, one of the other A&E nurses, and Lijah, the childhood sweetheart she'd recently reunited with. The fact that Lijah was also an internationally famous musician made that particular information all the more interesting. The time had sped by and, when Eden looked up to see Felix walking down the corridor towards her, she realised that almost an hour had passed. This was what she'd missed, laughing and chatting with like-minded people, and not constantly being on high alert in case Jesse took exception to her having fun and accused her of all kinds of things she hadn't done. It felt odd not to be constantly clock watching or thinking up excuses for why she was late, but the relief at not having to do any of that was like a huge weight had been lifted off her shoulders.

It had taken her a long time to get used to feeling free. Even eight months after coming home she still jumped when she heard a car door slam outside her parents' house and held her breath when she got a call from an unknown number, in case it was him. Despite the fact she'd ditched her old phone and got herself a new mobile number. If Jesse wanted to find her, he could do it easily enough. He knew where her parents lived and he'd almost certainly guess that's where she'd gone. He'd probably work out she'd go after a job at the local hospital too, but so far he hadn't come looking for her and she was finally starting to allow herself to believe that maybe he never would. He'd lied constantly in an attempt to control her, and all his threats about harming himself if she left had been empty; just one more way to assert power over her. Part of her hoped he'd found someone else to focus his attention on, but she wouldn't wish that on anybody. Maybe Sadie had finally persuaded him to get the help he needed, but she hadn't heard from her either and that was something else she was grateful for. 'I nearly didn't check you were still here, I thought you'd be at home by now.' Felix smiled and she knew without him having to say anything that he was pleased to see her hanging out with her colleagues and having fun.

'This is my brother, Felix. He's just had an interview as an OT.' Eden introduced each of the others to him in turn. When all the introductions were over, she turned back to her brother.

'So how did the interview go?'

'I'll tell you, if you show me proof that you've texted Drew and arranged to meet up.' Eden could have killed Felix for revealing that particular snippet of information in front of the others. They were bound to read too much into it, just like Felix was.

'Drew Redford, the pathologist?' Meg raised her eyebrows, but before she could ask any more questions and make it into far more than it was, Eden cut her off at the pass.

'Yes. We spoke about meeting up, because he's got some personal experience of ASD. I thought it might help me with understanding more about Teddie.' She didn't want to say that Drew was autistic too; that was for him to share or not as he saw fit.

'That's my Eddie's story and she's sticking to it.' Felix grinned and Eden flicked him on the arm.

'Sometimes I hate having a brother.'

'No you don't, you love me. Now are you going to send that text, or am I going to keep the details of how the interview went all to myself?'

'Well I'm invested now.' Isla leant forward in her seat. 'So I think you need to do it for all our sakes.'

'Okay, I'm doing it now.' Eden had already saved Drew's number in her phone, from when she'd made the promise to Felix before. It took less than a minute to send the text and she was determined not to make too big a deal of it, not least because of what Felix and the others would read into it if she did.

> Hi Drew. It's Eden, Teddie's mum. I wondered if you were still up for getting together? Let me know if so, but no pressure.

As the message flew off into the ether, she looked up at her brother again.

'Right, that's my side of the bargain fulfilled. So come on then, how did the interview go? And just so you know, there's a big part of me that hopes it was a toe-curlingly embarrassing experience.'

'Sorry to disappoint you, sis, but they offered me the job on the spot, subject to all the usual checks and references of course.'

'That's brilliant!' Eden jumped to her feet and hugged him. Despite the joke she'd made about hoping his interview hadn't gone to plan, she couldn't have been more thrilled to hear that he'd been offered the job and that he'd be staying in Cornwall. Things seemed to be looking up on so many fronts, she just hoped that arranging to meet up with Drew wouldn't turn out to be a big mistake. She'd made far too many of those in the past and the last thing she wanted was to make another one that would do anything to derail her fresh start.

6

Drew felt like a complete idiot. He'd been standing in the shop waiting for Gwen to come out of the stock room, where she'd insisted on checking whether she had another box of wine gums in stock, ready to fulfil his daily order for the next month or so. He'd already felt a bit awkward standing there, but then he'd spotted Eden and a group of others in the corridor outside the shop. Eden had her back to the doorway and she was good-naturedly bickering with one of her friends about who should buy the coffees. Suddenly the thought of bumping into her 'by chance' seemed ridiculous. She had his number and had clearly decided not to use it. Eden didn't want to bump into him, by chance or otherwise. He realised he had the opportunity to slip out of the door and head out of the main entrance before she saw him, and so that's what he did.

Drew had left the can of Coke and the Snickers bar that Saskia had requested on the counter, and had walked almost half a mile to the next nearest shop, before heading back to the hospital and going around to the side entrance. All just to avoid seeing Eden. He didn't just feel like an idiot, he was one. He must be if he couldn't act like a normal person. That was the mantra that was playing in his head for the rest of the day, and it wasn't until it was time to leave that he picked up his phone and saw a message from an unknown number.

Hi Drew. It's Eden, Teddie's mum. I wondered if you were still up for getting together? Let me know if so, but no pressure.

Drew stared at the message for a moment, trying to work out whether accepting her offer was a good idea, despite the fact that he really wanted to. What concerned him most was just how much her message had lifted his spirits. He'd done his best to hide his attraction to her when they were together, because even though he often wasn't very good at reading signals, let alone giving them out, he knew Eden didn't feel the same way. She'd been clear that her interest in him involved talking about Teddie. Drew wanted to help her and her little boy as much as he possibly could, but that wasn't the only reason he wanted to see her. He was worried that by saying yes, he wouldn't be being completely honest and that was incredibly important to him. Looking at the text again, he shook his head. He was being ridiculous. He'd been in his job at St Piran's for over a year, and he'd hardly done anything except work, this was his opportunity to alter that. Before he changed his mind, he sent Eden a reply.

Hi Eden. Yes, I'm still up for meeting. I don't know what your shifts are like, but I'm off this weekend if you're free either day?

As soon as Drew had sent the message he wondered if he should have been so honest about not having any plans for his weekend off. He was due to do some volunteer work, but nothing that couldn't be rescheduled, and Eden might as well get to know the real him. If she didn't like what she saw, they'd both be better off finding that out sooner rather than later and at least he wouldn't have lied. He'd had to contend with far too many lies in the past, and there was no way he was going to live one too.

* * *

Eden had thought carefully about where to meet Drew. Since their first encounter in the car park, she'd found out a bit more about him, mostly from Gwen, who seemed to know everyone and everything about life at St Piran's.

'He's a little bit quirky, but if I didn't have Barry and I was twenty years younger...' Gwen had paused and wrinkled her nose. 'Okay maybe more like forty years younger, I'd be very interested in getting to know Drew better. He's so interesting, I could talk to him all day long about his job. He might be quiet, but you know what they say about still waters running deep and all that. He looks like he could be living on a remote croft up in the Scottish mountains, striding through the heather back to the woman he loves. Like something out of *Highlander*. I bet there are hidden passions there.'

She'd winked then and Eden hadn't been able to stop herself from laughing, and telling Gwen that if she ever fancied a change of career she could try her hand at writing a steamy romance. She might be in her early seventies, but she never shied away from talking about any subject and she certainly seemed invested in other people's love lives. It was all done in good spirit, but she'd got the wrong idea this time. Despite her initial attraction to Drew, and Felix's insistence that she should keep an open mind, Eden still wasn't remotely interested in any kind of romantic relationship. The risk just wasn't worth it and she'd made sure Gwen knew where she stood.

'I don't care about his hidden passions, as long as they don't involve cutting up bodies when he's off the clock. I don't want to take Teddie with me to meet a serial killer in the middle of nowhere.' It had been a joke, of course, but his job was pretty unusual, and she had to wonder what kind of person chose to work with the dead. Maybe she'd watched too many crime dramas. There'd even been one recently where the forensic pathologist working on the case turned out to be the killer; it was the perfect cover for his crimes. Despite that, Eden had known that her comments about Drew were ridiculous and the expression on Gwen's face had confirmed it.

'I think what he does is amazing. Thank goodness someone is prepared to do a job like that and give answers to people who so desperately need them. He works with the police too, helping to get justice that might not be served any other way. As to the chances of him being violent' – Gwen had rolled her eyes – 'I'd bet my pension against that ever happening. I serve all kinds of people in here and in over forty years as a midwife I dealt with every personality type you can imagine, and Drew is one of the gentlest souls I've ever met.'

It had almost been as though she'd personally insulted Gwen and, much like the conversation with Felix, it had left Eden questioning herself for making assumptions about Drew. Just because he did a job she couldn't imagine doing, it didn't make him odd. She knew better than anyone how damaging labels and assumptions could be, and yet even the most basic of new experiences – like meeting a colleague – could feel almost overwhelming these days. The years with Jesse had made her that way, but that was no excuse for judging Drew before she even knew him, and she promised herself she was going to do better. She was determined to go back to being the girl she'd been before Jesse had attempted to mould her into someone else entirely. Maybe then she could finally put her relationship with him behind her, where it belonged.

In the end they'd arranged to meet at the coastal park between Port Kara and Port Tremellien. It started in a patch of woodland parallel to the beach and eventually led down towards the sea itself, just before the first row of beach huts that overlooked the main beach in Port Tremellien. There were slides, rope swings and tunnels, and even a zip line. Not to mention a café, with two huge sand pits outside, and a wooden pirate ship that had slides leading down from its deck. Teddie loved it there and there'd be enough going on around them to ensure that any lulls in the conversation weren't quite so awkward. Eden had borrowed her dad's car to drive to the car park close to where the trail began, and had then put Teddie into his buggy to walk down and meet Drew at the starting point. She just hoped the buggy would cope okay with the different terrain, now that Teddie was getting so much heavier than he'd been as a toddler.

'Thanks so much for agreeing to meet.' Eden was slightly breathless when she reached the point where Drew was standing. He was wearing an oatmeal-coloured Aran sweater, making him look exactly like the kind of sexy Highland farmer Gwen had described. She cursed the older woman as the thought popped into her head, Gwen and her ridiculous romantic notions had a lot to answer for.

'It's no trouble at all.' Drew smiled and Teddie started jabbering loudly in his made-up language. She'd described her son as non-verbal in the past, but recently she'd made the effort to stop doing that. He was very verbal and sometimes so loud that it made people around him jump. He just didn't speak, at least not in any language Eden recognised. She turned to Drew again, as Teddie's voice got louder.

'I'm sure he's fluent in Korean, and I just don't understand him. No wonder he gets so frustrated sometimes. He's started lashing out more, and the worst part is that it's usually towards himself. The last few days he's been slapping his head really hard. It makes me feel like the worst mother in the world.' Eden hadn't meant to say so much, especially not this quickly, but over the last couple of days Teddie's behaviour seemed to have escalated and she was desperate to talk to someone who might understand.

'All four-year-olds get frustrated. It's just that most of them can scream and shout about whatever is causing their meltdown. Teddie can't do that so he turns his frustration in on himself. I doubt it's because you're a bad mother, from what I've seen I suspect the opposite is true.' The matter-of-fact tone of Drew's voice made his words sound more believable than they might have done otherwise, and less like he was just saying what she wanted to hear. He'd already helped Eden more than she would have thought possible as a result. Sometimes she just needed to be able to voice her worst fears. She couldn't do that with her parents, not without her mother somehow making it all about her, even if she didn't mean to. She could probably have been more open with Felix than she was, but he'd only just come home and he had a lot on his plate trying to organise a permanent move back to Cornwall.

'Shall we take the woodland path down towards the beach? There's a café there and Teddie loves the pirate ship. Although he won't go near the sand pit, he hates the feel of it.'

'Me too. It's a sensory thing. When you think about it, sand and broken glass are different versions of the same thing.' Drew smiled again; it really did transform his whole face and she couldn't stop herself from thinking how nice it would be to make him smile like that more often. Bloody Gwen, she really had done a number on her. It wasn't just that, though, there was something about Drew that instantly made it feel like he understood her situation and, even more than that, a sense that he understood Teddie in a way almost no one else seemed to. He didn't see Teddie's stimming or his sensory issues as 'odd' the way many people did, he understood the reasons and that they were part of who Teddie was. Acceptance like that was far rarer than it should have been, and she already knew that arranging to meet Drew had been the right decision. Eden could almost feel her guard lowering, but her newfound openness still took her by surprise when her response came tumbling out.

'To be honest I'm not the biggest fan of sand either. Mum was always making us go to the beach for picnics when my brother Felix and I were kids. I think it's because she liked to be able to have the excuse to start on the wine early in the day and sit in the sunshine drinking it. All the while trying to convince herself that it was a lovely day out for our benefit. I never liked it, and not just because there always seemed to be more sand than filling in the sandwiches by the time we got to eat them. If we complained she always made the same joke about there being a reason why they're called SANDwiches.'

'Oh God, just thinking about the feel and sound of the grains between your teeth.' Drew shuddered. 'Tell me to mind my own business, if I shouldn't be asking, I'm not always great at judging these things... But I'm guessing from what you said that your mum had a problem with drinking?'

She hadn't meant to tell him that. It wasn't something she talked about with anyone except Felix, and yet with Drew she'd revealed a part of her past she usually kept hidden within minutes. Maybe it was because he didn't dive straight in with probing questions; even now he was giving her the option to shut down the conversation if she wanted to, but she didn't. For some reason she wanted to share this with Drew because she somehow knew he wouldn't sensationalise it, or revel in the drama of what had gone on. He must have seen everything in his job and nothing she said was likely to shock him; she'd have bet a month's salary that Drew wasn't the type to gossip either. She couldn't really explain it, but talking to him felt like a safe space and, after closing herself off to other people for so long, the flood gates seemed to be opening.

'She was an alcoholic for the first twenty-four years of my life. It's only in the last seven that she's been sober.'

'That must have been tough. Addiction can change a person into someone else entirely.'

'You sound like you're speaking from experience too?' Eden stopped walking, suddenly wondering if she was the one who'd overstepped the mark, as Drew came to a halt beside her. 'Sorry, you don't have to answer that.'

'It's okay. You mentioned wanting to talk to me about how my parents supported me with my ASD diagnosis and the answer is not well. I wasn't diagnosed until I left home and went to university. At the time I was told it was Asperger's, but it was recategorised to ASD when they scrapped that. It was actually a relief to have a reason for why I felt the way I did.' Drew shrugged. 'My parents had their own issues, and the problems I was having because of undiagnosed ASD went under their radar. My mother's addiction wasn't to alcohol, it was prescription painkillers. And as for my father... he was just never around.'

Drew sounded matter of fact and the expression on his face didn't give anything away either, but there was a flicker of something in his eyes that revealed how much this situation had hurt him, and she had to suppress the urge to reach out and comfort him because she had a feeling that was the last thing he'd want. Instead, revealing more of her own past felt like the best way of showing that she understood.

'I'm sorry, that sounds really difficult. My dad was always around, but he wouldn't accept that Mum had a problem, and I'm not sure what I'd have done if I hadn't had my brother to talk to. Have you got any siblings?' When Drew shook his head, Eden couldn't stop herself from reaching out and touching his arm, finding herself weirdly reluctant to remove her hand afterwards. 'You probably had it a lot tougher than me in that case.'

'I think...' Drew hesitated, almost as if his mind was somewhere else for a moment or two, before he continued. 'I think if I hadn't ended up as an only child things might have been different, but I was never the son my father wanted. The best thing about my diagnosis was understanding myself better, but I still don't think he gets it or wants to for that matter.'

'I can't believe they could be anything but proud of you.' Eden's chest ached at how misunderstood Drew clearly felt, even by his own parents, and it scared her too. His autism was high functioning, that was evident from how articulately he was discussing his own experiences, but the signs were that Teddie's ASD might be towards the opposite end of the spectrum. How would her beautiful boy ever make himself understood, if someone like Drew had struggled to do it?

'My father isn't proud of me.' Drew's honesty was breathtaking, and despite the fact his tone hadn't altered, Eden had seen the look in his eyes again that betrayed how he really felt. One of the stereotypes of autistic people was that they were emotionless, and it was yet another misguided notion Teddie would have to contend with. Eden already knew it wasn't true and she'd seen the pain in Drew's eyes, even if he didn't allow his voice to betray him. There were layers to him that she would guarantee most people missed, but Eden could see them. He was such a kind and understanding person, but he'd clearly been through a really tough time and she hated the thought that a lot of people wouldn't give him the chance to show the other side of himself, because he was different to them. She already felt a connection to Drew she couldn't explain, given the amount of time they'd spent together, but it was there all the same and she couldn't help smiling at what he said next. The whole world would benefit from being a bit more like Drew. 'It doesn't matter what my father thinks. I like what I do and I know I'm good at it.'

'I can well believe it.' She loved how refreshingly straightforward he was. After years with someone like Jesse, who'd spun so many stories that even he didn't know the truth from the lies, it was amazing to be with someone who told it like it was. Some of Drew's answers were succinct, but he was far from the monosyllabic, awkward person she'd feared he might be. It was clear that when he felt he had something worth saying, he was willing to open up and say far more than she'd expected him to. Although his responses were more honest and upfront than most people's might be, he wasn't as literal as she'd expected him to be either. The realisation hit her again that even with a child like Teddie, she was still carrying her own prejudices and assumptions of what ASD meant. But spending time with Drew was making her realise how ridiculous that was. Having autism didn't put someone into a neat little box. In a way that scared her, and yet it was reassuring too. Teddie and the abilities he was going to have couldn't be defined simply by his diagnosis, but that meant they couldn't be reliably predicted by it either. Things could get better than they were right now, whatever that might look like for Teddie. Even if she didn't get anything else from meeting up with Drew, she was determined never to forget that.

* * *

As it turned out, Drew had been able to open her eyes to a whole lot more. He'd told her about his experience of working with children who had autism during his medical training, and the benefits he'd seen of parents and carers who used Makaton to help communicate with their children. Makaton was a combination of signs, symbols and speech, and it was something Eden had been considering, but part of her had wondered whether it meant she was accepting that Teddie would never communicate the way other children did, and that by doing so she'd be giving up on him.

'Don't you think it would be better to have a way to communicate with him now, whether or not he eventually learns to speak?' There'd been no edge to Drew's voice when he'd said it. It wasn't accusatory, just a completely honest question that forced her to consider her motives and it was just one of many things that Drew had helped her look at differently.

When they'd reached the pirate ship, Eden had repeatedly lifted Teddie on to the platform at the top of the slide, so that he could come down. It was something experience had taught her he wouldn't bore of, even if they did it a thousand times, but it only took around ten or twelve lifts before she needed a break. When Teddie had tugged at her hand to let her know he was ready to go again she'd sighed.

'I'm sorry Ted, Mummy needs a rest, but I'll take you up again in a bit.'

'Do you want me to do it?' Drew's question had caught her by surprise – she hadn't wanted him to feel obliged and she wasn't sure how Teddie would react to someone he'd only just met.

'Do you really want to? He's surprisingly heavy to lift and he doesn't do much to help himself get up there. He can be a bit funny with people he doesn't know well too, so don't take it personally if he pushes you away.'

'Don't worry, I won't and I wouldn't have offered to take him on the slide if I didn't mean it.' It had been another reassuringly straightforward response and, when Drew had held out his hand, Teddie had taken it without hesitation. She should have been shocked, given how unusual that was for him, but somehow she wasn't. Teddie had recognised the same connection to Drew that she'd felt and her little boy was trying to tell her, in his own way, that she'd been right. After that, it had been Drew's hand Teddie had yanked on, to let him know that it was time to be lifted to the top of the slide again and, unlike Eden, Drew didn't show any signs of tiring. Eventually she'd suggested that they go to the café and almost as soon as Teddie was back in his buggy, he'd dropped off to sleep.

Drew had insisted on paying for the coffee and cake, despite Eden telling him that it should be her treat, considering he'd given up his time and lifted Teddie to the top of the slide at least twenty-five times. It was something else that marked him out as being completely different from Jesse. Her ex had been secretive about money as well as everything else. The lies he'd weaved had been so tangled that even now she wasn't sure she knew the whole story.

Now, as Drew walked back towards her, she found herself wondering how different her life might have been if she hadn't met Jesse. She would still be able to trust her instincts without overthinking and second-guessing everything, after years of gaslighting had made her doubt even the things she saw with her own eyes. She'd still have had the self-confidence that experience had robbed her of, which might have changed so many things, including how far she'd progressed in her career. Maybe she'd even have the happy little family she'd always envisaged, one that wasn't burdened with any of the issues she'd experienced in her own childhood. Eden would never regret meeting Jesse though, because she wouldn't have Teddie otherwise.

'There you go.' Drew set down the tray and put Eden's carrot cake and latte in front of her. The picnic table she'd chosen was furthest away from the others outside the café, and she hoped it would be quiet enough for Teddie to stay asleep.

'Thank you.' She looked up at him. 'Not just for this, but for everything today.'

'It's no problem.' It was the same thing he'd said when they first met up, but he wasn't finished. 'I enjoyed it, especially taking Teddie on the slide.'

'I think you're his new favourite person.' She really liked Drew and knowing how much her son liked him just intensified that feeling. It had been on the tip of her tongue to say that he was her new favourite person too, after how much he'd helped her to think things through, but she didn't want to make him uncomfortable. She hadn't really known what to expect from their meet up, and she'd had no idea that he'd worked with children with autism during his medical training. Or that he still did some volunteering in that area. It had meant they'd been able to talk about far wider issues than just his own experiences of autism, which were very different to Teddie's. She wasn't sure if there were additional insights he might still be able to share, but she knew she didn't want this to be the last time they met up.

'It'll be nice to be someone's favourite person.' Drew's comment wasn't self-pitying, just another example of the kind of total honesty she was finding so appealing. Although she wasn't sure what to say in response. She didn't want to say she was sure he was someone else's favourite person, because she had no way of knowing if that was true. Instead she decided to mirror his honesty and ask him the question she'd been wanting to ask for the last couple of hours.

'You haven't got someone waiting for you at home then?'

'Only my cat. Does that tick any ASD boxes do you think, living alone with a cat?'

'Far better than living with a total dickhead like I did for nearly seven years.' Eden hadn't meant to blurt that out and it took her by surprise again just how easy it was to be honest with Drew and tell him things she'd only usually share with the people closest to her. He probably didn't have the slightest interest in her personal life, but there was a hint of a smile playing around his mouth at her blunt choice of words, before his expression grew more serious again.

'Was he Teddie's father?' When Eden nodded, Drew was quiet for a moment and she found herself wanting to fill the silence and explain how she'd ended up with someone like Jesse. They were far enough away from everyone else for their conversation not to be overheard and suddenly the story was just pouring out of her. Every detail of it. She hardly paused for breath and she couldn't look at Drew, but she couldn't stop either.

'I met Jesse when I was working at a hospital in London, after university. He'd been in a car accident and was badly injured. The team caring for him weren't sure if he was going to walk again. I looked after him when he first came into the emergency department and he told me there was only one person in the world who'd care if he wasn't here any more, but it would be better even for his sister if he died. I couldn't believe he didn't have lots of people who cared about him, but when I went up to see him on the ward a few days later, one of the nurses told me I was his first visitor. After that I kept going to see him. I found out he'd been in care after his parents died, and that he'd gone to live in a bedsit at nineteen. He told me he'd faced cancer treatment alone that same year, because he hadn't wanted to burden his little sister with knowing just how ill he was. It was the same reason he hadn't told her about the accident. Or at least that's what he told me. I think now that it was all part of his plan to make me feel sorry for him and like he needed me, but all I could see at the time was someone vulnerable and alone. Jesse told me how hard he'd worked to move on from the start he'd had in life and that he was earning a good wage, but it wasn't enough. Eventually he confessed that he'd crashed his car deliberately because he didn't want to live. And despite what I know about him now, I think all of that was true. Somehow, over the weeks of going to visit Jesse, I found myself feeling responsible for him, and he told me I was the only reason he wanted to get better. He didn't want me to speak to his sister, because he said she'd had a lifetime of being burdened with his problems. I should probably have realised even then what I was setting myself up for, but somehow I couldn't see it.'

Eden paused, searching Drew's face and looking for signs of judgement or something that told her how stupid he thought she'd been, but there was no indication of that, and it made it easy for her to continue.

'I never intended to get into a relationship with Jesse, but before I knew it, I was already in too deep and I thought I could save him from himself. Growing up with a mother like mine made me want to save everyone, but Jesse didn't know how to be honest about anything. He'd tell me things I knew weren't true, but when I confronted him, he'd twist it back on to me and deny ever having said the things I accused him of lying about, until it felt like I was going mad. He checked up on me all the time, questioning what I was doing and accusing me of all kinds of things, telling me my behaviour was inappropriate and that everyone could see it but me. It filled me with so much doubt that I stopped trusting myself and I completely lost who I was for a while. I knew I needed to break things off. Except when I told him I was leaving, he said he had no reason to carry on. I couldn't be the one to tip him over the edge, despite the effect that living with him was having on me, so I stayed and it was a cycle that kept repeating, especially after his sister eventually got involved and begged me to stay. She said she couldn't lose him as well as her parents, and suddenly I felt responsible for Sadie too.'

Eden could barely catch her breath as she finished speaking and the realisation hit her that she'd told Drew things she hadn't even shared with Felix. It was as if he'd become her unpaid therapist, but the quiet way he listened and the complete lack of any judgement in his expression made it incredibly easy to talk to him. Saying those things out loud – some of them for the first time – made it feel as if the burden of what she'd been through had suddenly eased. The anger she'd felt for allowing those things to happen had lessened too. It was so much easier to forgive herself after explaining how she'd got sucked into the situation with Jesse, and it no longer felt like her dirty little secret as a result, or something she had to feel guilty about. Drew might actually be a miracle worker and, when he responded to what she'd told him, it was obvious he didn't blame Eden for anything that had happened with Jesse.

'I'm always amazed at how people can make someone else responsible for their lives and happiness, but I guess it's easier than facing up to your own shortcomings.' Something in Drew's tone told her he was speaking from personal experience and she waited for him to carry on speaking, but instead he left the space for her to continue her own story and she realised she needed to get to the end, as much for herself, as him.

'I should have got out much sooner than I did, but I kept hoping Jesse would change, or get the help he needed and that I'd no longer feel responsible for him and Sadie, but then I fell pregnant with Teddie. The last thing I wanted was to have a baby with someone like him. He'd told me from the start it wasn't even possible, because the cancer treatment had left him completely infertile. Looking back, I don't think he ever even had cancer. I think he lied to me and probably his sister too, creating a narrative where he was a victim, so no one would challenge him about his actions. I should have left before Teddie was born, but I was scared of what Jesse might do and I didn't want my baby to grow up and discover I was the reason his father was no longer around. It's ironic when I think about how much better off Teddie is without Jesse, but at the time I was so entrenched in saving Jesse from himself that I couldn't see it like that.'

'It wouldn't have been your fault if something had happened to Jesse.' Drew's response made it sound so simple. She knew it was just the straightforward way he had of seeing things, but she needed Drew to understand that it wasn't as simple as he seemed to think it was, but then he started talking and what he said couldn't have surprised her more. 'I know what it's like to live with that kind of threat hanging over you. For years my mother said she didn't want to live any more, and I thought if I could just be different, she might feel differently too. But I couldn't make her happiness my responsibility, even if I'd wanted to, and Jesse's wasn't yours. You can't make someone else happy.'

'I know, but it's not always that easy to stop trying, is it?' She searched his face again, and he shook his head.

'No, it isn't. The reason I love my job so much is because I like dealing in logic and facts; they make me comfortable and that's part of how my autism works. For every problem, there's a solution. Or at least there should be. It took me a long time to realise that emotions don't behave with that sort of predictability and that it didn't matter how many solutions I offered my mother to try and cure her unhappiness, I couldn't fix the problem.'

Despite all the things they'd discussed that day, this was the most personal thing Drew had told her, and it was also the most he'd said in one go. For a moment Eden wasn't sure how to respond, but she wanted him to know how grateful she was that he'd shared it with her.

'Thank you, that really helps to hear. I still feel guilty about Jesse and I worry about him too. Whichever parts of his past are the real story, they've damaged him, and it makes me sad that I couldn't put that right. But what you said is true; I never had the power to fix Jesse and it wasn't my job to try. The only thing that matters to me now is doing my best by Teddie.'

'You already are.' Drew held her gaze for a moment and the attraction between them was palpable. It wasn't just from her side either, she was almost certain of that. Eden could so easily have closed the gap between them and discovered how he'd respond if she did. She wanted to, and for a moment she thought she might actually do it, but then someone called her name.

'Eden!' Looking up, she saw Aidan waving furiously at her. Jase was with him, pushing baby Ellis in her pram. Letting go of a long breath and trying to shake herself out of the moment she'd so nearly had with Drew, Eden stood up as Aidan and Jase drew level with the table.

'Fancy seeing you here!' Aidan flung his arms around her. 'We're just off to meet Danni and Charlie, apparently Caleb is already in the sandpit eating his body weight in sand.'

'Oh no.' Eden shuddered. 'We were talking earlier about how much we dislike sand, weren't we, Drew?'

'Yes, we were.' He clearly wasn't intending to elaborate, and Eden had never been a fan of awkward silences, so she launched into an introduction.

'I don't know if you've met Drew before, have you? He's one of the pathologists at the hospital.' She didn't even wait for Aidan to answer, before turning towards Drew. 'And this is Aidan, who works with me, and his husband Jase.'

There was a round of polite hellos, before Aidan lowered his sunglasses and looked at Drew. 'A pathologist? I bet that's dead exciting!'

It was the kind of stupid joke he always made. Eden laughed and Jase let out an exaggerated groan, but Drew didn't seem to realise it wasn't actually a question.

'I don't know if I'd call it exciting, but it's interesting work.'

'Sorry Drew, just ignore my husband.' Jase shook his head. 'You can tell he's a father now, with dad jokes like that. I have to put up with that sort of thing all the time.'

Drew nodded in response, but he didn't reply and the silence suddenly felt even more awkward.

'Say hi to Danni and Charlie for me, won't you?' Eden had only met Danni a couple of times, but she was one of the A&E consultants she'd be working closely with in the future once Danni was back from maternity leave.

'Will do. You two have a good time.' Aidan raised his eyebrows, as if he wasn't sure that was possible and Eden had to admit how different Drew seemed around Aidan and Jase. As the two men disappeared down the path, she couldn't help wondering if this should be the last time she spent with Drew after all. She'd blamed Gwen for her unexpected attraction to him, but Eden knew the attraction between them was down to more than Gwen's romantic notions. She also knew that she didn't want to get into another complicated relationship. Until today, she hadn't wanted to consider another relationship of any kind and just the fact that she was thinking about it scared the hell out of her.

7

Drew pushed the door of the refrigerated cabinet closed and laid a hand against it. Postmortems were never easy, but some of them were far harder than others, and this had been a tough one. Whenever children were involved it was tragic, but this had been the most difficult for him personally since he'd taken on his role at St Piran's. The little girl had been nine when she'd died as a result of a brain tumour, the same illness that had taken Drew's sister. Flora was his reason for doing the job he did, and it killed him to think that in the more than twenty-five years since she'd died there hadn't been the kind of advances he'd desperately hoped for. He hadn't wanted any other children to die the way she had and naively he'd been certain that the work he and others like him did would have contributed to finding a cure by now. Even though he knew it didn't make sense to blame himself for the fact that children were still dying from this unutterably awful disease, for once Drew couldn't fall back on logic. He still felt as if he'd let Flora down, and all the children who'd suffered the same fate.

He wasn't sure yet whether he'd be asked to speak to the little girl's parents about the results of the postmortem. Occasionally he did talk to family members, but that was usually when the death had been unexpected or unexplained. In those instances the family needed answers and an explanation only the postmortem could give. Connie's parents knew why she'd died: an aggressive brain tumour that had taken her from them less than six months after diagnosis. The speed of Connie's decline was unusual even with glioblastoma, and they probably wanted to know whether an earlier diagnosis could have changed things and given them more time with their beloved daughter. But no matter what Drew was able to tell them, it wouldn't change the outcome and that's what he really wanted. He didn't want to see cases like this any more and his anger and frustration at the lack of progress in preventing deaths like Connie's was close to boiling over.

'You need to take a break, have at least an hour away from here before we do anything else.' Drew's instruction to Saskia left no room for argument, but his assistant clearly realised she wasn't the only one who needed to follow that advice.

'I will if you will.' The team had been short-staffed due to illness, and both he and Saskia had been working long hours for the past week, forgoing breaks as often as possible. But they couldn't push on through, not today.

'I will.' Drew nodded. He couldn't wait to get the PPE off and be outside in his normal clothes, breathing in air that didn't smell of formaldehyde, but there was something he needed to say to Saskia first. 'That was tough, but you did really well.'

'So did you.' She laid a hand on his shoulder for a moment and then turned away. There was nothing left to say, nothing more they could do for Connie, and Drew had to get out of there. He needed to go somewhere to find some peace and try to escape from the thoughts racing through his head, and he knew exactly where he wanted to go.

* * *

St Piran's was a busy hospital, but if you knew where to look there were a few places around the grounds where a bit of quiet contemplation was possible. Drew knew all of them. As someone with a neurodiversity that had gone undiagnosed for the first two decades of his life, he could do a good job of masking and pretending to be like everyone else if he tried. Sometimes it wasn't that difficult to understand the way that other people expected him to act, but sometimes it was, and either way it was exhausting keeping up the pretence. He'd been told during his medical training that he needed to smile more, and it had felt like his face was a mask he couldn't take off. He'd spent most of his life anticipating other people's expectations and trying to live up to them, instead of just being who he was. The environment he worked in and the life he'd chosen to lead, meant he didn't have to put on that act nearly so often these days. Yet there were still times when he did, and that's why he valued these quiet spaces so much, places he could come to and just be.

There was an area behind the Thornberry Centre, where the oncology unit was housed, which had been made into a memorial garden that was almost always quiet. Maybe it was a strange choice of place to decompress, given how much cancer had taken from Drew, but he always felt at peace in the garden. It was as if he could feel Flora's presence there somehow, despite the fact that she'd died hundreds of miles away, in a children's hospice near Edinburgh. Seeing Connie had been such a gut-wrenching reminder of the last time he'd seen his sister and all the pain he'd tried so hard to bury had threatened to come rushing to the surface. It had been almost unbearable, and it was the closest he'd ever come to not being able to do his job.

Three decades after her death, he still wished with all his heart that Flora was still around. The only part of his family Drew had left now was their father, and it was pushing the definition of family to even describe them that way. If Flora hadn't died, maybe their mother wouldn't have become addicted to prescription painkillers, finding dangerous ways to source more supplies when the prescribed medication was no longer enough. And maybe Drew wouldn't have felt the need to be her everything and try to fill all the gaps his sister had left behind. He wouldn't have had to try so hard to be the perfect son, and to push aside all of his quirks in order to be the 'normal' boy she so desperately wanted. Deep down he knew that no one could be responsible for someone else's happiness, just like he'd said to Eden. But that didn't stop him feeling guilty for not doing a good enough job of being the kind of boy his mother had wanted him to be, otherwise she wouldn't have continued spiralling in the way she had. It wasn't logical to blame himself for her unhappiness, but even someone who usually saw things as black and white as he did couldn't apply the rules in such a simple way. That was the trouble with feelings and emotions, they messed with logic, and it was why he had often found them so difficult to navigate.

'I need it to numb the pain of losing Flora.' Drew's mother had pleaded with him more than once to steal medication from the hospital where he was training to feed her habit. He'd seen what the pain of losing her daughter had done to her, and how his father's impatience at her inability to move on from that loss had compounded that pain. But Drew had never considered stealing the medication she desperately wanted – it was a line he couldn't cross even for her.

He had no way of knowing for sure whether his mother would still have died, even if Flora had lived. He doubted that she'd ever been happy in her marriage. His mother had been warm and loving, and had longed for their family unit to be the centre of everything, but she'd picked the wrong husband for that. That had probably been what had sealed her fate, long before her children were born, let alone before she'd so tragically lost her only daughter.

'Are you okay, Drew?' He recognised Eden's voice before he even looked up from the bench.

'I'm fine, thank you.' It wasn't true, but something else he'd learned over the years was that most people didn't want to hear how you really were and Drew had never been comfortable talking about emotions anyway. It had surprised him just how much he'd opened up to Eden when they'd gone to the country park. She'd shared so much with him about her relationship with Teddie's father and he'd felt he'd had to offer up something about his own life. Although there'd been more to it than that, because he'd found himself *wanting* to tell her, not just feeling as though he should. But he didn't want to offload on her now, she had problems of her own, she wouldn't want to know about his.

'I'm glad you're fine, but I'm not sure I am.' It was only when Eden responded that he realised he hadn't asked her how she was, another social cue he'd missed. 'Do you mind if I sit down? I won't be offended if you say no.'

'I think you might be.' Drew looked directly at her and raised his eyebrows, making her laugh.

'Alright you've got me, maybe I will be offended.'

'You'd better sit down in that case.' Drew's smile was genuine; he liked making her laugh. But then he remembered what she'd said about not being fine and the smile slid off his face. 'Are you having a bad day?'

'I got some sad news when I came on shift. I saw a patient not long after I started here, a little girl. She was being sick and complaining about pain in her head. I hoped at first that it might be a migraine, but I was scared it could be something far worse.' Eden swallowed so hard it was audible. 'And sadly it turned out to be the worst possible kind of something else: an inoperable brain tumour. I hoped so much that Connie might get longer than anyone thought, but I found out from one of the other nurses that she died the day before yesterday. I haven't been able to stop thinking about her and I know she was in the Thornberry Centre for her treatment, so I just wanted to be here on my break. It's silly really, there's nothing I can do to help her family, but it felt like the right thing to do. God, I'm sorry, I always seem to spill out all of my problems to you; maybe you should start charging me for your time.'

'I'm here because of Connie too.' Drew looked up at her, his vision blurring. He didn't want to cry. He had no right to tears. It was Connie's parents whose hearts had broken, but he didn't dare blink, because if he did there'd be no holding them back.

'Oh Drew, did you...' Eden didn't seem able to say the words.

'We took care of her like she was ours.' It was what Drew would tell Connie's parents if they asked to speak to him, because it was the truth, the least painful truth he could tell them.

'I can't imagine how hard that was.' Eden put her hand on his arm, and he didn't want her to take it off, but he shook his head.

'It's far harder for her parents and everyone who loved her. I was just doing my job.'

'I know, but it's hard for us too. We do the jobs we do because we want to help. I became a nurse to make people better and when I can't it breaks my heart, especially when it's a child.' Eden gave a shuddering sigh, her words catching in her throat as she continued. 'You're right though, I can't stop thinking about her parents, or how I'd feel if it was Teddie.'

She started to cry, although he could see she was trying not to, her shoulders shaking. He wasn't sure what to do, he knew what he wanted to do and what the 'normal' thing would be, but he had no idea if it was what Eden would want. Drew didn't trust his gut, it had let him down too many times in the past, but just for once he decided to risk it. He put his arm around Eden's shoulders and she leant into him, still sobbing. As hard as it was to see her hurting like that, it suddenly felt as if holding her was where they were both meant to be and part of him was already dreading having to let her go.

'It's just so awful.' He had to strain to hear, her voice choking with tears. 'I don't know how her parents will ever be able to get over something like that enough to carry on.'

'They'll never get over it. I just hope they can find some way to get through it and keep moving forward. My mother never really did after my sister died...'

Eden's head shot up in response to his words and he knew he had to tell her the rest. And just like before, he realised to his surprise that he wanted to. He hadn't told anyone about Flora in years, but today he needed to say her name out loud and to tell her story.

Eden listened without saying anything as he explained how Flora's illness had progressed, and how his mother had unravelled in the wake of her death. He told her about his father too, the respected barrister turned high court judge, who continued building his career without pausing for breath or appearing to mourn his daughter. He certainly didn't support his wife or son through their grief. By the time Drew had finished speaking, Eden was holding his hand, his other arm still around her shoulders, and the weirdest part was that it didn't feel awkward at all. It felt right.

'I'm so sorry, Drew, losing Flora must have been unimaginably painful. You were so young too, and you didn't have anyone to turn to.' She was crying again, letting go of him to wipe her eyes and he immediately missed the sensation of her hand in his. 'Looking after Connie must have brought it all back and you still did your best by her. I don't think you've got any idea how amazing that makes you.'

Knowing Eden thought that way about him made it feel as though a wave of warm water had washed over him, but he still didn't see what he'd done as anything special. Not compared to her. 'Like I said, I was just doing my job. You met Connie and her parents, and had to deal with all their emotions when they realised how ill she might be. That's the hard part, it's not something I could ever do.'

'I think you're wrong. Maybe you deal with your own emotions and other people's a bit differently on the surface, but I've been able to open up to you in a way I didn't know I could any more. You've helped me more than I can say. We might not have spent that long together, but every time we've met up it has taught me something and I'm so glad that fate put you in my path.' Eden moved closer, brushing her lips against his and his body responded, even as his mind raced, questioning everything about how he should react. But she pulled away again, before he stood any chance of working it out.

'I've got to get back to A&E. I wish I didn't have to.' Her fingers curled around his for a moment, and she squeezed his hand before she let go. 'Will you be okay?'

'Of course I will, we both will. We have to be in the jobs we do, don't we?'

He forced a smile, but it wasn't like the mask he used to hide behind. He wanted to smile whenever he looked at Eden, it was just much harder to do it on a day like today.

'We do.' She hesitated for a moment, her eyes searching his. 'Don't feel you have to say yes, but I wondered if we could meet up again?'

'I'd like that. It would be good to see Teddie.' He wanted to tell her that it would be good to see her too, but he still wasn't sure what it was she wanted from him. If it was just friendship, he didn't want to risk messing up the chance of that because he could use a good friend too.

'Great, I'll text you. Take care, Drew.' She touched his arm one final time before turning and walking away, and from the moment she disappeared from view, he missed her.

8

The patient Eden had just called through to the examination room for an assessment was shaking, and her eyes were glassy, as if she might burst into tears at any moment.

'Come through, Mei, take a seat.' The smile Eden offered the young woman wasn't returned. Her records showed she was twenty-three, but she could have been mistaken for someone ten years younger than that. She was small and very slim, without a trace of make-up evident on her face.

'It says here that you've been having strange sensations in your hands and feet, but can you tell me a bit more about what's been going on?' Eden's tone was gentle, but the threatened tears in Mei's eyes spilled over, nonetheless.

'I've been having these weird sensations and I think it's—' The words caught in Mei's throat and she started to sob. Rules on physical contact between staff and patients were set out in a list of guidelines, but sometimes there was only one thing to do in these situations, regardless of whether it aligned with protocol.

Getting up, Eden moved towards the young woman, crouching in front of her and taking her hand. 'It's okay, Mei, I know this is really scary. Whatever is wrong, we can help. Just take your time and breathe, then you can explain what's been happening.'

Mei nodded, taking slow shuddery breaths to try and regain control of her emotions. When she finally seemed ready, Eden asked her a question.

'Do you think you're okay to try and tell me what's been going on?'

'Yes.' Mei's voice was so quiet that Eden had to strain to hear it, and she gave her patient what she hoped was a reassuring smile.

'Okay, take your time, there's no hurry.' As Eden moved back to her seat, Mei started to speak. Her voice was still so quiet that if Eden had begun to make notes on the computer, the sound of her tapping on the keyboard would have drowned Mei's voice out.

'I've had pins and needles and numbness, and it's getting worse. It started in my hands and I thought it was because of my playing.'

'Playing?' Eden gave her a questioning look, all kinds of possibilities racing through her mind. If Mei was about to tell her that she made her living as an international poker player, it would qualify as one of the biggest surprises Eden had experienced working in A&E, and she'd seen a lot of very shocking things in her career.

'I'm a violinist and I've been studying and working in London. There aren't many opportunities to take master classes, or audition for orchestras in Cornwall, so moving there was the obvious solution.' For the first time Mei smiled. 'I love being back home and seeing my family, but I need to be in London if I've got any chance of having a career as a violinist. I was sure I was just overdoing it; I'd been playing so much and practising whenever I got the opportunity. I thought if I came home for a few weeks and rested, the pins and needles in my hands would go away, but if anything it's got worse and it's in my feet now too. I looked on Google and there were so many scary things it said it might be. I'm not registered with a GP down here any more and I didn't know where else to go.'

Mei looked close to tears again, and Eden kept her tone deliberately upbeat. 'You've done the right thing coming in, but there are lots of reasons for pins and needles and the vast majority of them aren't serious. I'm going to ask a few more questions. Try not to worry too much, although I know that's hard.'

'Okay.' Mei was biting her lip, clearly still terrified, but Eden needed to get as much information as possible to try and work out whether this was likely to be something as simple as a trapped nerve, or a far more complex condition. It wasn't her job to diagnose, but getting as much information as possible during the assessment would help ensure Mei saw the right specialist as soon as possible. Whatever was wrong wasn't immediately life threatening, and Eden wanted to give her colleagues as much detail as she possibly could.

'I need you to push your sleeve up please, Mei, and rest your arm on the desk, with your palm facing up to the ceiling, then close your eyes and tell me when you can feel me touching your arm.'

Mei did as she'd been instructed and Eden had to press harder than she would have expected before Mei responded.

'I can feel that, but only lightly.'

'Okay, you can open your eyes now. I just want to see what your balance is like when you're standing.'

Mei stood up.

'Great.' Eden was still conscious of the need to sound upbeat and hopeful. She didn't know what this was, but she knew that Mei was scared. Eden might not be qualified to treat whatever condition her patient was ultimately diagnosed with, but she could do her best to comfort and reassure her in the meantime. 'Okay, Mei, if you can try just standing on one leg for me.'

'Oh!' Mei reached out and grabbed the side of the desk to steady herself, as she lurched to one side. When she sat down again she knotted her hands together, almost as if she was praying.

'I can see it's affecting your balance. I'm going to speak to one of the doctors now and let them know what we've discussed, so they can work out what other tests you might need to help us get to the bottom of this.'

'It's motor neurone disease, isn't it?' Before the words were even out of Mei's mouth she was crying again, tears rolling down her face this time.

'Oh, sweetheart.' Eden was ignoring hospital protocols again. She didn't care what they said about using terms of endearment. Sometimes people needed to feel like they were more than just a patient, to believe that the staff looking after them cared on a deeper level. Using terms like that, with the right patients in the right situations really could help, Eden was certain of it. 'I know it must be terrifying not being sure what this is, but when you look your symptoms up online it's always the most serious ones that show up in the search. This could be so many things and the vast majority of them aren't anywhere near as serious as motor neurone disease.'

'I know, but my paternal grandmother died from it last year.' Another tear rolled off Mei's face and plopped onto her trouser leg, leaving a darker stain where it had landed.

'I'm really sorry to hear that.' Eden swallowed against the bubble of concern rising in her own throat. Her first job after qualifying had been on a neurological ward, and she knew there could be a genetic link with MND, but she also knew that was only true for a relatively small number of cases. Either way, statistics couldn't comfort Mei, the only thing that would ease her fears right now was certainty, and that was something Eden couldn't give her. She wished she could promise Mei that she didn't have the same disease as her grandmother, but all she could do for now was try to give her hope.

'MND would be very rare in someone of your age, but I understand why you're so worried. I'm going to ask some of my colleagues, who know a lot more about this kind of thing than I do, to come and talk to you and organise whatever tests you might need.' Eden reached out and took Mei's hand again. The young woman's face was wet with tears, and she hated the thought of her facing whatever might be to come on her own. 'Is there someone you can call to come in and be with you? There could be a bit of a wait if you're going to be sent down for scans and you might feel better if you've got someone to talk to.'

'I didn't want to tell my parents I was coming in. Losing my grandmother hit them both so hard, if they think there's even a chance...' Mei couldn't finish the sentence, but she didn't need to. Eden knew how terrified she'd be if she thought Teddie was facing a life-threatening diagnosis, but there was something else she knew too.

'If you were my child, I'd want to be there, no matter what.' She was probably overstepping the mark again, but she couldn't help it.

Mei nodded slowly. 'Can I use my mobile phone in here?'

'Of course you can.' Eden released her hand. 'I'm going to speak to one of the doctors, if you want to make the call while I'm gone. Then I'll be straight back to let you know what's happening.'

'Thank you.' Mei gave her a watery smile. 'You've been so kind.'

'I won't be long.' Eden needed to leave before the words she was so desperate to say came out of her mouth. She wanted to tell Mei it was all going to be okay, but she couldn't know that for sure and lying to her patient was one protocol she definitely didn't want to break.

* * *

Eden hadn't been able to get Mei off her mind for the rest of the shift. Her mother, Xiang, had arrived within half an hour of her daughter's call, and by then one of the team from neurology was already with her, outlining the series of tests she would need to determine what was causing her issues. It wasn't going to be a quick diagnosis and not even a consultant neurologist could promise Mei straight away that she didn't have the same disease that had killed her grandmother. There'd be MRI scans, blood tests, and possibly a lumbar puncture before they'd have the answers. It was going to be a scary wait for the outcome, and Eden was just glad Mei had her mother by her side. For a good chunk of her life, Eden hadn't had that kind of support. Karen's alcoholism wasn't something she could ever have imagined when she was a small child. Karen had been a doting mother, until the loss of both of her own parents in quick succession had seen her turn to alcohol in an attempt to numb her grief. It had quickly escalated into an addiction that had seen Eden's mother putting her own life, and the lives of her children at risk. Vodka had been her go-to drink, because it was the easiest to disguise, but if she was desperate she'd drink almost anything. Eden's father had enabled it by covering up for Karen even after she'd crashed the car with both children as passengers. Despite the fact that she was still a child, it had felt as if she and Felix were the only ones who could rescue their mother from what would almost certainly kill her in the end. It shouldn't have been their responsibility – it *wasn't* their responsibility – but it had still fallen to them to seek out the help that had eventually put their mother on the path to recovery. When Eden was sixteen and Felix was eighteen, and finally confident that they wouldn't be taken into care, they'd gone to their mother's GP together to report their concerns, and a referral had been made to a social worker. It had still taken another seven years of attempts by Karen to quit drinking, followed by relapses back into her addiction, before she'd eventually stopped for good.

Thankfully Mei seemed to have a far more conventional relationship with her mother and she'd seemed a lot calmer by the time Eden had last seen her. It had been a tough shift all the same, and when Meg had said she'd ordered in end-of-shift doughnuts to be delivered from *Americana*, Eden hadn't needed a lot of persuading to join the others in the staff room. Her parents had taken Teddie swimming again, so there was nothing to rush home for.

'I can't believe you've barely got back from being off for ages with your broken ankle, and now we've got your going-away party next Saturday.' Isla was pretending to berate Amy, as Eden walked into the staff room, just ahead of Eve. Meg was already there too.

'Remind me who it was that disappeared to Australia and New Zealand for months on end, not caring about leaving the rest of us behind in the emergency department?' Amy wagged a finger at her best friend. 'Anyway, it's not a farewell party, it's bon voyage. I'll be back.'

'Oh of course you will,' Eden interjected. 'I mean who wouldn't want to leave behind a rock and roll lifestyle to deal with belligerent binge drinkers in A&E on a Saturday night.'

'Eden's right.' Eve nodded. 'If something's going to get thrown when you're in the vicinity, surely you'd much rather it was underwear being flung at the stage, than a chair being chucked at your head?'

'The size of my knickers, it could be a close-run thing.' Amy grinned, before putting on her best schoolteacher voice. 'And surely Dr Bellingham, Nurse Grainger, you're not suggesting there's a life preferable to one in A&E.'

'Of course not.' Eve shook her head, an expression of mock outrage on her face. 'What could possibly be better than cleaning up vomit and dealing with people who think they're entitled to behave however they like.'

'You do know what a rock star lifestyle looks like, don't you?' Meg pulled back the lid on the box of doughnuts. 'I think there's plenty of entitled behaviour and intoxication involved. You might not get drunks trying to throw chairs, but you could see a TV or two hurled out of the window. All rock stars are divas.'

'Not Lijah.' Amy and Isla said the same words at the same time, making them both laugh.

'Okay, I'll grant you that, from what I've seen at least.' Meg shrugged, as Esther and Zahir came into the staff room together. It was almost a full house. It was nice to see Meg and Eve opening up a bit more and joining in with the kind of joking around that got the team through the day. Eden was starting to feel much more at home too. A&E staff tended to bond quickly, and the three of them had all joined in fairly quick succession, but it was only just starting to feel as if their personalities were coming to the fore. She still didn't know that much about Eve or Meg's lives before they started at St Piran's, but she guessed they had their reasons for holding back. She understood that and there were definitely parts of her own story she was happy to keep to herself. For a moment her thoughts turned to Drew, as they often did, and the realisation hit her that he was the only person at St Piran's who knew her whole story.

Eden was still putting on a bit of a front with her colleagues, because deep down she wasn't the same happy-go-lucky version of herself she'd have been ten years before. Life had a way of changing people, not always for the better. Despite what she'd been through with her parents, she'd still been an optimist before Jesse had come into her life. He'd been the one to take that away and she was determined to get it back. In the meantime, she was going to fake it until she made it, even if that meant hiding a part of herself from most of the people around her. Just being able to have a chat and a laugh in the staffroom made her feel more like her old self.

'Okay, even if it really is just bon voyage and not farewell, we have to do something to mark the occasion. The question is what?' Isla passed Amy a doughnut from the box as she spoke.

'Oh, we're still having a party. I'm not going to see any of you guys for two or three months at least, and I never had a leaving party when I switched from permanent staff to agency, because I was still on sick leave. I think that gives us more than enough of an excuse to have a get-together. I don't think we've had one since Gary and Wendy's wedding.'

'Did I hear my name mentioned?' Gary, another of the A&E nurses, who was in his early fifties, pushed open the door of the staffroom at that precise moment. 'Or was it just that the doughnuts were calling to me.'

'Both.' Eden smiled. 'Amy was just outlining what's going to happen at her leaving do… sorry, I mean her I'm-off-but-I'll-be-back party.'

'Will there be doughnuts from *Americana*? If so, I'm in, regardless of the rest of the plans.' Gary licked his lips, as he pulled a chocolate glazed doughnut from the box.

'There'll definitely be doughnuts, and plenty of other food. Plus music and drinks, partners are welcome too. The more the merrier.'

'Are you going to bring Felix, Eden?' Eve was clearly attempting to sound like she wasn't bothered either way, but Eden had seen the way she'd looked at Felix on the day she'd introduced them. She was used to people noticing her brother, it happened all the time, but before she could even answer Meg responded for her.

'Of course Eden isn't bringing her brother, she'll be bringing her mysterious Scot instead. That's if he's allowed out of the underbelly of the hospital.'

'Now you've got me intrigued.' Gary obviously meant what he'd said, because he'd even put down his doughnut.

'Meg's just letting her imagination run away with her.' Eden shrugged. 'She's talking about Drew, one of the pathologists. He's been giving me some advice about Teddie, that's all. He's got family experience of autism, so it's been helpful.'

'Well, romance or no romance, you're welcome to bring him and your brother along with you. The question is, should we have a barbecue or get a food truck in, or both?' Amy smiled and Eden's shoulders relaxed. She was grateful to her for changing the subject, because she really didn't want to get into a conversation about whether she might be interested in Drew *like that*. Conversations of that sort naturally led to questions about past relationships, which was a subject she definitely didn't want to get into. It was pointless talking to them about Drew anyway, he wouldn't want to go to the party with her even if she invited him. She was sure of it, from the things they'd talked about and the difficulty he'd admitted having in certain social situations. What she didn't want to admit to herself, let alone to her friends, was that she'd have loved to ask him along, if she hadn't already known what the answer would be.

9

Drew often left work later than planned. He barely noticed the passing of time when he was engrossed in something. He might realise he was due to finish if Saskia headed off at the end of the day, but often, after that, Drew would start writing up notes from a postmortem. Sometimes hours passed before he looked at his watch again. He worked hundreds of hours of unpaid overtime like that, but he didn't care. There was no one waiting at home for him. Only Marmalade, his ginger Persian cat, who frankly couldn't care less whether or not Drew was in, as long as there was food left out for him. Today, though, Drew would be leaving the hospital two hours early, having for once in his life taken some time off in lieu of additional hours worked, but he needed to pop into the shop on the way out.

'Extra wine gums mid-afternoon?' Gwen furrowed her brow at the sight of him. 'It feels like Armageddon might be coming.'

'You might be even more worried when you discover I'm not here for wine gums.'

'I must be having a dream.' Gwen pretended to pinch herself, in an over-exaggerated way. 'Just don't tell me you're here for something frivolous and flighty like Skittles, or Starbursts.'

'I'm after something suitable for a child. I was thinking about a Freddo or a Curly Wurly.' They were sweets Drew could remember from his own child-hood and he couldn't imagine Teddie not liking them. He and Eden had met up five times now, and it had quickly become obvious that Teddie was a bit of a chocoholic. Eden had confided that she'd been worried about her son's diet before his diagnosis, because he was only willing to eat a very narrow range of foods. She'd said the paediatrician had reassured her that Teddie was getting the nutrients he needed from the food he was eating, and the dietician had explained it was the textures of many other foods that Teddie couldn't cope with. Fruit and vegetables could be inconsistent. The texture of a banana on one day, at one level of ripeness, could be very different to the next. Teddie's autism meant he found that kind of unpredictability difficult. Eden had smiled when she'd been explaining it to Drew, holding up one of the fun-size bars of milk chocolate that she seemed to have a limitless supply of.

'It seems chocolate can be relied upon, it never lets Teddie down. It never lets me down either when I come to think of it. I can't tell you how many difficult days Dairy Milk has got me through. There's no situation it can't make better.' She'd wrinkled her nose. 'Oh God, I'm giving myself away, aren't I? I could at least be classier and go for Green & Black's.'

'I've got a friend from uni days, Matt. He has autism too.' Drew had found himself opening up to Eden once again, still amazed at how much personal information he was willing to share with her. 'For years he'd only eat Bournville chocolate, or Wotsits. His mother was always insistent that on Christmas Day he had to sit with the rest of the family. She'd put a bar of chocolate on Matt's plate and he'd sit and eat it with a knife and fork.'

'At least she didn't make him have gravy on it.' Eden had laughed then, the sound of it making him smile too. He really enjoyed her company, and if he'd had to bet on it, he'd have said she felt the same way. He'd grown very fond of Teddie in a short amount of time too, and those feelings were definitely reciprocated. The little boy would often put his arms out towards Drew, which was no small thing for a child with autism, and it felt like they were kindred spirits in a way that he wouldn't have been able to put into words.

'The packets of giant chocolate buttons are always a safe bet for children.' Gwen's voice broke into his thoughts. 'And Eden will be able to ration them more easily, if she doesn't want Teddie to have them all in one go.'

'How do you know the chocolate's for Teddie?' It was all Drew could do not to let his mouth drop open. He had no idea how Gwen had guessed who the chocolate was for, and even less idea how he felt about her doing so.

'Because I've got ears like a bat, eyes in the back of my head, and a nose like

Pinocchio's, according to my husband.' Gwen laughed. 'If there's something going on in this hospital, I know about it.'

'I can well believe it.' Drew suspected it would be impossible to keep a secret from Gwen, so what she said next surprised him.

'There is one thing that's a real mystery to me, though.'

'Is there?'

'Yes, and I'm going to tell you what it is, even though you didn't ask me.' Gwen gave him a level look. 'What puzzles me is why you don't ask Eden if she'd like to go out with you.'

Drew furrowed his brow. 'We have been out together. Five times.'

'I mean without Teddie. It's obvious you like her, and that she feels the same.'

'I don't think she likes me like that. We're friends.' The final part of his statement took him by surprise too, but he realised it was the truth. They had become friends. Drew had looked up the meaning of friendship when he was much younger, at a time when he was finding it difficult to form lasting relationships at school. He'd known there must be a logical answer, and that researching more about friendship was the best way to find a solution to the problem. In the end the definition had been far more straightforward than the solution, which had taken a lot of trial and error to come to. The dictionary he'd consulted had described friendship as 'an attachment between people based on personal regard'. He had high regard for Eden, and she seemed to value the insight he'd been able to offer her into Teddie's autism. So by that definition alone they were friends. There was more to it than that, though; it was a feeling he wasn't sure it was possible to quantify. He couldn't have put his bond with Teddie into words either, let alone have looked up a definition for either of those things in the dictionary.

'The best relationships are based on friendship and I'm willing to bet if you ask her out, she'll say yes.'

Apprehension fluttered in his chest at the thought of risking his friendship with Eden, because of how much it meant to him. But an even bigger part of Drew still wanted to take the chance. The easiest way to cope with that was to focus on the bet that Gwen was offering, rather than everything he had to lose. 'What's the wager?'

'If she says no, I'll pay for your wine gums for the next year.'

'And what will I have to give you if she says yes?'

'A front row seat for the wedding.' Gwen dropped the perfect wink, and much to Drew's surprise once again, he found himself nodding, but then something hit him.

'I think what I might really need is a penalty to pay, if I lose my nerve before I ask her.'

'You have to come to my belly dancing class. Only once, but joining in will be compulsory.'

Drew looked at her for a long moment, picturing just how awful it would be to have to go through with a forfeit like that, but then he surprised himself for a third time. 'Okay, you've got a bet.'

Gwen reached out and shook his hand. 'We have indeed and no welching on it, Drew, because I'll find out if you do.'

'I know you will.' Drew picked up two packets of the chocolate buttons Gwen had recommended, and two bars of Dairy Milk. However Eden responded when he finally got up the nerve to ask her out, he didn't want to lose her friendship. She'd said chocolate could make any difficult situation better, and he might just need all the help he could get.

* * *

The Spotted Pig may have sounded like the kind of gastro pub Drew might have suggested taking Eden to, if they'd gone out on their own, but it was actually a newly opened children's farm a few miles inland from Port Kara. Drew had suggested they take Teddie there because the pathways around the farm had been specially designed to facilitate wheelchair access. He'd seen how Eden had struggled with Teddie's buggy sometimes and, although the little boy could be a runner when the mood struck him, most of the time he didn't want to walk far. The farm was open until 7 p.m. in the summer months, so they'd decided to head over for a couple of hours after work.

'It's so lovely to be out in the sunshine.' Eden smiled at Drew as they stopped by one of the paddocks where a fat little Shetland pony, who was almost as wide as it was tall, was scratching its bottom against a fence post. The view beyond the field looked out on to open farmland with just a glimpse of turquoise-coloured sea in the distance. It was a beautiful day and it felt a world away from how Drew spent his days at work. He'd never have come somewhere like this without Eden and Teddie, but she was right, it was good to be outside and feel the sun on his skin.

'My mother used to take me to the farm up the road to see the animals. She'd been at school with the farmer, and he never minded us roaming about on his land.' When Drew thought about the times his mother had been happiest, after Flora's death, it was always on days like that – trips out where it had just been the two of them. He didn't remember ever hearing his father make his mother laugh and there was something very wrong about that. 'I don't think there were places like this when I was a child.'

'What, in the olden days?' Eden grinned and he raised his eyebrows, smiling too.

'And the seven years between us makes all the difference I suppose?'

'How do you know how old I am?' She narrowed her eyes for a moment, as if him knowing that kind of information made her uneasy for some reason, and he wished he hadn't said it. It made him feel as if any kind of exchange between them that didn't centre around Teddie was off limits, but surely that couldn't be true. They'd shared a lot about their lives during their meet ups, and yet suddenly it felt as though the rules might be changing. Drew was almost tempted to ask Eden if she could define the rules for him, because it would make him more comfortable, except he knew he wasn't supposed to ask questions like that. He was supposed to just be able to pick up on the trajectory of a conversation, or the dynamics of a relationship, without having them spelt out to him. The trouble was, autism didn't work like that, at least not for Drew.

'You said that your thirtieth birthday was possibly the saddest milestone birthday anyone has ever had.' Drew shrugged. 'And that at least your mum had bought you a cake for your next birthday, now that you're home again.'

'I'd forgotten I'd told you that. It's just I wondered if...' Eden shook her head, seeming to answer her own question before she'd even asked it. 'It doesn't matter; I'm being silly.'

'You thought I'd been looking you up on the hospital system?' Drew could see in her eyes that he was right. Eden told him that she didn't have social media accounts because of Jesse. She'd said her ex could find her if he really wanted to, but that she didn't want to give him any motivation to try. If she was out of sight, she might be out of mind. It was obvious how worried she was about what might happen if Jesse did decide to find her, and that she might not be able to stop him from seeing Teddie. After all, he hadn't committed any crimes as far as social services were concerned. She'd told Drew there was a chance she might be able to make a case for coercive control, but it would be hard to prove and there was no way of knowing what a court would decide. Drew could understand why that made social media feel like an unnecessary risk, which could give Jesse access to the life Eden was living now, so she knew he wouldn't have been able to look up the details of her age that way. He tried not to feel hurt that she'd assumed the worst of him, looking up private information about her in the hospital's online records. He understood how hard it was for her to trust anyone and he had to accept that sometimes she might doubt him too.

'I'm sorry.' Eden cast her eyes down towards the floor for a moment before looking up again, giving him a half smile. 'I forget just how much stuff I've told you. Like I said before, I seem to have found myself an unpaid therapist, whether you like it or not.'

'I like it.' He wasn't sure whether it was a good idea to admit that, but seeing as he had no idea what the rules of their interactions were supposed to be, all he could do was fall back on what felt safest and tell the truth.

'I'm glad, because I like it too.'

It was almost as if Drew could feel Gwen standing next to him, whispering in his ear that now was exactly the right moment to ask Eden if she'd like to go out with him some time, just the two of them, but he couldn't seem to get his mouth to form the words. In the end, it was Eden who broke the silence.

'Apparently there are some newborn calves in the barn. Maybe we could take Teddie over to have a look at them?'

'Actually that's why I suggested coming here.' Drew was still second-guessing the boundaries of their conversation, but she'd asked for any insight he might be able to give her about growing up with autism, and what he was about to say fell into that category. 'My speech wasn't delayed in the same way Teddie's is, but for a long time I found it difficult to get people to understand what I was saying. Sounds were easier to connect with than words, I liked the repetition of them. There was this book my mother read me, about monkeys. I must have only been about four or five, and she asked me what sound a monkey made. I can still remember the feel of the ooh ooh ooh sound and I couldn't seem to stop doing it. I don't know if it was because of how it made me feel, or the fact that my mother understood the sound I was making so much more easily than she did some of my words when I spoke. I just wondered if it might help Teddie too. Focusing on making sounds that mean something, like the noise that cows make, might work better than trying to push him towards saying actual words... Sorry, no, push is the wrong word, I wasn't saying that's what you're doing.'

Drew was tying himself up in knots and he was beginning to wish he hadn't said anything at all, but then Eden put a hand on his arm. 'It's okay, I know exactly what you mean. I want him to speak, of course I do, and I can see how frustrated it makes him not being able to tell me what he needs. Right now him speaking seems impossible, but I can see how him being able to repeat the sound an animal makes in response to a question could be a bridge between understanding and language. And I think you might be a genius.'

Drew couldn't help smiling at Eden's words. He was still getting used to someone having that much of an effect on him. He might not have received much praise from his parents, but he'd had plenty about his work over the years. This was different though, this was personal, and it meant far more when it came from Eden than from anyone else. Even so, he couldn't just accept the compliment and say thanks, it would have made him feel far too awkward. So he made light of it to take the focus off himself, the way he always did. 'I'd like to pretend this is a new breakthrough that's all my idea, and that I'm some kind of expert on the best methods of communication, but there's a reason I chose to work with patients who are already dead.'

For a moment they just looked at each other and then they both started to laugh, harder than Drew could remember laughing in a very long time. He could have been disappointed that he hadn't found a way to take Gwen's advice and ask Eden out, but he decided to focus on the positives instead and feel grateful for having spent the afternoon with her and Teddie. It felt amazing to have met someone who still seemed to like him, even when he was being wholly and unapologetically himself.

* * *

'I need some one-on-one bonding time with Teddie before I go back to the States to pack stuff up and tie up the final loose ends.' Felix came into the kitchen where Eden was stacking the dishwasher. They'd had dinner together, just the two of them. Their parents were out with friends at a restaurant in Padstow, and Teddie was already in bed.

'I'm sure Teddie would like some one-on-one time with his uncle too. When were you thinking of?'

'Saturday afternoon and into the evening.' Felix gave her a knowing look. 'A little birdy tells me you've been invited to a party, but you're not going because with Mum and Dad away with their golfing buddies, you've got no one to look after Teddie.'

'Who told you that?' She'd have bet her money on Gwen passing that information on to their mother, when they were at book club together, and it getting back to Felix that way, but he clearly wasn't giving up his source.

'It doesn't matter who I heard it from, what matters is that you should be going. You told me you wanted to make a life for yourself back here, for you and for Teddie, and that you want to make new friends. What better way is there to turn colleagues into friends than socialising together?'

'In my experience it can go the other way.' She wrinkled her nose, hoping it might be enough to make Felix back off, but he knew her too well.

'Yes, but you won't know until you try.'

'I suppose I could go to the party, although the idea would have been much more appealing if I could have taken you with me. Amy said I could bring you along and I hate going to things like that on my own.' Eden wasn't just making excuses any more. The idea of trying to force her way into conversation between groups of existing friends did make her cringe, but standing on her own with a drink in hand wasn't exactly appealing either. A big part of her knew it wouldn't be like that, because of how friendly the team were, and the fact that Meg and Eve were fairly new too, but she still didn't like the idea of going alone.

'So don't go on your own. Take Drew with you.'

'I can't do that.' She was shaking her head so hard it hurt. Felix could read her like a book and if she gave any indication of how much her feelings for Drew had grown, he'd pounce on that and tell her that she needed to follow her heart. She hadn't meant to let Drew get under her skin as much as he had, because she'd had no intention whatsoever of developing feelings for someone, but she hadn't been able to help it. Watching him with Teddie had made it inevitable. The bond between them, and her little boy's total trust in Drew, was enough to convince her that she could trust her instincts about him.

When he'd taken Teddie to see the cows, with the hope that repeating the mooing sound might help her son's language development, he'd shown Eden just how well he understood Teddie and how much he wanted to be a part of making a difference to his life. He had insights and ways of connecting with Teddie that she didn't possess. It wasn't that it superseded her bond with her son in any way, that was unique and incredibly special in its own right. It was more like they were part of a team, each with their own strengths, and both of them able to enrich Teddie's life more together than they could alone. All of those things deepened the feelings she had for Drew even further. Eden loved having him as a part of both of their lives, and she could no longer pretend that she didn't want him to play an even bigger role. But the self-doubt that Jesse had fostered in her was still there in so many senses. She might be able to trust her gut about Drew being a good guy, but she still couldn't rely of her instincts when it came to interpreting how he felt about her. She knew her brother wouldn't see it that way, though, even before he answered.

'I don't see why not, if you've been told you can take a plus one.'

'I didn't say I *couldn't* take him with me, but I'd have to ask him first. That's the part I can't do. I'd be mortified if he said no.' Eden shook her head again. She couldn't risk it; she didn't want to lose Drew's friendship or his support, and she didn't want Teddie to lose the bond he'd built with him either. It wasn't worth it, not just so she'd have company to a party she knew would be Drew's idea of hell anyway.

'Yes, you can ask him, because you, my darling little sister, can do anything you put your mind to. You got yourself and Teddie out of an abusive relationship, and before that you carried on working and kept a roof over your heads through all the years of hell Jesse put you through. Asking Drew out is nothing in comparison and, from what I've heard, he's far too nice a guy to make a big thing out of it even if he decides it's not something he wants to do.'

'I don't think it's his kind of thing.'

'But what if it is? I can tell you like him and don't even try to tell me I've got that wrong, because I know you far too well.' Felix didn't break eye contact. 'Just ask him, Eddie, I think you'll be glad you did. But, if it all goes horribly wrong, I promise to be the one who takes Mum out for her next three Mother's Day lunches, on my own if necessary, without a single complaint.'

'How can I turn down a deal like that?' Laughing, Eden shook her head.

She knew Felix wouldn't give up until she'd at least agreed to try, and maybe he was right, she might just end up being glad that she did.

10

When Eden spotted Ali, one of their regular patients in A&E, just before the start of a late shift, her heart sank. She'd been on a high at the end of her previous shift, after a visit from Mei's mother, Xiang, who had brought in a card and a huge box of chocolates to thank Eden for the care she'd given her daughter and to let her know that Mei had been diagnosed with Guillain-Barré Syndrome. Although it could be an extremely serious condition, Mei's symptoms had been relatively mild and she was already showing positive signs of progress, with the neurologists confident that she'd eventually make a full recovery.

Seeing Xiang and hearing Mei's news had been a lovely reminder that sometimes everything worked out okay, and that the A&E team were often able to help patients take the first steps towards completely recovering. She'd probably never see Mei again and for the young woman's sake, she hoped that was true, but every emergency department had patients they knew by name, because of how regularly they used the service. Sometimes it was because of genuine medical issues that necessitated recurrent admissions to hospital, but more often than not it was because of social problems or mental health issues. The very worst kind of patients, though, were the ones who fell into the entitled category. The type who'd go to A&E because they couldn't get a GP appointment for a minor complaint. Eden had seen them all, from patients with tiny splinters, to one who was too afraid to remove a plaster because of the pain and wanted someone to do it for her. The key to surviving the difficult days in her job was being able to talk to the people who really understood it: her colleagues. Back before she'd met Jesse, it had been normal for her to go to the pub with them after work, to debrief on the day. Sometimes there'd be laughter and sometimes there'd be tears, but those times at the end of a shift were where colleagues could become friends, and it was something Eden wanted to have again.

When she'd lived with Jesse, he'd done his best to isolate her from not just her friends but her family too. He'd tell her he couldn't cope without her if she went to visit family, and his jealousy, paranoia and almost total reliance on Eden had made it difficult to maintain friendships. She'd lost touch with her old friends from Port Kara, and many of them had moved away in the time she'd lived in London. The new friends she'd made down there had slowly been driven away too, Jesse had made sure of it, and there'd been no more going out to the pub at the end of a shift. The only person Eden had remained close to was one of the paramedics, Paul. He'd entertain Jesse with stories about some of the patients they'd picked up. One of the most ridiculous had been a woman who'd lost her bracelet and had phoned the ambulance and told the call centre operator she couldn't breathe. When Paul and his crew mate arrived, it had turned out she was stressed because of the lost bracelet and wanted someone to help her find it. Thankfully that kind of thing was the exception. The backgrounds of most of the regular patients were quite sad, people who were so lonely and desperate that calling an ambulance felt like their only chance of human connection. Towards the end of her relationship with Jesse, Eden could see how that might happen to people. If he'd had his way he'd have driven everyone else away. He'd flown into a rage when she'd mentioned one of her conversations with Paul, in the hope that sharing an anecdote might raise a smile, in the midst of yet another one of his moods. She should have known better.

'I bet you'd rather be with Paul, wouldn't you? I bet you're already shagging him every chance you get.' Jesse's face had been just inches from hers, spittle flying out of his mouth as he screamed the accusation. She should have walked out then, just as she should have done a thousand times before, but even as she told him she couldn't take this any more and that they couldn't carry on like this, she knew what was coming. It had been scarily predictable, and yet it had held so much power over her.

'I might as well kill myself. There's no point to me being here if I'm not with you. I just hope you can live with it. Normal girlfriends don't behave like you do and hang out with other men. It's no wonder I'm so depressed. I'm going to end it this time and it's you who's driven me to it.' The gaslighting had come as naturally to Jesse as breathing in and out, and he'd started acting as if he was going to carry out his threat, the same way he aways did. Grabbing packets of painkillers from the bathroom cabinet and even holding a knife against his skin on the inside of his wrist. He never went through with it, but she had no way of knowing if that was because she always stayed. If she left him and he ended his life it would be her fault, he made sure she was in no doubt of that. The only person at work she'd confided in was Paul, but she'd been careful never to mention his name to Jesse again. Ironically Paul had been the only person, apart from Felix, who'd been able to help her see that she needed to put herself first in the end.

'I lived a lie for years, Eden. Tried to make my marriage work with Jane, even though all I was doing was making us both miserable. I felt terrible leaving and coming out, and I'm not going to say it wasn't painful for both of us, but she's remarried now too we're all much happier now. You only get one life and you can't live it for anyone else.' Paul's words had hit home. Eden giving up her life for Jesse wasn't making him happy, he seemed incapable of even feeling that emotion, and it certainly wasn't making her happy. She desperately wanted to leave, but even after Paul's sage advice, she couldn't seem to take the final step. It was only when Jesse began losing patience with Teddie that something in Eden snapped.

'The little shit bit me.' Jesse had taken their son by the shoulders and shaken him. It wasn't the first time Jesse had shown a flash of anger towards Teddie, but it was the first – and last – time he'd ever been physical. Eden had called Felix in floods of tears and he'd told her that he was getting on the earliest flight back home and that she needed to do whatever it took to get herself and Teddie to safety in the meantime. She'd left the same day, heading straight to Paul's house, not caring in that moment what happened to Jesse, as long as Teddie was safe. Her love for her son eclipsed the guilt she felt about leaving his father, and she didn't look back. Paul and his husband, Alastair, would have let them stay indefinitely, but Eden knew she needed to get far away from Jesse, and go home to Cornwall. She'd called her parents and her father had driven straight to get her. Felix had tried to insist that he would still fly over, but she'd told him that everything was okay and she was going back to Port Kara for good. In the end it had been that simple and, looking back, it seemed like the woman who'd stayed with Jesse for all those years had been someone else. She'd thought she could save him, but the only person capable of doing that had been Jesse. She still worried about what he might be doing, and who else he might be drawing into his twisted world, but he wasn't her problem any more. He couldn't be, because Teddie needed her more than he ever had.

It had been more than nine months since she'd come home and Jesse hadn't come to find her or even attempted to contact her parents. In the beginning, she'd been sure it was just a matter of time before he turned up and, when he didn't, guilt and doubt had started to creep in. What if he'd followed through on his threat and it hadn't all just been a way of guilt tripping her into staying? She didn't want to initiate contact with either Jesse or Sadie, so she'd emailed her old landlord, who'd confirmed that Jesse was still living at the flat. He was alive, she knew that much, and that was enough to know she'd made the right decision. Teddie had been the one to save her and he was still showing her the way even now. Eden knew how lucky she was to have the support of her family, especially given the distance that had grown between them during her time with Jesse. Not everyone was that lucky.

Seeing Ali now, waiting in A&E, she was reminded of some of the conversations she'd had with Paul about how sad and lonely some people's lives were. Ali deliberately neglected his injuries to get treatment and medication, because that seemed like a better option than being ignored, or fully aware of the world around him, without the edge somehow being taken off. It broke Eden's heart that he felt that way.

'Hi Ali, are you okay?' Her shift wasn't due to start for another twenty minutes, so she had time to chat to him. Maybe she could brief whoever was triaging patients and give them a bit of background. She really liked Ali, he wasn't a bad person, just a very damaged one.

'Hi Eden.' A smile lit up his face as he spoke, and he looked different somehow. His hygiene was undoubtedly better than it had often been in the past, and his clothes were cleaner too, but there was something else she couldn't put her finger on, a look in his eyes she couldn't quite define. 'Actually, I'm doing okay.'

'I can see that.' She returned his smile, still trying to figure out why he looked so different. 'So why are you here?'

'I was hoping to see you.' Ali was still smiling.

'For medical reasons?' Eden suddenly felt wary. Her desire to want to fix people's problems for them had cost her so much in the past, and she'd actively fought against slipping back into that pattern since finally breaking away from Jesse. Despite that, it was only ever just below the surface, and she knew others could see it in her too. She liked Ali, she really did, but she couldn't allow herself to be sucked into anything outside of her role.

'I wanted to say sorry. For wasting so much of your time. I wasn't looking after myself and because of that I was taking up time and resources that could have been used on other people. But you were always so kind, so I wanted to say thank you too.'

Eden was taken aback; apologies and a thank you were the last things she'd been expecting. 'I was just doing my job, Ali.'

'No, you weren't.' He shook his head. 'You went above and beyond every time, and I'm not saying I won't ever be back here, asking you to do that again, but right now I'm doing better than I have been in a long time. I'm trying to make a permanent change and part of that is accepting that I've behaved badly in the past and making amends. It's early days, but you're one of the first people I want to thank and say sorry to.'

'Oh Ali, you don't need to thank me, or apologise, I'm just so happy you're trying to get better.' She wanted to reach out and take hold of his hand, but she knew she had to maintain the boundary between them. 'Can I ask you what's changed?'

'I got a place at Domusamare, the charity you told me about.' Ali pressed his hands together, as if in prayer. 'I can't thank you enough. They gave me a bed in one of their hostels, and I'm being mentored by a member of the volunteer team. He goes with me to some of my support group meetings. He virtually had to carry me to the first couple, and I can call him if I need someone in between times. Because of you, my mentor, and the rest of the team at the charity, I feel like I might actually have a chance this time.'

Eden's eye's pricked with tears. There were so many days in her job where it felt like she was just trying to hold back the tide and that she couldn't really change anything for her patients, especially those with social and emotional problems. It made her so happy to hear him sounding optimistic and actually looking forward to the future, and he deserved credit for his own role in making that possible. 'It's because of you too, Ali, you're doing far more for yourself than I could ever have done. I'm so pleased you've got a mentor to call on and to be there for you, no one can get by without someone they can rely on.' Ali had never had that before, she knew that from some of the things he'd told her and it was exactly what he needed. This was such incredible news and Eden had to curl her fist into a ball to stop herself from reaching out to him.

'Yeah, I'm really lucky and Drew's amazing. Actually you might know him, he works here as a pathologist, I think.' Ali laughed, as Eden's eyebrows shot up in surprise. 'Sorry, that's probably a really stupid thing to say in a place as big as this, but you should try and get to know him if you don't already. I wasn't sure about him at first, he's quiet and he seemed really serious, but he's calm and incredibly kind, like you, and he has a great sense of humour once you get to know him a bit.'

'He does sound amazing.' Eden nodded. She already knew just how true that was, and the chances of Ali describing anyone but her Drew were almost non-existent. *Her Drew*. They were just two little words, but they said a lot and they scared the hell out of Eden, because he wasn't hers and she didn't want to find herself wishing he was, but that's exactly what was starting to happen. She'd had no idea he was a mentor, but it didn't really surprise her. Despite an admission that he sometimes found it hard to read people, Drew had a way of understanding how to help them. He'd done it with her and Teddie, and she could easily imagine how much of a difference he'd made to Ali's life too.

'I'm meeting him now, actually. He's taking a couple of hours off work to drive me to an appointment with a dentist to see whether there's anything they can do about these awful gnashers.' Ali grinned, showing off a smile that had more gaps than teeth. 'Who knows, if I end up with a set of Turkey teeth, someone might even give me a job eventually.'

'I won't recognise you next time I see you.'

'That's the plan.' He dropped her a wink and then got up to leave, hugging her tightly but so briefly that she didn't have the chance to feel uncomfortable. 'Thank you so much, Eden. You're one of the best. Don't ever forget that.'

With a raise of his hand, he was gone, disappearing out of the doors and off to meet Drew no doubt. She wanted to run after Ali and throw her arms around him, telling him how incredible he was for finding the strength to take these first steps. She wanted to tell him that Drew had helped her too, and that his assessment of the man who'd supported them both had been spot on. She could have confessed to Ali that she was developing feelings of more than friendship for Drew, it would have been a relief to tell someone, but she didn't do any of those things. Instead, she decided to be brave too. Pulling her phone out of her pocket, she tapped out a text.

> Hi Drew. I just wondered if you were free on Saturday afternoon/evening? There's a going-away party for one of the nurses in A&E, and I really don't want to go on my own.

Looking at the text before she pressed send, she deleted the part about not wanting to go on her own and retyped it.

> I know I'd enjoy it a lot more if you came with me.

Before she had a chance to overthink it, or edit the message again, she pressed send. She probably wouldn't hear from him for a while, and she needed to brace herself to expect a polite 'thanks, but no thanks' when he did respond. She'd hardly had time to put her phone back in her pocket when it pinged with a text from Drew.

> It would be really nice to spend some time with you and, yes, I'm free on Saturday.

Eden smiled to herself, a frisson of what felt a lot like excitement bubbling up inside her. As she shoved the phone back into her pocket and headed through to the department, she was already looking forward to Saturday evening far more than she had been just a few minutes earlier.

11

Felix had taken Teddie to a new trampoline park about five miles the other side of Port Tremellien. There was nothing Teddie liked better than bouncing, and he'd attempt it on any surface with even the slightest bit of give. If the springs on his grandparents' sofa hadn't collapsed by the time Eden and Teddie finally got their own place, it would be a miracle. After the trampoline park, Felix was going to take Teddie for dinner. It would inevitably involve nuggets or sausages, with chips. They could only be the right sort of chips, too thick or too crunchy and they'd be rejected with a level of force that had to be seen to be believed. If Teddie ever tried out for the Olympics, he'd have a damn good chance at qualifying for the shot put, if the effectiveness of his food-throwing technique was anything to go by.

After dinner, Felix would be bringing Teddie home, to keep to his normal bedtime routine as much as possible, and he'd stay on to babysit until either Eden or their parents got home to take over. She didn't need to worry about whether Teddie would be okay with Felix in charge, so the nerves looping in her stomach had nothing to do with leaving her son in her brother's care.

Looking in the mirror, Eden tried to decide if the outfit she was wearing was too much. It was a wide-legged, teal-coloured jump suit, which she couldn't deny brought out the colour of her eyes. The V-neck was low enough to give a hint of cleavage and make her look far less like the harassed working mother who usually stared back at her from the mirror. Almost every other time she'd met up with Drew, she'd worn jeans and a T-shirt, only once opting for a summer dress and even then it had been the loose kind that could easily have concealed another small person beneath it. The jumpsuit revealed arms which were far more toned than any workout could achieve – carrying Teddie when he was doing his paving slab impression had that effect. The outfit was perfect for a party that was going from afternoon to evening, but it wasn't the sort of thing she'd have worn for a catch up with a friend. Today was supposed to be both of those things, which was why she was still wondering if she ought to change and opt for something more casual. She didn't want to look like she was trying too hard, especially as she still wasn't sure how Drew felt about her. Deep down Eden knew she was overthinking it and that he probably wouldn't pay the slightest attention to what she was wearing. Looking at her reflection again, she gave herself a talking to.

'It's fine, it's not like I'm wearing a ball gown.' Turning away, she grabbed her bag and a denim jacket to cover up in case she became self-conscious later, and headed out of the bedroom door.

Drew was waiting outside the house for her when she emerged, a full five minutes before they were due to meet. She'd planned to hang around until he turned up and enjoy the cooler air outside, although it was unseasonably warm for an autumn afternoon, almost as if Amy had ordered the weather for her party. Eden smiled when she saw Drew. She should have known he'd be early, he wouldn't have wanted to keep her waiting even for a moment.

'You look great.' The words were out of her mouth before she could stop them, because he really did look great. Drew was wearing an olive-coloured linen shirt, over navy-blue trousers. The shirt was untucked and the sleeves casually pushed up to the elbows, giving him the look of an ever so slightly crumpled, but undeniably sexy leading man, straight out of a TV drama. Gwen was going to have plenty to say when she saw him.

'So do you.' She might have taken Drew's words as the kind of meaningless compliment that was expected in response to what she'd said to him, if he hadn't added more. 'You look beautiful, in fact.'

'Thank you.' It had been on the tip of her tongue to ask him when he'd last got his eyes tested, or to make some other self-deprecating remark, but she knew Drew was telling the truth. As far as he was concerned, she did look beautiful. If she batted away his compliment, he'd probably feel he had to repeat it, in an attempt to convince her that he meant it. An exchange like that would have left them both feeling awkward. So it was easier just to say thank you, even if she didn't think she looked anything close to beautiful.

Eden kept her arms by her sides as they walked down the hill towards the beach. If this had been an *official* date, she might have linked her arm through his, but she still wasn't even sure what it was. She'd asked him to a party and he'd said yes, that was all she knew for certain. Whatever this was, she was glad Felix had pushed her into asking Drew and she'd meant what she'd said in her text, she was looking forward to it far more than she would have been without him.

Amy was hosting the party in a new restaurant that had huge bifold doors which opened onto a boardwalk, with steps down to the beach. When the tide was out, the restaurant's guests could play games on the sand. Amy had explained her decision to have the party there when she, Isla and Eden had been having a coffee outside the hospital shop.

'It sounds fabulous.' Gwen's eyes had glittered. As the lynchpin that unofficially held the entire hospital together, it had been inevitable that she would be invited to the farewell party too and she was never going to be a wallflower. 'If this Indian summer keeps on, we might even be able to go for a swim.'

'Should I pack my swimsuit just in case?' Isla had pulled a face, clearly thinking Gwen was joking, but she should have known better.

'No need for that. Undies will work just as well if the mood takes you.'

Eden might be wearing her very best matching underwear beneath her jumpsuit, but that was just to make herself feel more confident about the way she looked, even if no one could see it. In fact, there was absolutely no way anyone would see it, because she'd rather pull her own fingernails out than strip off in front of her colleagues and run into the sea. She had a feeling Drew would be even less keen to get involved in an impromptu dip in his underwear, but it wouldn't surprise her at all if Gwen led the charge. That woman wasn't frightened of anything, or at least she didn't seem to be. Eden on the other hand was an expert at second-guessing everything and worrying about things that hadn't even happened. She'd spent so much time worrying about how today would go that she hadn't even allowed herself to imagine a scenario where it might just be lovely. Although now that she was walking side by side with Drew, it suddenly seemed like a strong possibility.

There was a question she'd been dying to ask him, but she only felt able to do it now that they were face to face. 'I saw Ali Wilson the other day when he came into the hospital. He said he knows you.'

'Ah yes, we met at… Yes, I know, Ali.' Drew clearly didn't want to break any confidences without being certain of how much Eden knew and she felt another surge of affection for him. He was such a good man and he just kept on proving it.

'I couldn't believe how much better Ali looked than the last time I saw him. The mentoring is obviously paying off, but I had no idea you volunteered with Domusamare.'

'He told you that I'm his mentor?'

'Yes, and how much difference it's made to him. With your job it must be hard to fit it all in.' She wanted to tell him how impressed she was that he made time for volunteering, but before she even got the chance he did his best to make it sound like nothing much at all.

'It's no big deal. Just a couple of hours a week face to face, but most of it's done on the phone. I work with a couple of local charities, ones that are close to my heart.' For a moment it looked as if that might be the end of the conversation, but then Drew took a deep breath. 'I started volunteering with a homelessness charity when I was still in Scotland. I got involved after someone I knew used their services and I saw what a difference they make. I wanted to work with a similar charity when I moved here and when someone told me about Domusamare, I knew it would be a good fit. I do some work with one of the local autism support charities too.'

'That's great. I still can't understand how you fit it all in.' Every time she found out something else about Drew she liked him even more than she had before. Nothing about him was a disappointment, or a red flag that made her want to back off. After what she'd been through with Jesse, that was nothing short of a miracle.

'I'm sure it won't surprise you to hear this, but I'm not exactly a party animal, which means when I'm not working, I have more free time than anyone probably ought to.'

'Oh no and there I was counting on you to be the first on the dance floor.' Eden laughed, just to make sure he knew she was joking. 'Anyway, never mind the dancing, I don't know about you but I'm ready for a couple of drinks. It's been a long day of wrangling with bureaucracy and pulling together everything I need to try and get Teddie a place at the right school. Thanks again for all the information you sent me by the way, but please tell me your day has been more exciting than mine.'

'It's been okay. I was on call overnight and into this morning, but nothing came in.' He'd told her before that he was part of an area-wide team providing 24/7 cover for forensic cases, as part of his broader hospital role. Living and working in such a rural area meant that skills like Drew's were in high demand, and although the kind of blended role he had was unusual, his qualifications and experience made it possible.

'How do you fill your time while you're waiting to see if you get a call out?'

'It depends. This time I spent it catching up on some paperwork, and wondering why you'd invited me to a party. I'm not exactly the obvious choice.'

'You are to me.' She didn't look at him as she answered, and she didn't stop walking either. It was easier that way.

'I'm glad.' His tone was gentle, but he didn't reach for her hand even though her fingers twitched with the desire for him to do so, and she kept her arms clamped to her sides as they continued their journey down the hill towards the beach. Talk soon turned to Teddie, and Eden relaxed again as she realised just how easy it was to tell him all the things that worried her.

Stealing a glance at Drew as they continued walking, she felt a wave of gratitude for him coming into her life. Here was someone who understood her son in a way that perhaps even she didn't. Their autism was at opposite ends of a vast spectrum, and the paediatrician still wasn't certain whether there were more complexities to Teddie's diagnosis than ASD only. Eden had her suspicions, but she'd been trying to let the specialists lead her, rather than becoming one of those infuriating people who relied on Doctor Google. The trouble was the system was overloaded, and if she didn't fight for Teddie every step of the way he wouldn't get the help he needed. Eden was already beginning to gather evidence for the next stage of the fight, filming Teddie's behaviour, including his stimming and emotional outbursts, both of which were still escalating. The hardest part of the whole situation was not being able to predict anything about the future. She had no idea what level of ability or disability Teddie would have in the longer term, and that was scary, especially when she thought about the prospect of anything happening to her. When she was talking to Drew about Teddie, it was clear he understood that too.

'I know it's not the same for me, but when I got my diagnosis it helped me to understand why I was the way I was and that was a relief.' Drew breathed out slowly. 'My mother was heartbroken. She thought it meant the end of all the dreams she'd had for me. I think she kept hoping that I'd change, settle down and buy a house around the corner from her, get married and give her the grandchildren she was longing for. She probably thought that would make up for losing Flora, but it never would have done. And that kind of life wouldn't have happened for me either, whether I was diagnosed or not.'

'What makes you say that? Why don't you think you'd ever have got married and had a family?' Eden's question sounded pointed, even to her own ears, as if his dismissal of marriage and settling down somehow affected her personally. It didn't, of course, but she cared far more about what his answer might be than she wanted to admit.

'It's not that I don't want to.' He turned and caught her eye for a moment, before looking away again. 'I just could never envisage it happening for me and, even if I did find someone, I wouldn't have bought a place around the corner from my parents. I couldn't wait to put some distance between myself and my father for a start.'

'I can understand that. There was a time when getting away from my mother was my greatest wish.' Eden was trying to push down the sense of relief that had welled up inside her when Drew had admitted he did want a relationship. It shouldn't have mattered to her nearly as much as it did. 'It must have been really hard to feel that kind of pressure to fulfil your mum's hopes and expectations.'

'It was, especially as I knew it was never going to happen. Her getting upset about it didn't help either of us, it just made me feel even more like I'd let her down.'

Eden glanced at Drew again. Even after all this time he seemed weighed down by the feeling that he'd somehow fallen short of what his mother needed, but she could see it from the other side. Drew's mother should have wanted her son to do what was best for him, not what was best for her. Eden didn't want to make that same mistake with Teddie, so she had to ask Drew another question. 'What do you wish your mum had done instead?'

'I wish she'd used the information she had about my diagnosis to reframe her thinking and what she wanted for me. She knew I had a passion for medicine, that my studying was going really well and that I had a plan to go into pathology. She could have seen the hyper fixation that autism gave me as a positive in that respect. It meant I kept going no matter how tough the studying got, because I knew it was the path to making that ambition a reality, but my mother couldn't let go of her own dreams for me.' Drew suddenly stopped and turned to look at Eden. 'You're nothing like her, and Teddie's lucky, but for your own sake I'd suggest trying to let go of all the dreams you had for him when he was born and find some new ones based on who Teddie really is. Otherwise you'll torture yourself, and you won't be able to celebrate any of Teddie's achievements.'

Eden paused for a moment, temporarily winded by the raw honesty of Drew's words. She knew he was right, but it was a hell of a lot to get her head around and she had no idea what those new dreams for Teddie might look like. There was only one thing she knew for certain, and she met Drew's gaze as she finally spoke. 'I just want him to be happy, and feel safe and loved.'

'He already is. Nobody is happy all the time, but Teddie experiences the kind of pure joy that most people will never know.'

'Thank you.' Eden's eyes filled with tears. Drew had no idea how much his words helped and she couldn't stop herself from leaning forward and kissing him on the cheek. It was about as chaste as kisses came, but somehow it still made her lips tingle.

'Thank you, Drew. I'm so glad we met.' She didn't want him to feel like he had to say anything in response, so she didn't leave a gap for him to speak. 'But we'd better hurry up or we'll be the last to the party, and Gwen will probably have our names down for beach volleyball, or something crazy she's come up with, like a limbo competition.'

Eden turned back towards the path and started walking again. Part of her wanted to ask Drew whether he still thought his mother's dream of him getting married and settling down was as unlikely as he'd made it sound, but she wasn't sure she wanted to hear the answer.

* * *

As Eden had suspected, the party was already in full swing by the time they got there. Once upon a time, before her relationship with Jesse, she'd have thrown herself right into the thick of things. She wouldn't have been afraid to walk up to people she didn't know well and join in with their conversations, or introduce herself to people she'd never met before. Jesse had changed all of that. He didn't like her talking to other people, and he would sulk and accuse of her of all kinds of things. He was so good at twisting the truth that in the end she almost believed she had been inappropriate. He'd told her on multiple occasions that she'd embarrassed herself and everyone else with the way she'd been acting. In the end she didn't trust herself to read social situations any more, and she wondered if that was how Drew felt. He'd told her how difficult he'd found university at first, and the self-imposed isolation that had finally led to his diagnosis.

Looking at him now, she'd never have believed he found it so hard, because there were a circle of people around him who appeared to be hanging off his every word. It might have had something to do with Gwen loudly introducing him as a pathologist, who worked for the police as well as the hospital. It was the kind of job that fascinated people and Drew seemed to be in his comfort zone when he was talking about work. He'd told her it was small talk he struggled with the most, but she could hear him now talking to Isla and her partner, Reuben, about a case he'd been involved with. He could only discuss it because the trial he'd presented his findings to was already over. Eden had barely focused on the conversation going on around her, because she was too busy listening in to what Drew was saying, and it made her jump when Aidan suddenly prised her glass out of her hand.

'I can imagine what you might see in him.' Aidan topped up Eden's glass with champagne as he spoke and passed it back to her. 'I'm a very happily married man, but I've always found intelligence to be an aphrodisiac and everything Drew says sounds clever.'

'Oh that's charming isn't it, you used to say I was the cleverest man you knew.' Jase shot his husband a look of mock outrage, but then he smiled and gave himself away. He wasn't remotely threatened and Eden had a strong suspicion that the two of them ribbed each other all the time. What Aidan said next immediately proved her right.

'I used to think like that, my darling, but that was before your main topics of conversation centred around the colour and consistency of our baby's poo, or whether five pages of instructions are enough for your parents to be able to look after Ellis, despite raising two children of their own. I'm sure they really needed reminding not to leave her unattended on the kitchen worktop. We better ramp it up when she gets a bit older, otherwise they might let her play with a knife block instead of a shape sorter.'

'I'm not that bad.' Jason pulled a face, but then he laughed again. 'Alright so I'm a baby bore, but Ellis is far too clever for her own good and she's already turning herself over. The way she's babbling, she'll be talking before we know it too and then I'll have both of you bossing me around.'

'What are you hoping her first word will be. Daddy or Papa?' Eden knew the names Aidan and Jase had chosen for themselves and she did her best not to let her voice betray the tightness in her throat. She'd have given the world for Teddie to say anything, and she tried not to think too much about the possibility that he never would.

'Let's just say I've heard Jase coaching her by repeating Papa over and over again, when he thinks I'm not listening.'

'Don't turn it into a competition.' Gwen suddenly appeared out of nowhere. 'Because, trust me, as soon as she starts talking, it'll be Daddy this and Papa that non-stop. Don't rush through all the stages, they each have their own magic. The connection in the way your child looks at you before they learn to speak is something that's never quite the same once they start talking.'

She caught Eden's eye for a moment, an understanding passing between them that needed no words. Gwen had told Eden about her magic act, and sometimes she wondered if it might not be an act at all. If it wasn't magic, then Gwen must at least be able to read minds. She seemed to know just what advice to give, even when it hadn't been asked for.

'You're right, Gwen, and we are trying to treasure every moment.' Aidan nodded, looking serious for once. 'I said more or less the same thing to Esther and Joe about making the most of the pre-kids' stage of their relationship too. Me and Jase know better than anyone how hard it is to think about anything else when all you want is a family, but it's important to remember all the upsides of it just being the two of you.'

Eden hadn't even realised that the most senior nurse on the team was trying for a family with her husband. She could see Esther and Joe now, down on the sand, playing a very energetic game of volleyball against Eve and Meg.

'You can tell they haven't got kids yet; they've certainly got more energy than any parents I know,' Eden said, laughing at the expression that crossed Aidan's face in response.

'Absolutely. That's why they've thrashed Wendy and Gary, and Danni and Charlie at volleyball already. They tried to get me and Jase to give them a game, or to join in with the five-a-side football match they're organising between A&E and the mental health team, but the last thing I want to do is spend my evening off chasing balls up and down the beach.'

Jase grinned. 'And you've got the cheek to say I'm the boring one.'

'I'm sure you two don't need any advice about playing with balls.' Gwen's tone was deadpan and it was impossible to know whether the innuendo was intentional or not, although they usually were when it came to Gwen. 'But in my experience the couple that plays together stays together. If you make it a priority to have fun as a couple, you can cope with all the challenges that parenthood throws at you, as a team.'

Suddenly the tightness in Eden's throat was back. When she'd thought about having a child with someone, long before Teddie had arrived, she'd wanted exactly the kind of partnership Gwen had just described. She'd imagined being part of a couple who parented together, a united front able to tackle whatever came along. Eden had wanted to do things so differently to her own parents, to raise a child with a stable foundation and with the guarantee that both parents would be there whenever they were needed. For a long time it had felt like she'd failed Teddie by not providing that, but as she looked up and caught another glimpse of Drew, she couldn't help wondering if it was something else she needed to reframe. The dream she'd had of what parenthood might be like, hadn't come true, but maybe there was a different dream out there just waiting for her to discover it.

* * *

'Thanks so much for coming with me.' Eden felt strangely shy as she and Drew finally managed to get some time away from everyone else at the party. She'd wanted to be on her own with him all evening, but now that she was, it felt almost too intimate. Now there was nothing stopping her from acting on the impulse she'd had to reach out for his hand, almost from the moment she'd seen him waiting outside her house, but she still wasn't sure how he'd react if she did. They were on the concrete pier that flanked one side of the beach, a hundred metres or so away from the restaurant. The tide was still far enough out to offer up a wide stretch of sand, but she hadn't suggested going down there, because she knew how much he hated it. There were shouts of laughter and the buzz of conversation in the distance, but it was far enough away from where they were walking to be able to hear the sound of the waves lapping against the shore too. The soft autumn light of the afternoon had faded into darkness, and the sky was filled with a blanket of stars that somehow made all her worries seem a lot smaller. She felt calmer and more content than she had in a very long time, and Drew had undoubtedly played a big part in that.

'Thank you for asking me along. I've really enjoyed it.'

'I'm glad.'

'I didn't expect to, but it was a nice surprise. It was good to meet some more of the staff, and it helped that we could all talk about work. I'm sure I'd have found it far more difficult to make conversation if we didn't have the hospital in common.' Drew stopped walking and turned towards her. 'But this has still been the best part of the night, just talking to you.'

'It's been my favourite part too.' Heat flooded her cheeks and she was glad it was probably too dark for him to tell she was blushing, but she'd wanted to be as honest with him as he was with her.

'I was going to ask you out, before you asked me to come to the party. I've been wanting to do it for ages, but I kept losing my nerve. It was only when Gwen made a bet with me that I promised myself I'd do it.'

'You have a bet with Gwen about asking me out?' She was smiling now, imagining how that had gone down, but Drew shook his head.

'Well not a bet exactly, more of a forfeit if I didn't do it. She knew I kept losing my nerve, so she said I had to join in with a belly dancing class if I wimped out again.'

'That's a pretty serious threat.' Eden laughed, unable to stop herself from picturing just how mortified Drew would be to have to go through with that. 'So do you still have to pay a forfeit, seeing as I was the one to ask you out?'

'No, thank goodness. We agreed to come to a compromise and voided the bet. She said all she cared about was that we'd finally got our acts together to go on a date.' Drew looked down at the floor and then back up at her. 'I didn't tell her I wasn't sure if that's what this was. I'm still not sure, but I know I want it to be.'

Eden could sense how hard it had been for Drew to admit how he felt, and the urge to kiss him was almost overwhelming. She'd wanted him to kiss her from the start of the evening, but she hadn't been sure it had even crossed his mind. Now she knew he wanted to, but she was just as certain he still wouldn't do it because he didn't trust himself to have read the situation right. One of them had to make the first move. Stepping forward, she laid a hand against Drew's face, giving him the chance to step back if she'd somehow got things wrong, but he didn't. Instead she moved even closer, pressing her lips against his, and suddenly he was kissing her back with the sort of passion that left her in no doubt about how he felt. He'd been waiting for this and wanting it just as much as she had.

'Can we go out again?' Drew's tone was more urgent than she'd ever known it to be.

'Are you sure you're not just trying to avoid having to put on a pair of harem pants and jiggle your hips like you mean it?' She raised her eyebrows and he laughed, shaking his head.

'Having you say yes is the only thing I want.'

'In that case, yes, I'd really like to go out again, but right now I think we'd better get back to the party and say our goodbyes, before we become the main source of gossip. You know what they're like, and I've got to get home soon, in case Teddie is having a rough night.' She shrugged regretfully, but Drew nodded.

'Of course, Teddie will always come first.' There was no edge to his tone, or any hint of bitterness in his words. He understood her situation completely.

It would have been so easy to rush headlong in to things with Drew, but they needed to take this slowly, for both of their sakes and more importantly for Teddie. Just like Drew had said, her son was always going to be her priority, but she had a strong suspicion that he'd be Drew's priority too, and the thought made her smile into the darkness as they made their way back.

12

Eden was incredibly grateful for the support her parents had given her since her return to Port Kara. They worked well together as a team, her mother always coming up with different ways to try to engage Teddie. Although it wasn't completely straightforward, despite Karen's sobriety she could still be unpredictable at times, her mind seeming to wander off on a tangent mid-conversation, if something else more interesting caught her attention, or popped into head. It was why Eden's father had given his wife the nickname Goldie, having likened her attention span to that of a goldfish. Karen wasn't in the least offended, she seemed to revel in her reputation as a scatty, slightly eccentric middle-aged woman, and would often loudly pronounce that 'no one wants to be a boring grandma, do they?' Eden could certainly never accuse her mother of being boring, but it was also why she'd never want to leave her in sole charge of Teddie for any length of time. Especially as he had no concept of risk or danger, and he wasn't the sort of child you could leave to his own devices, even for a moment.

Karen's obsession with conspiracy theories showed no sign of abating, and the internet was both her friend and downfall. She could disappear down rabbit holes of misinformation and crackpot ideas, and by the time she emerged nothing could convince her that they weren't undeniable facts. The theories that drove Eden insane were the ones about the potential 'cures' for autism, as if it was a disease, rather than a difference in the connections between the nerve cells in the brain. Her mother's inability to separate fact and fiction, combined with spending an unhealthy amount of time on TikTok was a dangerous combination. But when Karen had sent Eden a link to a technique called bleach therapy, which was every bit as terrifying as it sounded, they'd had a blazing row which had almost been enough to persuade her to head back to London.

'Stop sending me all this stuff, Mum.' Eden had held up her phone and jabbed a finger at the message her mother had just sent her via WhatsApp. She'd been doing her very best to remain calm, even if it was the six hundredth time she'd asked her mother not to send her any more ridiculous links about so-called 'cures' for autism.

'I don't know why you're so resistant to these alternative ideas. What's the harm in trying them?' Karen's bottom lip had jutted out like a sulky toddler. 'Don't you want Teddie to get better?'

'He can't get better, Mum, because he isn't ill. Autism isn't an illness.' She'd said the last part really slowly, as if her mother really was a toddler.

'That's just a word, you know what I mean.' Karen had folded her arms tightly across her body, and Eden's scalp had started to bristle.

'I'm not sure I do know what you mean, why don't you tell me?' There had been an edge to Eden's voice that should have been a warning to her mother, but if Karen realised, she ignored it.

'It's just such a shame, isn't it, that Teddie's the way he is. And I just don't think you should give up on trying to find a solution.' Her mother's words had hit her like bullets. It wasn't as if she hadn't heard that kind of thing before, but coming from Teddie's own grandmother it felt far worse.

'So you wish Teddie was different?' She hadn't waited for her mother to answer. 'Would you love him any more if he didn't have autism? Because I wouldn't, I couldn't possibly love him any more than I already do.'

'Of course not. That's not what I'm saying and you know it isn't.'

'What are you saying then? That because he has autism he somehow has less value than a child who doesn't have autism?' Even in the moment a part of Eden had known that her mother wasn't being deliberately cruel, just thoughtless and clumsy, with no real understanding of the impact of her words, like so many people Eden encountered. It was exhausting, and the real reason she was lashing out at her mother was because of all the other conversations like this, the sideways looks, and heavy tutting. She'd seen and heard it all.

Comments about her letting Teddie watch *Paddington* on her phone, in an attempt to keep him calm. *Lazy parenting. Just look at her using her phone as a babysitter*. Words like that rang in her ears for days afterwards, and they imprinted on her brain forever. People were so quick to judge and were often incredibly vicious in delivering those judgements. They didn't stop to think whether there might be reasons why Teddie was noisy and made repetitive sounds, or why his behaviour and her parenting didn't seem acceptable within the narrow constraints of what complete strangers thought was right or wrong. They'd never walked a mile in her shoes and they had no idea what they were talking about. She'd had plenty of well-intentioned comments too, but they were often just as ignorant. *He's far too handsome to have autism, I'm sure he'll grow out of it, all toddlers have tantrums*. She couldn't blame people in a way. There were damaging stereotypes about all kinds of diversity, and people were good at being blinkered, not bothering to look beyond the superficial. Maybe Teddie's behaviour did look like that of any other toddler tantrum from the outside, but if the people watching had ever been in the eye of the storm during the meltdown of a child with autism, they'd know it was like comparing a stiff breeze with a tsunami.

Eden had lived with other people's judgement for years, but she'd never expected it to come from her mother and sometimes it felt like no one understood Teddie the way she did or saw all the joy he brought to the world, because it didn't look the same as the joy other children brought. Then Drew had come along, and seemed able to see all of that right from the start. She couldn't help reflecting on her mother's attitude as a result, and in a way it hurt even more than it had in the past to realise that Karen still couldn't see her grandson the way Drew did. It wasn't that Eden didn't want Teddie's life to be easier than it was, and there was no denying that his autism presented challenges that would be there for the rest of his life. Deep down she understood that's where her mother's comments were coming from; if they could just find a way to make Teddie's life a bit easier for him then that had to be worth pursuing. Except Eden knew it didn't work like that. There'd be no magic wand that took Teddie's autism away, and she wanted the people around him to stop wishing for that, and to appreciate her son the way he was. Otherwise, just like Drew had said, they'd never accept Teddie and would always think of him as somehow less than he could have been, when for Eden he was everything.

Before she'd met Drew, it had felt as if no one was truly on her side, not even her own family. It was the pain of thinking she was the only one who loved Teddie unconditionally – exactly the way he was – that had made the row with her mother escalate into the kind of argument that went down in history, the sort that rattled the plates in the kitchen cupboards and was never forgotten by anyone who'd witnessed it. The only upside of such an angry and tearful exchange was that it had stopped Karen sharing most of her crazy ideas about autism with Eden. It was also the reason why she could trust her mother not to get it into her head to try out any of those ideas herself. Eden had left her in absolutely no doubt about how she felt about it.

Despite Karen keeping her outrageous ideas about autism to herself more often since the row, it had done nothing to dampen her obsession with other ridiculous theories. And the second Eden brought Teddie down for breakfast, she launched into the latest one.

'When's your next dental appointment?' Karen looked at her from over the top of her glasses which had slid down her nose. She had the laptop open on the kitchen table, and a cup of coffee next to her, which had gone so cold that it had formed a kind of skin. This was never a good sign, because it meant her mother had lost all track of time online, which only ever meant one thing.

'Why's that?' Eden put a piece of seeded bread into the toaster as she spoke. Teddie didn't like white bread, or brown, the consistency of either was never quite right. He'd only eat multi-seeded bread, and even then only one particular brand. It was like the bakery version of the princess and the pea, and there was no fooling Teddie, he'd know if she didn't get it right.

'Because you should ask your dentist what they think about root canal treatment and if they've seen all the research on the problems it can cause. You don't want to be with the wrong dental practice if there's an emergency.'

'Frankly I'm glad to be with any dental practice.' When Eden had moved back to Cornwall, it had taken what felt like three hundred phone calls and some unashamed begging to get herself and Teddie registered with a dentist who eventually found the space to take them. 'And I'd imagine all dentists have the same view on root canal treatment, and when it is and isn't recommended.'

'That's just it!' Her mother's eyes flashed with passion, she was getting into her stride now and nothing Eden said was going to stop her. 'Dentists shouldn't ever be recommending root canal surgery, because it's causing all sorts of terrible illnesses like breast—'

Eden cut her mother off. 'Mum, just don't, okay? We're never going to agree on what I've learned from my training versus what someone on TikTok has told you, and whatever it is I don't want to hear it.'

'Sometimes it worries me how closed-minded you are.' Karen shook her head, and Eden was tempted to tell her that it worried her constantly just how much utter nonsense her mother allowed into her mind, but she didn't want another row. Karen wasn't harming anyone, and this was just part of the addictive behaviour she'd spiralled through over the years. If she had to have an addiction to something, this was almost certainly the lesser of a wide range of potential evils.

'But wouldn't it be boring if we were all the same.' As she spoke, Eden walked over to where her mother was sitting and slid an arm around her shoulders, squeezing her tightly for a moment, just like Teddie did. 'Even if I do think some of your ideas are – how shall I put it? – let's just say *interesting*, I still really love you.'

'I love you too.' Karen looked across to where Teddie was playing with a bowl of plastic food clips, opening and closing them repeatedly. 'And I love that little boy with all my heart.'

In the first couple of years of his life, before his diagnosis, he'd been bought all kinds of toys. Eden's parents hadn't got to see him as much as she knew they would have liked, partly because of the distance, but mostly because of Jesse. He'd made such a fuss about Eden going home to visit, and she hadn't wanted her parents to see how bad things were if they'd come to stay with her. It had meant the gifts that Karen and Dave bought Teddie were all the more lavish, but he'd never played with any of them. He didn't do any kind of creative play, that involved imagination or make believe, he preferred what the paediatrician had described as exploration. He'd take tubs of Play-Doh out of the slots in the box they came in, and spend what felt like hours putting them back in those same slots, before repeating the process. He wasn't interested in the Play-Doh itself. Since Eden and Teddie had been home, Karen had launched herself into finding ideas that might engage her grandson. It was a good use of her research skills and it almost made up for all her crackpot theories. Teddie's favourite way to pass the time right now was with one of Karen's creations: a series of empty cardboard toilet rolls, taped to the end of the row of kitchen cabinets, through which he could post small objects. It was repetitive and predictable, and it gave Teddie an undeniable sense of contentment.

'He loves you too.' Eden stepped back from her mother's chair. 'He might not be able to say it, but you know it's true, otherwise you wouldn't be in the very small group of people he wants to hug.'

'And those hugs are officially the best thing in the world. I swear there's nothing they can't fix.' Karen put her hand over her heart for a moment, and then looked up at Eden. 'Where are you two off to today? Out with Drew again?'

'Yes, we're taking Teddie to the park before the weather finally realises it's supposed to be autumn and then we're going back to Drew's place for lunch.'

'Oooh very nice.' There was a twinkle in Karen's eyes, but she knew better than to ask Eden if there was any romance on the cards. They'd never really had the kind of relationship where they discussed things like they were friends. The years of Karen's addiction had robbed them of the easy closeness they might have had otherwise, and she probably knew that Eden would just have dismissed the idea anyway. She'd been telling herself ever since she left Jesse that she didn't have time for romance, and that she didn't want it; except, even as the thought came into her head, she realised that wasn't true. The kiss she'd shared with Drew by the beach, under a blanket of stars, had probably been the most romantic moment of her life. She couldn't let her thoughts linger on that for too long, though. If she did, she'd undoubtedly want more from him than Drew might be willing to give. She'd had enough disappointment in her life, and there was no way she was setting herself up for more.

'I'm not sure how nice lunch will be. Drew knows about Teddie's very selective palate, so no doubt we'll have a delightful beige banquet to look forward to.' Eden exchanged a look with her mother and they both laughed. The beige banquet was a term they'd come up with after Teddie's fourth birthday, when Eden had prepared all his favourite foods and every single one of them had been beige. Chicken nuggets, garlic bread, pizza and chips, not a single bit of greenery in sight.

'Just enjoy yourself, darling. You deserve it and remember that not everything you do has to be about Teddie. You are allowed to have a life for yourself too.' Karen stood up and planted a kiss on Eden's cheek.

'Thanks, Mum.' She knew her mother meant well, but she couldn't agree with what she'd just said. In her world everything was about Teddie, and one of the best things about Drew was that he understood that. It was also one of the reasons why it would be so easy to fall for him, but she couldn't risk putting her heart on the line. She'd thought about it a lot since the party, and as much as she wanted to go on another date with Drew, she didn't think it was a good idea. She could end up losing Drew's friendship and getting her heart broken in the process, which was just too much of a risk. It was far safer to make their interactions all about Teddie, and that's what she intended to do from now on.

* * *

The trip to the park was a huge success. Teddie had squealed with laughter when he and Eden had gone on the rope-nest swing together, and Drew had pushed them higher and higher, until Teddie had begun clinging to her like a koala, communicating in his own way that they'd now gone a little bit too high. Afterwards they'd put a picnic blanket on the ground, and Teddie had run his hands over the grass, enjoying the sensation of pulling clumps of it up and throwing them on the ground again. That was when Eden had found herself making another confession to Drew, as they watched a little girl riding a tiny pink bike with stabilisers.

'I need a bike like that.'

'I don't think even a fully trained clown could ride a bike that small.' Drew had furrowed his brow and she'd smiled in response.

'A *fully* trained clown? That sounds like one hell of a commitment to make to the vocation.' They'd both laughed then, and she'd thought about how nice it was just to be sitting there with him, talking nonsense and teasing each other. But she wanted to open up to him too, and for him to know more about why she wanted Teddie's childhood to be so different to her own. 'The real reason I need a bike like that is because I can't ride one, not without stabilisers. I never learnt.'

'Why not?' His tone had been gentle, and Eden suspected it was because he already knew the answer.

'Because Mum and Dad were a bit too wrapped up in her problems to make time for stuff like that. My brother managed to teach himself, but it involved borrowing a friend's bike and more cuts and bruises than we get in

A&E on some Saturday nights. So when he offered to teach me too, I decided against it. I know it's silly, but teaching Teddie to ride a bike was one of the things I was looking forward to doing. I wanted to watch him learn to do something I've never been able to do. Except now I'm not sure he'll ever have the coordination or motivation to manage it.'

'You'll find a way and so will he. It might not look exactly the same way everyone else does it, but maybe a trike would work for him eventually. Or maybe Teddie will just decide to become the coolest kid in Port Kara and get a segway. Whatever he wants you'll make it happen.'

Drew had sounded so certain, and suddenly it had been far easier for Eden to believe it was true. He made her feel like she was a better mother than she'd ever given herself credit for, because of his ability to make her see herself through his eyes. It was something she was coming to value more than she'd ever have thought possible.

When Teddie had decided he'd pulled up enough clumps of grass they'd gone back into the playground. He'd been fascinated by the puzzle toy where he could push discs along rows and thread them up and down a series of zigzagging metal rods. The only slightly awkward moment had occurred when a very overweight lady and her daughter had walked past them, while Teddie had been in the midst of making his latest favourite repetitive sound, which unfortunately sounded a lot like he was saying the word 'fat', over and over again.

'I still don't know whether I should have explained, or if that might have made things worse.' Eden bit her lip as she stood in the sunny kitchen of Drew's house, half an hour after they'd left the park. His cottage had a modern glass extension on the back, which made it feel almost as if the kitchen was part of the garden. The sensation was heightened by the fact that Drew had lots of house plants, almost like he was trying to create his own mini Eden Project, just twenty miles from the real thing.

'Maybe she didn't hear him.' Drew's voice was muffled as he reached into the kitchen cabinets to get out some plates.

'Sadly I think she did; her face went scarlet and I hate the thought she might have been upset.'

'If there'd been other children there, they might have said it for real. They're brutally honest and I still remember my father flying into a rage when my younger cousin came for a visit and asked him if the reason he didn't have any hair on his head was because it was growing out of his nose instead.' Drew laughed as he set the plates down on the kitchen worktop, his warm brown eyes crinkling in the corners in a way that made it very hard for Eden to remember she was only here for Teddie's sake. 'He's such a vain man and it really hit him where it hurt. It made Mum and I laugh for ages afterwards. Whenever he started another affair, she'd make the same comment about him making an extra effort to keep his stray hairs under control for his latest girlfriend. God knows what she saw in him, or any of the other women for that matter.'

'You're clearly nothing like your dad.' Dangerous feelings were welling up inside Eden again. She didn't want her feelings for Drew to deepen any more than they already had, but she seemed powerless to stop them. She loved it when he opened up to her like this. He'd gone from a buttoned-up, very measured person, who'd communicated with the fewest words possible, to someone she could have long, meaningful conversations with. He also had a knack of sharing snapshots of his life with her in a way that made it feel as if she knew him better, and liked him more and more, every time they met. But she couldn't afford to let him get under her skin if she was going to stick with her plan of keeping this all about Teddie, so she had to try her hardest to keep things light. 'At least you're nothing like him in the nose hair department, thank goodness.'

'Well, that's a relief.' Drew laughed again and, despite all her good intentions, Eden's eyes were drawn to his mouth, remembering what it felt like to kiss him. She'd considered telling him it couldn't happen again, because she valued their friendship far too much to risk losing it. But he hadn't brought up the topic of them going on another date again, so the kiss might not have meant nearly as much to him as it had to her. She suspected he'd only asked her out for a second time because it was what was expected of him. If she mentioned the kiss, she could end up making things far more awkward than they'd be if they just pretended it had never happened.

'I can't believe how well Teddie and Marmalade are getting along.' Eden turned to look at where Teddie was sitting on the floor, playing with the bubble tubes that Drew had bought for him, drops of coloured liquid flowing from one end to the other, like a lava lamp, when he turned them over. Drew's cat, Marmalade, was stretched out on the floor next to Teddie, basking in the sunlight streaming through the windows, and every so often Teddie would reach out and rub a hand against his fur. Eden had been worried that the cat would react as cats often did to unwanted affection and sink his claws into Teddie's hand, but Marmalade just lay there, purring softly, and soaking up whatever attention Teddie wanted to direct his way.

'I think they're kindred spirits.' Drew looked across at Teddie and Marmalade. 'Cats are the perfect pets for people with autism; they're not as needy as dogs, and they're happy to exist in their own little bubble for a lot of the time, as long as they get their basic needs met, although they can be really affectionate. Marmalade does sometimes bring me the most disgusting gifts, though. This morning it was a disembowelled mouse.'

Eden wrinkled her nose at the thought. 'It's a good job you're not squeamish.'

'I don't think I'd be very good at my job if I was.' Drew laughed again and a wave of contentment washed over Eden that felt almost more dangerous than the attraction she had towards him. It was such a perfect moment and she wanted this, for her and Teddie. A warm kitchen, ringing to the sound of laughter, a happy little boy busy with the things that brought him joy, and someone who loved them both, who they loved in return. Except Drew didn't love them, and she couldn't let herself build up a fantasy where he was part of that picture, otherwise she'd be getting ideas that were just as ridiculous as her mum's crackpot conspiracies. She turned away from Drew so her face didn't give her away.

'His gifts might leave a lot to be desired, but Marmalade is a very handsome cat and you chose the perfect name for him.'

'Strictly speaking he's Marmalade the Second. Flora always wanted a ginger cat and she'd already chosen the name Marmalade for when she eventually got one. But she died before she had the chance, so as soon as I had my own place I bought one. Marmalade the First lived for fifteen years and the one over there is his replacement. It's probably weird to give both cats the same name, but it makes it feel like Flora is still around in some way.'

'It's not weird, and you're a really lovely man, Drew, and I like you more than I've liked anyone in a very long time.' The words came out before she could stop them, but they were true and it didn't matter how risky it was, her feelings for him had already tipped over into something she could no longer control. She'd tried to keep the conversation light, but no matter how hard she tried to push down the feelings she had for him, they just kept coming back up. She couldn't pretend any more that this was just friendship, not on her part at least.

'Thank you. You're...' He was obviously struggling with what to say in response, and she held up her hand. The last thing she wanted was to make him feel awkward and she knew how hard this kind of thing was for him, but suddenly it felt incredibly hard for her too.

'You don't have to say anything in response. I just wanted you to know.' Eden didn't want him to look at her and see the emotion betrayed in her eyes. She'd put her feelings on the line and his response hadn't been what she'd hoped for, exactly as she'd feared all along. Embarrassment burned in her throat, but she needed to act as if her comments had been no big deal, otherwise the risk of losing his friendship could become very real. Turning away from him, she crouched down on the floor next to her son. 'What have you got there, Teddie, look at the pretty colours.'

Tipping the bubble tube upside down, she focused on the droplets of liquid falling in slow motion, doing her best not to think about anything else. She'd told him the truth and she couldn't take it back. Deep down she didn't want to, because it would have come out one way or another and he'd always told her how much he valued honesty. All she could do was hope that it hadn't ruined their friendship, because she wasn't sure what she'd do if she lost that.

13

Ever since the new hospital had opened, the Friends of St Piran's had run at least two fundraisers a year. This time around, for the autumn event, they'd decided to involve the wider community and raise funds in conjunction with two local charities. Members of staff at the hospital had been asked to put forward suggestions about which charities should be supported, and Eden had proposed the Three Ports' Autism Trust. She couldn't have been the only one who'd suggested it, because it had been one of the two charities selected, along with one that supported cancer patients and their families in the local area.

When Gwen, who was chairperson of the Friends of St Piran's, had asked Eden to help out by running a stall, she'd been desperate to do her bit, not least because her charity had been chosen. She'd just had to make sure that both her parents would be around to look after Teddie. Felix was already home from his brief trip back to the US and he would happily have done it, if he hadn't already booked to view some flats so that he had everything in place before starting his new job. It was only after he got offered the position that he admitted he'd already worked his notice in San Francisco and instructed a realtor to proceed with the sale of his condo in Potrero Hill. Her brother had clearly made his mind up a while ago to come home for good, and she knew he'd support her with Teddie in whatever ways she needed him to, but for today she'd have to rely on her mum and dad.

Once her parents had confirmed they were free to look after Teddie, Eden had been offered the choice between the hook-a-duck stall and the tombola. She'd opted for the latter, in case anyone had asked her to demonstrate how the ducks should be hooked. She had the kind of coordination that meant she found it impossible to thread cotton through a needle, without missing the eye altogether. So her chances of hooking a duck while it bobbed about on the water were probably non-existent.

The tombola stall was one of the biggest at the fair. Prizes had been collected over a number of months, and anyone who got a ticket ending in either a zero or five would win a prize. It meant that for every five tickets someone purchased, there was a very good chance of winning. Eden was running the stall along with Meg and Eve, so there could be two of them there at one time, just in case someone needed to make an emergency dash to the loo. It was a strong possibility after being plied with drinks by Gwen, who was marching from stall to stall reminding her volunteers of the need to stay hydrated in the sunshine, despite the fact that it was now well into October. The Indian summer seemed determined to stretch itself out as far as possible and despite a few autumnal-feeling days, the day of the fundraiser had dawned sunny and far warmer than anyone could have anticipated, even Gwen.

'I think it's all the praying I've been doing for good weather, but I didn't expect it to be hotter than it sometimes is in August. You'll be on your feet all day, talking to customers and your mouth will as dry as a camel's backside in a sandstorm if you don't drink enough water.' Gwen's face had been completely deadpan when Eden and Eve had tried to refuse the water she'd brought round to their stall on her second round of drinks deliveries.

'You paint a vivid picture with your words, Gwen.' Eve had laughed, taking the proffered bottle of water. 'And seeing as I already look like a camel's backside, I don't want to feel like one too.'

'You're beautiful, Eve, and I've never heard anything so ridiculous, which says a lot when I'm on a committee with a certain parish councillor who rang the police when someone put two of his gnomes in a compromising position.' Gwen had a twinkle in her eye that would have been a dead giveaway if she'd been questioned by police about the incident. 'I've got no idea how that could possibly have happened. It could have been anyone who didn't like the fact he voted against upgrading the children's playground. All that aside, if I hear you talking about yourself like that again, Eve, you'll have me to answer to. You should never doubt how lovely you are, but I think you might feel better if you cut back a bit on working extra hours.'

'It comes with the territory, doesn't it?' Eve's tone was casual as she shrugged, but the muscles in her neck looked strained. It always seemed as if she was holding something in. She smiled at all the right moments, but it never quite reached her eyes and Eden suspected her tiredness was down to more than just the job. She looked like one of those people being interviewed on the news, who'd survived a major trauma, but who were never going to shake that haunted look from their eyes. It was strange that both the new doctors on the team had that same slight air of melancholy, despite being friendly and warm. Although everyone had their baggage, Eden knew that better than anyone, and for all she knew she shared that same haunted look too. It might feel as if she hadn't really got below the surface with her new colleagues, because they hadn't opened up to her about their pasts, but the same was true of her. Drew was the only one who knew the full extent of what she'd been through with Jesse, so it was no wonder she felt closer to him than she did to anyone else at the hospital.

'You just make sure you don't let yourself get burnt out, Eve. Life isn't all about work, don't learn that the hard way. You need to make room for letting your hair down and having some fun.' Gwen set down the second bottle of water on the edge of the stall. 'And drink lots of water if you want your face to look like a baby's bum, instead of a camel's!'

With her trademark wink and hoot of laughter, Gwen disappeared into the growing crowd of people milling around the fair. Eden and Eve barely had a moment to stop after that, especially once Meg had been roped into helping out on another stall, but there was a great atmosphere, and everyone who came to the stall to buy tickets seemed to be in good spirits. Eden's parents had said they'd bring Teddie along at some point, but she hadn't seen them yet. If Teddie was having one of his more emotional days, she'd rather they didn't bring him anyway, it might all be a bit too overwhelming for him. Some people with autism struggled with crowds and loud noises, but it didn't seem to affect Teddie. It was just hard for him to be anywhere but home on a day when his emotions were heightened.

'Right then, Benji, this is the stall you wanted to come to, where you can win a prize.' She recognised Drew's voice before she even turned around from rearranging the remaining prizes, and saw him standing there. He was next to a young lad who must have been a least six feet tall and who immediately stuck out his hand to Eden.

'I'm Benji, and I like planes, and trains, and lions, and rabbits, and seahorses and bears.'

'Hi Benji.' A smile spread across Eden's face as she took the young man's hand. He was like a walking ball of energy. 'My name's Eden and I like all of those things too, I also like elephants and giraffes, and big bowls of ice cream.' They were the first things that came into Eden's head, but Benji seemed to approve.

'Me too. My favourite flavour is chocolate, but I like vanilla, and caramel, and mint choc chip, but definitely not coffee and I don't like dogs. I got chased by a dog when I went to see my auntie.' Benji screwed up his face. 'I live at forty-three Polperro Drive, Port Tremellien and my postcode is—'

'I don't think Eden needs to know your postcode, Benji.' Drew smiled, his tone gentle. 'Why don't we buy some tickets and see if you're lucky enough to win a prize. Remember, you need a ticket that has a zero or a five at the end to be a winner.'

'A zero or a five, a zero or a five, a zero or a five.' Benji repeated the mantra as he handed over a ten-pound note. 'Ten tickets please, Eden.'

'Okay Benji, I'm going to get you to spin the drum and then you can pick your tickets out. If you get a ticket with a five or a zero at the end, we can match it up with the prize that has the same number.'

'Let's do it!' Benji gave a shout of excitement and then spun the drum so vigorously that it was in danger of flying off the table, before pulling out the tickets one by one. By the time he was at ticket number eight without a winner and getting more and more disappointed, Eden found herself silently praying that the next one would end in the right number.

'Look at the ticket, Benji, what does it say?' Drew's face lit up with a smile as he pointed at the number Benji had just picked out and all the feelings that Eden had for him, which she'd tried to push down over and over again, came flooding back to the surface.

'It's a five, it's a five!' Benji was jumping up and down on the spot, waving his ticket as if he'd won the lottery, and Eden caught sight of the number 115. Turning behind her, she spotted the matching ticket, stuck to the chest of a soft toy dog. The one animal Benji said he didn't like. With a sleight of hand that any magician would be proud of, she whipped off the number and stuck it to a box containing a Lego plane, pulling off the plane's original ticket and shoving it in her pocket.

'Congratulations, Benji, do you want to see what prize you've won?' Standing back, she couldn't help smiling again as he scanned the prizes behind her, his face still a picture of excitement.

'Look just over there, Benji.' Drew pointed in the direction of the plane, and the whoop of joy that Benji omitted a split second later made her jump.

'I've got a plane. Look Drew, it's a plane!'

'I know, isn't that lucky?'

'Here you go, Benji.' He beamed with delight as Eden handed him his prize.

'Thank you, Eden. It's the best plane ever.'

'I think it might be.' She caught Drew's eye then and he was looking at her in a way she didn't think he ever had before, a surge of hope and excitement rising up inside her as he did.

'Thank you.' He mouthed the word silently and she nodded in response. She wanted to thank him for so many things too, most of all for how differently he'd helped her see things these past few weeks, and in the last few moments too. She had no idea what twist of fate had made her cross paths with Drew, all she knew was that she wanted to thank fate too.

* * *

By three o'clock the fair was starting to wind down. Eden had seen her parents arrive with Teddie about an hour before, but they hadn't brought him over to see her. They knew it could cause problems, because if he saw his mum he might well want to be with her.

'Right, you've done your bit now, you can let me and Eve finish up here.' Meg's tone was insistent. 'Go and spend time with your family.'

'I can come back and help you pack up.'

'No way.' Eve shook her head, the two of them all but pushing Eden away from the stall. 'You did all the setting up, and if you go over there now, you can watch the tail end of the dance display.'

'I must admit I'd like to see Gwen dance. She makes me tired just watching her, but she's such an inspiration.' Eden meant what she said. Gwen must have been at least forty years older than she was, but her energy was boundless, and no one could possibly have described her as old. Her enthusiasm for life kept her young on the inside, and it showed on the outside. The advice she'd given Eve earlier about making time in her life to have some fun had hit home for Eden too, and it was something she was determined to do. She couldn't see herself joining a dance troupe, but she wanted to find something beyond work and motherhood. Something just for her.

'She's a force of nature, but I'm happy to hang back here. I don't want her dragging me up to dance.' Eve shuddered at the thought. 'I have to have a few drinks before I can dance in public, otherwise I'm about as relaxed as the Tin Man, with about the same amount of rhythm. I've got to go back to the hospital this evening anyway.'

'Are you working?' Meg's question took the words out of Eden's mouth.

'Mmm, sort of. I've just got a patient I want to check up on.' Eve shrugged, quickly changing the subject. 'You two could have a drink, though. They're selling cocktails half price in the beer tent.'

'Did you see the names someone came up with?' Eden grinned. 'There's a Piran's Star Martini, a Hospital Wallbanger, and a St Agnes Island Iced Tea. Although that seems pretty tame; if it had been Gwen who'd made up the names I dread to think what they'd have been called. What do you reckon, Meg, do you fancy a Cornish Cosmopolitan later?'

'I don't drink. Well not alcohol anyway.'

'What, never?' Eden hadn't meant to sound so surprised, but she had to admit that was fairly unusual amongst the hospital staff. As someone with an alcoholic in the family, she wished she hadn't made it sound so weird for someone to choose not to drink, but if it bothered Meg she wasn't showing it.

'I gave up three years ago, I just didn't want to get too reliant on it at the end of a long shift. They're doing a nojito mocktail, so I might grab one later, but you should go and get yourself a well-earned drink and enjoy the rest of the fair. You haven't stopped all day and I bet Teddie can't wait to see you.' Meg smiled, making it feel a bit less like she was just desperate for Eden to move off in the direction of her parents and Teddie. It had been good working side by side with Eve and Meg, and Eden was determined not to read too much into them encouraging her to leave them to it. She felt as if she'd got to know them both a little bit better over the course of the day and she liked their company. It was something she hoped she could build on in the future, but she could see

Drew standing over near her parents and Teddie, which meant all the people she most wanted to spend time with were now on the other side of the fair. So she didn't need any more persuasion to leave.

'I'll see you both later then. Just let me know if you decide you need a hand with packing up.'

'Thank you, but we won't. Just go and have some fun! Otherwise I'll get Gwen to come and drag you over there.'

'I'm going, I'm going.' Eden gave a wave of her hand and headed towards where her parents were standing with Teddie. At that very moment Drew turned to look at her, and something fluttered in her chest. So much for constantly reminding herself that they were only friends; her body still didn't seem to have got the message.

14

'Teddie looks like he's having fun.' Eden smiled at the sight of her son walking along the bales of straw that created a border for the 'dance floor'. He was holding his grandfather's hand, and jumping off the corner bale, and then dragging Dave back further down the row of bales, climbing up again and repeating the process.

'He's keeping your dad busy!' Karen laughed. 'He's been such a sweetheart, no trouble at all.'

'Thank you.' Eden squeezed her mother's arm. 'Do you fancy a drink? I thought I could grab us all one before Gwen's dance display. They do a mocktail apparently, a nojito. It sounds a bit fancier than a Diet Coke and I feel like I've earned it. I'm sure you and Dad have too, running after Teddie.'

'Ooh, that sounds good. Gwen's amazing, isn't she? I'm thinking of starting the belly dancing class she runs. She said it's good for your pelvic floor and for your...' Karen broke off then. 'You probably don't want to hear the rest.'

'If it's about you and Dad I definitely don't.' Eden pulled a face. She really didn't want to hear about her parents' sex life, even if she was secretly glad that them having one meant their relationship was probably healthier than it had been in years. There'd been a time when she was almost certain their marriage wouldn't last. Things had become more strained between them when her mother had eventually accepted she had a problem and her father had finally faced up to it too, but it all seemed to be behind them now. 'I'll be right back.'

'Okay sweetheart, no hurry. Teddie's having the time of his life.' Her mother smiled and it was lovely to see her just enjoying the day and not staring at her phone, engrossed in researching whatever her latest obsession might be.

'Thanks, but I won't be long, I don't want to miss the dancing.' Eden walked in the direction of the bar, until she got to where Drew was standing. He wasn't with Benji any more, and she couldn't resist the urge to stop and talk to him.

'It was lovely to meet Benji, he's great.' Eden smiled as she spoke, and Drew mirrored her expression.

'He is, isn't he? I always say he's like sunshine in human form. I wish I had half that joie de vivre.'

'Me too.'

'I think you've got plenty of joie de vivre. I always feel happier when I'm around you.' Drew widened his eyes, as if he realised he'd said too much and wished he could take it back, but his honesty was so refreshing. After all those years of barely being able to recognise what the truth was with Jesse, it was so nice to know that Drew meant what he said. She'd taken his comment as a huge compliment, and she loved the idea that she made Drew happier, because he made her happier too. She still didn't know if that meant they'd only ever be friends, but even if that was their destiny, she was incredibly grateful she had him in her life. She couldn't stop herself from hoping that it might be something more, but the ball was in his court and, even if she had wanted to test the waters again, now wasn't the right time.

'I think that might be the nicest thing anyone's ever said to me.' Eden touched his arm, wishing they were alone again, on the beach at nightfall, where all their inhibitions could had been obscured by the darkness. Maybe then she would have been ready to risk putting herself on the line and kissing him for a second time. She had a feeling she'd know how he really felt then, even if Drew still couldn't put it into words, but the light hadn't faded yet and they were surrounded by people, some of whom would be watching their every move. So she dropped her hand and maintained her distance, changing the subject back to something far more neutral. 'Do you know Benji from volunteering?'

'Yes, he goes to the day centre run by the Three Ports Autism Trust.' Drew smiled again. 'I could be having the worst day I've ever had, but if I see Benji suddenly everything's okay again.'

'I can imagine, he seems so happy.' Eden couldn't stop the shuddering sigh escaping from her lips. A familiar sensation of fear creeping up her spine. 'That's all I want for Teddie. I just want him to be happy, but sometimes I'm so scared of what the future might bring and of other people being unkind to him, especially when I'm not around to protect him.'

'I understand why that might scare you, but he'll be okay because you'll fight his corner for him whenever he needs you to. I'm not saying you can protect him from everything, but he will be happy. You'll make sure of it.' Drew's response was so resolute, it made it easier to believe. Eden's greatest fear, far beyond how Teddie's diagnosis might affect her own life, was that it might impact upon his happiness and she meant what she said: all she wanted was for her little boy to be happy.

'Thank you.' Eden wanted to reach out more than ever, but she curled her hand into a ball instead. 'I'm going to get my parents a drink; one of Gwen's volunteers has come up with some interesting sounding cocktails and mocktails. Can I get you one?'

'I'll get them.'

'No, you won't!' He laughed at the look of determination of Eden's face, and held up his hands.

'Okay, okay, at least let me help you.'

'I'll allow that.' She smiled and they walked the rest of the way to the bar together. Less than ten minutes later, they were heading back towards Karen and Dave with four of the nojito mocktails, the smell of mint and lime mingling in the air. There were still a few minutes until the final dance performance, and Karen was deep in conversation with Gwen, but her father and son were nowhere to be seen. No doubt Teddie had got fed up with the climbing on the straw bales and her father had probably taken him off in his buggy to make sure he didn't get agitated.

'Here's your nojito, they smell delicious.' Eden handed her mother the drink. It was in a proper cocktail glass, even if it was made from plastic. 'These were a great idea Gwen, do you want me to get you one?'

'Thank you, lovely girl, but I think I better wait until after the final dance, otherwise I might need to stop for a comfort break halfway through. I need to go and round up the others now too.' Gwen blew Eden a kiss, before heading off.

'She really is an amazing woman.' Karen turned toward Eden, after Gwen walked away. 'I'm definitely signing up for one of her classes.'

'I think it's a great idea.' Eden was glad to hear her mother's plans; joining Gwen's dance troupe would be far healthier than spending hours online. 'Where's Dad?'

'He needed to go to the toilet, but he said he'd rather nip home than use one of the portaloos.' Karen shrugged. Her parents lived opposite the hospital, and the fair was being held in one of the fields behind St Piran's.

'Where's Teddie?' Even as Eden asked the question her blood seemed to cool in her veins. There was no reason for her father to take Teddie home with him. Her son was still in nappies, and it wasn't as if Teddie could have asked to go to the toilet. Despite the fear already making goose pimples crop up on her skin, every part of her was willing her mother to tell her that Teddie was with her father. But even before Karen spoke, she knew with a crushing sense of horror what was coming.

'He's over there on the straw bales.' Her mother's eyes widened when she turned to look and realised there was no sign of her grandson in the place she'd last seen him. Eden's stomach lurched as a wave of nausea washed over her.

'Oh my God, Teddie!' The drinks she was holding slipped out of her hands. There was no build up to the panic; the desperation to find him and the sheer terror of not being able to, rose up in an instant, yet Eden couldn't move. She was frozen with fear.

'When did you last see him, Karen?' Drew's voice was urgent, but somehow still calm. When Eden's mother didn't answer immediately, he took hold of her by the shoulders. Not roughly, but firmly enough to get her to focus. 'It's really important.'

'A minute ago at the most. I just turned away to talk to Gwen. I can't believe he went so quickly, no one could expect that to happen.' Karen was visibly trembling, but Eden wanted to shake her even harder, and shout at her for turning her back on her grandson, even for a moment, but she still couldn't move or even speak. She was terrified that if she did it would make his disappearance real. There was a chance that if she didn't react, she'd look again and he'd suddenly appear, from behind one of the straw bales, because the alternative was too awful to think about.

'He can't have got far. You go towards the tombola in case he saw you over there and went looking for you.' Drew put his hand in the small of Eden's back, forcing her forward and out of her reverie. 'I'll go to the other side of the fair, and Karen can get an alert put out on the loud speaker in case Teddie is mixed in with the crowd, and no one realises he's actually on his own.'

'He can't be lost.' A sob caught in Eden's throat as the realisation hit her that it was the only way to describe her son's whereabouts. Nausea rose up again inside her making her stomach roil so violently that for a moment she thought she was going to throw up. Her little boy, her baby, who couldn't utter a word to anyone even if they tried to help him, was out there alone. Her breath started to come in shuddering rasps. Then Drew grabbed her hand, squeezing it tight.

'We'll find him, I promise, but you've got to slow down and breathe so we can do what we need to do.' Squeezing her hand again for the briefest of moments, Drew turned his back on her and moved quickly in the direction he said he'd look. When she turned to move off too, her mother was standing in front of her, her chin trembling with emotion.

'Eden, I'm so sorry, I—'

'Just get the announcement done. Now!' Eden shouted the words and broke into a run, nausea still lurching in her stomach as she fought to do what Drew had told her to do and keep her breathing steady. Teddie was nowhere to be seen and a series of unbearable scenarios were already racing through her head. All she could do was repeatedly call out his name as she ran in the direction of the tombola stall, tears streaming down her face and the worst sense of dread she'd ever felt in her life making it almost impossible to keep going. If Teddie really was gone, she didn't even want to try to carry on.

* * *

Drew had told Eden that she needed to stay calm, but the truth was he was struggling not to lose himself to panic too and the thought of Teddie being somewhere on his own made bile rise in his throat. Even worse was the thought that someone might have taken him. The only comfort was that Teddie hadn't cried out. Drew had seen how the little boy reacted to strangers. He was a beautiful child, with cherubic blond curls and big, blue eyes. People often seemed to think it was okay to reach out to him and touch his hair, just because they wanted to. He'd seen Teddie cry on several occasions, when an over enthusiastic stranger got too close to him. It was almost impossible to believe that someone he didn't know would have been able to lure him away, much less snatch him, without anyone hearing Teddie offer up a cacophony of protests. Almost impossible wasn't enough though. Drew had to know for certain that he was safe, and it felt as if his heart was beating out of his chest as he ran between the stalls, desperately hoping to catch sight of the little boy who had come to mean more to him in such a short time than he'd ever dreamt possible.

'He's got to be here somewhere.' Drew whispered the words under his breath, as his eyes darted from side to side, desperately hoping for a glimpse of that golden blond hair. He ran along all the stalls on the far side of the land where the fundraiser was taking place, but there was no sign of Teddie. Looking across to where Eden had gone, on the other side of the field, he could see her gesticulating wildly, as Meg and Eve attempted to comfort her. It was clear she hadn't been able to find Teddie either.

Doubling back on himself, Drew scanned the stalls again. Trying not to let the worst-case scenario overwhelm him. What if Teddie had somehow got out of the gate and onto the road? There was a volunteer collecting donations on the gate, so it didn't seem likely, but what if they'd turned their back for a few seconds, just like Karen had? Maybe Teddie had tried to follow his grandfather. If he'd got out on to the road... Drew shook his head, trying to dislodge the terrifying image that was threatening to take up space there.

'Come on, Teddie, show me where you are.' Drew tried to think about where he could possibly be and then it came to him. Benji had insisted on walking behind the stalls when he'd asked Drew to take him around the fair, so that he could see 'everything' as he'd put it. One of the stalls had a carnival-style game, where you could throw balls at a target to win, or attempt to loop a small hoop over other prizes. Behind the stall, there'd been two plastic boxes, one with some extra balls in it, and one with some colourful bean bags, which clearly weren't being used for any of the games on offer. Drew's fingers had given an involuntary twitch at the sight of the bean bags. He'd imagined the feel of them in his hands, their weightiness and the sensation of the beans moving beneath the material. He'd been given a juggling game as a child, which had consisted of three bean bags and he'd loved the way it had felt to hold them in his hands. If Teddie had seen the brightly coloured balls, or had picked up one of the bean bags, maybe he'd had the same reaction, that same desire to hold them in his hands. As Drew darted between the stalls again, he prayed he was right, because with every second that Teddie was missing, the chances of something bad happening was increasing.

As he reached the back of the carnival stall, his heart sank. There was no sign of Teddie and Drew was finding it hard to swallow. He was so tiny and so vulnerable, and Eden loved him with a force that was impossible to convey. This was killing her, and it felt as if it was killing Drew too. This couldn't be happening, Teddie needed his mum, and she needed Teddie even more, but it was as if he'd disappeared off the face of the earth. Drew blinked, unable to hold back the tears that had been filling his eyes, his throat burning at the thought of how scared the little boy must be. Then he saw it – a flash of colour in the corner of his eye. He turned his head sharply and Teddie crawled out from the back of the stall, a yellow ball in one hand and a red bean bag in the other.

'Oh my God, Teddie, you're okay.' Drew wasn't sure how the little boy would react to him scooping him up, but he couldn't stop himself. It didn't matter if he screamed at the top of his lungs, because he'd be safe in Drew's arms. Holding Teddie tightly, as if his whole life depended on it, Drew breathed out, and the little boy hugged him back, burrowing his face into Drew's shoulder.

'You're okay, darling, you're okay.' Drew was crying hard now, from sheer relief and the realisation of just how much Teddie meant to him. He wasn't sure he'd ever called anyone darling, but it was the term of endearment his mother had used with him when he was small, before Flora died and everything changed. The swell of love he felt as he held the little boy in his arms made it feel like the only thing he could say.

Still holding Teddie tightly, Drew turned and ran back between the gap in the stalls, just as an announcement came over the sound system about Teddie being lost, audible gasps sounding from the people around him, at the prospect of a lost child. Drew couldn't stop, he couldn't explain to the worried people in the crowd that it was all going to be okay, because he had to get to Eden.

'I've got him! Teddie's okay, he's here and he's okay.' He ran towards her, calling out, and then she looked up and started running too, tears streaming down her face.

'Oh Teddie, oh thank God, Teddie! Teddie.' She took him out of Drew's arms, kissing his head repeatedly and saying his name over and over again. Finally she looked up at Drew. 'I don't know how to thank you, he's everything to me and I don't know what I would have done if—'

A sob choked her words, and Drew broke the habit of a lifetime and didn't stop to second-guess whether what he was about to do was the right thing or not. Wrapping his arms around them both, as Eden continued to sob, he held them tight, whispering assurances that it was going to be okay now. He was vaguely aware of people watching them and of other people clamouring to comfort Eden, including her mother, but she didn't move away from him. Instead she leant in closer, as if she didn't want him to let her go. So he didn't. He wasn't sure he ever wanted to let her go, and the thought should have terrified him, because he'd never wanted to care this much about someone again. Not after what had happened to his mother and Flora. But if his work had taught him anything, it was that there were things in life that no one could control and, much to his surprise, this time he didn't even want to try.

15

For the first week after the fundraiser, Eden kept having nightmares that Teddie had gone missing again, but in those scenarios, he was never found safe and well. She'd dreamt about him being dragged into the sea by a wave, and knocked off his feet by a speeding vehicle. Each time she'd wake herself up screaming, and clawing at the sheets, sweat pouring off her as she fought to save her son. It would take her a few moments to realise that it wasn't real, relief flooding her body and her ragged, panicked breathing eventually slowing down again. She had to creep into Teddie's room each time, to check that he really was in his bed, safe and well. Eden would lay a hand against his chest, checking the rhythm of his breathing, in a way she hadn't done since he was a baby. She'd been scared of something terrible happening to him back then, too. After he was born she'd suddenly realised she had complete responsibility for another person and that it was her job to keep Teddie alive, and to make sure he was happy and healthy, and she'd been really worried that she wasn't up to the job.

Eden had been terrified and it had been made worse by the fact that she had felt so very alone. If she hadn't already known that her relationship with Jesse was doomed, the way she felt after Teddie was born would have told her all she needed to know about their future. Their relationship should never have happened. Jesse had come into her life at a time when Karen had finally stopped needing to be rescued, and Eden hadn't been sure what her purpose was any more. When Jesse had shown up needing the kind of help and support Eden was so used to giving it had created a perfect storm, making it feel like love, when in reality it had only ever been co-dependence.

Covering up for Jesse's shortcomings had felt like second nature to Eden, because it was all she'd ever known. If she hadn't had Teddie, there was still a good chance she'd have stayed with him even longer than she had. Jesse had made her feel useful and wanted, but something changed when Teddie came along because he was all that mattered. Putting him first had been like breathing in and out, and every bit as natural. Jesse's days as a feature in her life had been numbered from that moment onwards, and every time he'd put his own needs and desires above their son's, Eden had pulled away from him a little bit more. In the end, she had completely detached from him, long before she'd finally left.

The fact that Drew had taken charge of the situation when Teddie had gone missing was just one more thing that set him apart. Her mother had been desperate to find him too, Eden didn't doubt that, but she'd still wasted precious time and energy in the wake of his disappearance on trying to make sure she couldn't be blamed. She probably hadn't even been aware she was doing it, but a lifetime of making excuses was hard to undo. If Jesse had been there, he'd have been assigning blame to anyone but himself too, and she couldn't imagine him swinging into action with the pace that Drew had. She was almost certain that Jesse wouldn't have found their son as quickly either, because he didn't know or understand him the way Drew did.

Perhaps all of that explained why the only time the panic inside her had completely subsided since the fundraiser was when she and Teddie were with Drew. It felt like where they were supposed to be, the three of them all together. Yet in a way that was scary too, because she still didn't know how things between her and Drew would turn out, she only knew how she wanted them to. They'd kissed again, several times, which had proven the strength of her attraction towards him, but they hadn't gone beyond that, and they hadn't spoken about how to define what was going on between them. It felt like the start of a relationship that had the potential to become something serious, but she was worried that labelling it might be too much too soon for Drew, and the last thing she wanted was to make him feel uncomfortable. He'd had relationships before, but none of them had lasted long and he'd told her that he'd come to terms with the fact that he might be on his own forever. It was obvious he enjoyed spending time with her and Teddie, as much as they enjoyed being with him, but that didn't mean he was looking for some kind of happy ever after, and she wasn't even sure he believed in it.

She was trying to go with the flow, but that wasn't easy for Eden. Living with so much uncertainty growing up had made her crave something solid. One of the things that had attracted her to Jesse had been his undisguised desire for them to be completely committed to one another right from the beginning. At the start of their relationship she'd felt certain that he loved her and wanted to be with her; he'd left her in no doubt of that with the things he'd said and done. It was only later that she'd learned what it really was – love bombing was what psychologists called it. Jesse had showered her with affection and compliments to move the relationship on far more quickly than it should have done and to suck her in to a co-dependency that almost made her forget who she was on her own. Combining the love bombing with his difficult past, and Eden's desire to fix things, had been a lethal combination.

All of that meant she was trying to see the slow pace of things between her and Drew as a good thing. They weren't making each other any promises, or making declarations of love far too early on in their relationship, but not knowing where this was going was new territory for Eden, and she couldn't help wondering if that was adding to her anxiety and whether that in turn was contributing to the nightmares she'd been experiencing. After all, she knew that Teddie was safe, but she still couldn't shake the feeling of what might have happened and how easily everything could change in a heartbeat.

The nightmares hadn't been the only fall out from Teddie going missing, it had changed the dynamic between Eden and her mother too and some of the tentative trust that had built up between them had been lost. Karen had promised she'd never take her eyes off her grandson again if she was looking after him, and Eden knew she meant what she said. Her mother hadn't stopped crying for hours after he'd been found, but they could so easily have lost him due to a moment's carelessness and it felt like too big of a risk to take. Despite being in recovery for seven years, Eden knew how fragile her mother still was, and she didn't want to do anything that would send her spiralling. Instead she'd spoken to her father and Felix on their own and they'd agreed to double down on making sure at least one of them would always be around if her mother was involved in taking care of Teddie. At least until Eden was certain there was absolutely no chance of repeating what had happened. She knew it might be unreasonable, and deep down she accepted that it was probably unfair on her mum because anyone could make a mistake, but when it came to Teddie she wasn't taking any chances.

It had been difficult to come back to work and leave Teddie in the care of the nursery staff, especially knowing her parents would be picking him up at the end of his session. But if she didn't force herself to do it, she might never be able to and not working wasn't a choice she had. She'd asked her father to text her regularly to let her know what was going on, and she was just heading back from her break when he sent her a message.

> Hello sweetheart, just to let you know that Teddie's fine. We're at the garden centre, he's been to see the fish and now we're in the café, and he's trying to post all the sugar packets through the slots in the back of his chair! Xx

The garden centre was one of Teddie's favourite places. If Eden ever drove past it and didn't turn into the car park, her son would start to cry. There was an aquatic section, which was his idea of heaven, lots of bubbling water, brightly coloured fish and calming blue lights that made Eden feel relaxed too. Teddie was also quite keen on the café and if he could have spoken he'd probably have given his compliments to the chef for the choices on the children's menu, all of which fitted in very well with Teddie's love of beige food. Eden smiled and quickly typed a reply to her father.

> Thanks Dad. He tried eating the brown sugar last time we were there, packet and all. Probably because it's made of beige paper! See you all later and give Teddie a big squeeze from me xx

Eden slipped her phone into her pocket and headed back through the double doors that led from the waiting room to the emergency department.

'I swear to God if I didn't love that man so much and I wasn't making allowances for sleep deprivation with Ellis's teething, it might have been enough for me to divorce him.' Aidan who was clearly mid-conversation with Esther and Eve, pulled a face. 'Mistaking soy sauce for maple syrup and then pouring it all over my pancakes. I still gag when I think about the taste.'

'It could have been worse, it could have been WD40.' Esther laughed. 'And to be honest I probably haven't got much room to talk. I made Joe a cup of coffee last week, when I came in from a nightshift and he was just getting up, and I forgot that the packet of table salt had split the week before. I didn't want to throw it away, so I tipped it into a Tupperware container and put it in the cupboard. On the morning I made Joe's coffee, the sugar pot was almost empty, so I decided to top it up... with salt. I didn't realise until Joe spat the first mouthful all over the duvet. It wasn't quite the loving gesture I'd planned for, but it certainly woke him up!'

'Makes me glad I'm single.' Eve smiled, but there was something in her tone that didn't quite ring true. It was either because she wasn't as glad about that as she was making out, or maybe that she wasn't single at all. Eden knew she'd turned Zahir down when he'd asked her to go to the cinema with him, not long after she'd returned to work. Aidan had overheard the conversation and discretion wasn't exactly his strong point. Whatever the reason, if Eve didn't want her colleagues to know the truth about her personal life, Eden could hardly blame her. There was plenty of stuff from her own past that she didn't want to drag up.

'What about you, Eden? Would you be willing to risk another relationship, even if it meant being on the receiving end of salty coffee, or pancakes soaked in soy sauce?' Aidan gave her a questioning look. 'Or are the rumours true that you and a certain brooding Scot are already in a relationship? Come on, spill the beans and tell us what's been happening.'

'There's really nothing to—' Eden's response was cut off by the sound of the red phone ringing, which meant a call from the ambulance service to warn them about the imminent arrival of the most serious category of emergency. Esther got to the phone first, but the rest of them fell silent, as they listened to the details of what they were about to face. Even after all this time in the job, it still made Eden's blood run cold when there was an emergency of that type. It meant someone was in a critical condition, and that their loved ones were about to hear terrifying news, if they hadn't already. She'd far rather have faced Aidan's awkward question. She knew plenty of staff in A&E lived for the adrenaline rush of that sort of life and death situation, but Eden had been on the other end of it. Just before her mother had finally got sober, she'd relapsed from a previous attempt to stop drinking and gone on such a bender that her blood alcohol levels had become life threatening and she'd ended up in A&E, and subsequently intensive care. She'd got the call when she'd been hundreds of miles and a six-hour drive from her mother's bedside and she'd never forgotten how it had felt to be that helpless. Since Teddie had arrived, her greatest fear had become anything happening to him. That could so easily have happened at the fundraiser, and she shivered again thinking about the horror some poor family were about to go through. Esther's summary of the call did nothing to reassure her.

'There's an eighteen-year-old male on the way in. He collapsed on the rugby field at school. The staff gave him CPR and defibrillation, which the paramedics repeated after they arrived. But he's arrested again en route. ETA to resus five minutes.'

'Oh God.' The words slipped from Eden's lips, but she was already moving towards resus, ready to play her part. This kind of situation was when the A&E staff came into their own, a well-practised team who knew their roles and were ready to deliver the best possible care whatever they might face. Eden couldn't allow herself to think too much about the boy or his loved ones, otherwise she wouldn't be able to do her job. For now she had to think of him as a patient, someone who needed her help and she couldn't allow her feelings to get in the way of that. There'd be time enough for that later. Right now she had a job to do and like every single member of the team, she was determined to give it everything she had.

* * *

As soon as the paramedics rushed Callum Sinclair through to resus, it was apparent that the chances of saving the teenager's life were extremely slim. He was still in his rugby kit, his physique like an advert for physical health, as if running a marathon wouldn't have been beyond him. But the rest of Callum's appearance gave away just how serious his condition was. His lips were tinged with blue and his face beneath the oxygen mask looked grey. He was only a boy and Eden's heart was aching even before she heard the sound of someone wailing just beyond the doors that led into resus. Zahir, Esther and Aidan were continuing the resuscitation attempts and Eden felt useless. There were only so many people who could work on a patient at the same time, but she wanted to be there if one of the others had to step back to rest.

'That's his mother.' Jeff, one of the paramedics, looked close to tears himself as he turned and spoke to Eve. 'She was there to watch the match and she's in pieces. Her husband's on his way, but I think she needs someone with her in the meantime, or at least to give her an update.'

'I don't think I can.' Eve took in a couple of gulping breaths and widened her eyes. It almost looked like the start of a panic attack, but then she managed to gain control, fixing her gaze on Eden. 'Would you be okay to go and talk to her? I can stay here in case... in case...'

She couldn't finish the sentence and Eden knew there was something going on with Eve. She wasn't entirely sure her friend would be capable of stepping in to help out with resuscitation if the need arose, but what was crystal clear was that she wouldn't be able to do anything to support Callum's mother when she was clearly struggling so much herself.

'Of course. Do you know her name, Jeff?'

'It's Rachael.' Jeff swallowed hard as he looked at her. 'He's not going to make it, is he? I should leave him now that he's here, but I just need to know. He's the same age as my son and I keep thinking that could be Finn lying there. How can that just happen?'

'It's not fair.' Eden hugged him for just a moment; she couldn't hear Callum's mother sobbing any more, but the pull to be there for her was overwhelming, this other mother whose pain she could already feel. She couldn't do anything for Callum while her colleagues fought for his life, but Rachael needed someone and Eden wanted it to be her.

Coming out of resus, she couldn't see Callum's mother at first, but then she spotted Isla.

'Have you seen the woman who was out here crying? Her son's in resus.'

'One of the agency HCAs took her to the relatives' room.' Isla bit her lip. 'It's heartbreaking. Is there any update?'

'Not yet, but I want to see if I can do anything to help. Although God knows what.'

'Sometimes just being there is all you can do.'

'It just doesn't seem enough, does it?' Eden tried to smile at Isla, but her face refused to comply. Instead she raised a hand in thanks and moved off towards the relatives' room, her mouth suddenly feeling as if it was full of sawdust. She just hoped she could find the words when she got there, but she already knew what Callum's mother was going to ask, and there was no way she'd be able to provide the response Rachael wanted so desperately to hear.

Standing outside for a moment, Eden placed her hand against the door and looked through the pane of glass. A woman with ash blonde hair had her head in her hands and another woman, who was wearing a health care assistant's uniform, was sitting opposite her. Neither of them were speaking from what Eden could see. Pushing open the door, she introduced herself, trying to keep her tone even and her voice from shaking.

'I'm Eden, one of the A&E nurses. You're Rachael, aren't you, Callum's mum?'

The woman's head shot up in response. 'Is he okay? Please tell me he's okay!'

'The team are with him now. They're the best doctors and nurses I've ever worked with and they all want to help Callum.' Eden had rehearsed what she was going to say, as she'd walked towards the room. Rachael had asked the question she'd known she would, because of course that was all she cared about, that her boy was okay.

'I just don't understand how it could happen. He was running for a try, like he does all the time, and all of the St Barts crowd were cheering. Then he just dropped to the ground.' Rachael's face was streaked with tears as she looked up at Eden, a look of utter desolation in her eyes. 'How can he go from that to just not breathing? I've worried about him getting an injury playing rugby before, being badly hurt in a tackle, but never something like this. I'm so scared they're going to give up on him; I thought the paramedics were going to do that before they even brought him in.'

'I can't imagine how terrifying it was to see him like that, but I promise you that Callum is getting the best care possible and no one will give up on him.' Sitting down beside Rachael, Eden took her hand. She could have added words *until they're certain there's no hope* to the end of her sentence, but she didn't. There'd come a point when the team might stop trying to bring Callum back, but it wouldn't be because they'd given up on him. Eden had been with patients when the team had been forced to 'call it', making the decision that continuing to try to save the patient's life was futile. It was always a painful and difficult decision, but it would be even more so with a young person like Callum. All she could do was pray that in resus a miracle was happening, and that someone would walk along the corridor soon and say the words that Rachael wanted with every fibre of her being to hear.

'Thank you.' Callum's mother gripped her hand and for a moment the only sound was the clock ticking above their heads.

'Should I stay?' The health care assistant looked up at Eden. The young woman's leg was jigging constantly and it was clear she was finding the situation difficult. Sickness, and a more general shortfall in staffing, meant the team had been forced to rely on agency staff far too often lately. It made a difficult job even more challenging, when those staff were unfamiliar with how the team worked and often quite inexperienced too. The young woman opposite Eden barely appeared to be out of her teens, and she looked as if she'd love to make a bolt for it. Giving her permission to leave was an easy decision to make, because Eden was certain she could be of more use elsewhere.

'You can go. I'll stay with Rachael.' Having a nurse with her experience sitting with a relative might be deemed a waste of resources, and it would mean patients who needed less urgent treatment experiencing a longer wait time, but right now Eden didn't care as much about that as she did about Rachael. Callum's mother was in the hospital all by herself, going through the worst possible scenario any parent could ever imagine, and Eden could feel her torment almost as if it was her own. The thought of something ever happening to Teddie had been her greatest fear from the moment he was born. Nothing that his diagnosis could throw at them would ever come close to the sheer terror she'd experienced in those few minutes he'd been missing. The way the nightmares had made her feel in the days since then were just a fraction of what Rachael was going through right now, and Callum's mother couldn't wake up from the horror and realise it was all okay.

When the health care assistant left the room, Rachael began to sob again and for a few moments Eden just held her, but then Callum's mother began to speak.

'He's always been sporty, and he was kicking a ball almost from the moment he could walk.' As she pulled away to look at Eden, her eyes were still full of tears. 'He discovered rugby when he was about seven and that was it, we knew he'd found his thing. He's the captain of the school team and he's got a place to go to uni in Bath, to play there. My husband's convinced we'll see him start for England one day.'

'He sounds incredibly talented, you must be really proud of him.' Eden wished she could picture Callum, full of life on the pitch, but the way he'd looked when he'd been brought in made that almost impossible.

'We are. Cal works so hard and he's such a loving boy. He still gives me hugs like he did when he was little, but he's almost eight inches taller than me now, and they're great big bear hugs. I'd give anything to have another one of them.' A sob escaped from Rachael's throat, and Eden wished she could tell her that she'd be able to hug her son again, but she had a horrible, heart-breaking feeling that Callum's mum would never get to do that again and her throat was burning with the effort of stopping herself from crying too. All she could do was try to show Rachael that she understood how precious those moments had been.

'Hugs between mums and sons are incredibly special, aren't they? My little boy's only four, but his hugs are the best thing in the world to me.'

'I knew you'd understand, I don't know how but I could just tell.' Rachael gave her the briefest of smiles through her tears. Before Eden could even reply, the door to the relatives' room burst open, making her heart lurch in response. She'd expected to look up and see one of the team standing there, a grave expression on their face, but it was a man she didn't recognise.

'Oh James, thank God you're here.' Rachael stood up and flung herself against the man, who held her up as she sobbed against his chest.

'It's alright, darling. He's going to be okay.' Despite his words, worry was etched on his face as he looked towards Eden. 'Is there any more news?'

'The team are with him now and, as soon as they can, someone will come and talk to you about what's going on.' Eden felt almost robotic as she parroted the words she knew would bring Callum's father no comfort at all. Not knowing what was going on with their son must feel like hell, but there was a very real possibility that a new kind of hell was coming, one that would never end if they lost their son.

'I'll give you a moment together.' She said the words quietly, but they must have shocked Rachael, because she let go of her husband and whirled around to look at Eden.

'Please don't go. I don't want them to come and speak to us when you're not here. If there are long-term repercussions because of how long Callum wasn't breathing, we need someone here who understands what he means to us. I need a friendly face.' The situation Rachael was outlining was almost certainly the best-case scenario, but Eden understood what she was asking. She wanted someone in the room who saw Callum as more than just a patient.

'I'll get you both some water, just to give you a few moments alone, and then I'll be right back, I promise.' Eden put a hand on the other woman's arm, and Rachael nodded. The truth was, she needed a few moments to gather her own emotions. Heading down the corridor, she filled two paper cups from the water dispenser and turned back towards the relatives' room, just in time to see Eve heading towards her. The expression on her friend's face said more than words ever could. All the colour seemed to have drained out of her, and her mouth was trembling.

'He didn't make it.' Eve whispered the words as they reached one another, and they hit Eden like a punch to the gut; the drinks she was holding almost slipping out of her hands, the way they had on the day Teddie had disappeared.

'Are you okay?' It was a stupid question, because it was obvious Eve was far from being okay.

'I couldn't hold it together. It was too much like... I almost lost someone I love in the same way; he made it through, or at least a version of him did. But it brought it all back.'

'Oh, Eve.' Eden wanted to do something to comfort her, but Rachael and James were waiting for her, and any minute now someone would arrive to give them the awful news.

'I'm okay. Zahir told me to go home and that's what I'm going to do. I'll be worse than useless here.' Eve managed to give her a watery smile. 'He's going to come and speak to Callum's parents.'

'I promised to be with them.' The words seemed to wedge themselves in Eden's throat. A huge part of her wanted to follow Eve out of the door and not have to face the couple who were about to be told the most devastating thing imaginable. But this was all she could do for them and Callum now, and as hard as it was she knew she'd never forgive herself if she didn't keep that promise. She just hoped her face wouldn't give her away the moment she walked back into the relatives' room. Zahir needed to be the one to tell them the news, to explain to them what had happened and all the things the team had done to try and save their son's life. If Eden broke the news that he was gone, they wouldn't hear anything else, and they'd be left with questions that might make the torture they were about to face even worse. They needed to hear from someone who'd been there with Callum at the end.

'Take care of yourself, Eve, and ring me later if you want to talk.'

'I will and you too. They'll appreciate what you're doing for them, even if they don't realise it straight away.' Eve touched her hand briefly and then moved off down the corridor, leaving Eden to take the final few steps to the relatives' room. She couldn't make eye contact with Rachael as she set the cups of water down, the words she couldn't say bubbling up inside her. *I'm so sorry*. It was almost impossible to swallow them down and she was certain she'd have lost the battle if Zahir hadn't pushed open the door behind her within a matter of seconds and said the very words she'd been fighting to hold back, words no one ever wanted to hear.

'Mr and Mrs Buckingham, I'm Zahir, one of the doctors. I'm so sorry to tell you that despite all our attempts Callum couldn't be resuscitated and he died a few moments ago.'

The sound Rachael made was unearthly, Eden couldn't compare it to anything she'd ever heard, not even a wounded animal. Words couldn't describe it, but she could feel it, deep down inside her, in a place she might have called her soul because there was no other word to explain what it was. It was a sound she'd never forget and one she hoped she'd never have to hear again for as long as she lived.

16

Callum's parents had asked to see their son after Zahir had delivered the devastating news of his death. When Rachael had asked Eden to be the one to accompany them, part of her hadn't wanted to do it. Witnessing their pain had been almost unbearable, but an even bigger part of her had seen Rachael's request as a privilege. She had wanted Eden with her at the most difficult time of her life, and the very least Eden could do was step up and be there. Callum's parents would remember every aspect of this day for the rest of their lives. The memories would be indescribably painful, but if Eden could do anything to make that even a tiny fraction less awful, she was willing to do whatever it took.

'Can we stay with him? I don't want him to be on his own.' Rachael looked at Eden, almost twenty minutes after they'd gone into a viewing room to see Callum. He'd been moved out of resus, because the never-ending stream of patients needing emergency care didn't stop, not even for the dead. For the second time that day, Rachael's eyes pleaded for an answer Eden couldn't give her.

She wanted to tell Callum's mother she could spend as much time with her son as she needed, but she knew that even forever wouldn't be long enough. 'You can stay with Callum until they let us know what's happening, I'll stay here with you, too.'

'What do you mean what's happening?' Rachael's voice was thick with emotion.

'Callum will need to be seen by one of the pathologists, so that they can determine his cause of death.'

She'd been careful to avoid the words mortuary or postmortem, but Rachael wasn't stupid. She knew exactly what Eden meant.

'A pathologist?' Her face was a mask of horror. 'That means they'll cut him open and...' She couldn't finish the sentence, sobs overtaking her body and her husband wrapped an arm around her shoulders.

'Surely we have to give our permission?' Callum's father didn't need to tell Eden that was never going to happen, for her to know that's what his response was likely to be. Except they had no say in what happened to their son next, and she was going to have to find a way of telling them that.

'In the case of a sudden and unexpected death like Callum's, there needs to be a postmortem to determine the cause and to give you the answers you need.'

'What we need is for Callum to wake up and open his eyes.' James shot her a look that could have melted ice, but Eden knew it wasn't personal.

'I know that right now nothing feels as if it will make a difference, but understanding why and how Callum died could do in the future. It might also mean that it changes the outcome for other people too.'

'I don't give a shit about the outcome for anyone else! We still won't have our son. There are waste-of-space arseholes out on the street, who spend their whole lives hurting other people, walking around without a care in the world and our son is lying here dead.' James's anger was tangible, and Eden wanted to tell him he was right, that there should be some kind of natural justice, but the world didn't work like that. If life was fair, Callum would be sitting at home with them now, regaling his father with a story about how he'd scored the winning try, his mother looking on proudly, having witnessed it all. Instead they were side by side, an air of unbearable sadness enveloping the whole room as they stood beside their beloved son's lifeless body.

'Callum would have cared. He'd have wanted something good to come out of this, he'd want to change things for other people.' Tears were still running down Rachael's face, but her words were filled with tenderness. Her crying seemed to ramp up again as she turned towards Eden. 'I just can't bear the thought of our beautiful boy being cut up, like a piece of meat.'

'It isn't like that, I promise you the pathologist will look after Callum and care for him every step of the way.' An image of Drew came into Eden's mind, and she knew without a doubt she could make that promise.

'I can't stand the thought of him being in the mortuary all by himself either.' Rachael swayed, and for a moment Eden was worried she might faint. She probably would have done if James hadn't been there to hold her up.

'Do you think it would help if you spoke to the pathologist first? He'll be able to reassure you that Callum will be looked after exactly the way you'd want him to be if you were there with him.'

'Would they do that?' It was James who answered, the look of surprise on his face overriding the expression of devastation for just a second or two, before the pain took over again.

'I know one of the pathologists who definitely would.' Eden was certain Drew would be willing to help Rachael and James in whatever way he could.

'I think I might be able to cope with it a bit better if I knew who was going to be...' Rachael's face crumpled, the words too much for her to say out loud, and James drew her towards him.

'I'll go and speak to one of the team, and I'll ask that Callum isn't moved until you've had a chance to discuss it.' Eden rested a hand on Rachael's shoulder, knowing she'd fight tooth and nail to make sure things weren't made any more difficult for Callum's parents than they already were.

* * *

'I'm so glad you managed to get away.' Eden had called Drew to see if he was at work and available to talk. When he'd said he could make himself free in fifteen minutes, she'd asked him to meet her at the entrance to the hospital.

'I told you I would.' He made it sound so simple, but his response made her smile through the tears that had been threatening to start again. She loved the fact that if he promised to do something he'd follow through with it.

'Thank you for coming, I know I probably wasn't making a lot of sense when I called.'

'I think I got the gist of it.' Drew took hold of her hand and it was the weirdest sensation. Like a jolt of electricity passing through her body, at the same time as making her feel safer than she had before he'd taken her hand. She'd experienced that frisson of excitement before, but never quite so strongly, and certainly never at the same time as the certainty that she could put her complete trust in the other person. Drew let go of a long breath. 'From what you said you lost a young patient and his parents are understandably devastated, but the thought of him having to undergo a postmortem is making that even worse and you'd like me to reassure them about the process. Is that right?'

'That's exactly it.' Eden didn't want him to let go of her hand, but she knew he was going to. 'Is that something you can do?'

'Of course. When do they want to meet?'

'Would you be able to do it now? I don't think Rachael will be able to leave Callum until she can be sure he'll be taken care of.' Eden swallowed against the lump in her throat that felt as if it might choke her. How could Rachael ever be expected to walk away and leave her son behind? Eden was certain she wouldn't be able to do it, and even the thought made it hard for her to catch her breath.

'I've got some reports to write up, but I can do them later. This is far more important.' Drew's hand brushed against hers again, and she had to fight the urge to curl her fingers around his. It would have been inappropriate and unprofessional, but that didn't stop her wishing she could.

The walk back to the viewing room, where Callum's parents were waiting, passed in silence, but it wasn't the uncomfortable kind. It felt as if there was an unspoken understanding between them that needed no words. The hospital chaplain had arrived just as Eden was leaving to meet Drew, and she'd asked Isla to arrange for another one of the team to wait outside the viewing room, in case the chaplain had to leave before she got back. It was the protocol they had to follow, with an unexplained and unexpected death, and hospital policy meant they couldn't leave Callum alone with his parents. It seemed completely ridiculous as if anyone looking at Rachael and James could possibly imagine they might have had something to do with their son's death, but as far as the law was concerned nothing could be ruled out completely until the postmortem was over and an official cause of death had been determined.

Isla, whose shift had been due to end when Eden had spoken to her, had obviously decided to undertake the task of staying with Callum's parents herself. It was a mark of the kind of person she was and Eden felt lucky that she had so many colleagues who shared her values, especially on days like today.

'Thank you so much for staying on, but I can take over now.' Eden hugged Isla, whispering the words in her ear. They'd all been affected by the events of the day, and Isla's body seemed to sag with relief at the prospect of getting off home. Cases like Callum's always made the staff count their blessings and forget about all the stupid minor niggles and inconveniences of life, at least for a little while. Isla would be hugging the people she loved all the tighter when she next got the chance, and it was exactly what Eden would be doing too, once she was reunited with Teddie.

'See you later.' Isla mouthed the words to her and slipped silently out of the room. James and Rachael remained by their son's side, as the hospital chaplain looked on; even she must have felt powerless at a moment like this. There was nothing any of them could say that would make things any better for Callum's parents, but they were going to have to let their son go soon. As much as they might want to sit by his side for the rest of their lives, there were legal processes to follow. They'd be able to see him again after the post-mortem, but that first initial wrench from his side was going to be agonising.

'Rachael, James, this is Drew, one of the pathologists.' Eden's voice was quiet and it felt wrong to talk at all in the stillness of the room, but they needed to hear what Drew had to say.

'Thank you for coming to talk to us.' James held out his hand and Drew shook it. It was amazing how social norms could come to the fore, even in the most extraordinary circumstances.

'I'm so sorry about Callum.' Drew's use of his name immediately broke down the first barrier, Eden could see it in Rachael's eyes. He could just have said *I'm so sorry for your loss*, but using his name made it clear he was talking about their son as a person and not just a body on a bed. It was a tiny gesture that made a world of difference. Drew might not think he always read social situations right, but he had this time.

'Thank you.' Rachael's voice was little more than a whisper and silent tears rolled down her cheeks, as she turned back towards her son, resting her head against his chest for a moment.

'I can't even imagine how difficult this is for you, and I know the last thing you want is for Callum to be put through anything else.' Drew's voice was steady, but there was an unmistakable empathy there too. 'The reason we need to do the postmortem is so that we can be certain what caused Callum's death. It might seem futile, when it can't bring him back to you, but it might give you information that can safeguard you or other members of your family, if it turns out there are any hereditary factors involved. What we discover when we examine Callum could also contribute to preventing the same thing happening to other people.'

'We understand why you need to do it, but what his mum... what we both need to know is what will happen to Callum while he's with you?'

'We'll examine Callum thoroughly and undertake a physical and chemical analysis to identify any diseases or abnormalities that may have contributed to his death. I'll be with Callum for around four hours and I can promise you that my team will treat him with the utmost dignity and respect. We all want to find the answers for you, but I know nothing we can do will make this any less painful.'

'Callum would have wanted his death to eventually help someone else, wouldn't he?' Rachael looked at her husband, who nodded, his eyes red-rimmed and swollen. Although James wasn't crying right now, it was obvious the tears could start again at any moment. Rachael turned back towards Drew. 'Will you... Will he look like Callum again when you're finished? We won't be able to see where you've opened him up, will we?'

'No, we'll make sure of that.'

'Will we be able to make the arrangements for the undertakers to take Callum to the chapel of rest after that, so we can keep visiting him until the funeral? That's what I want.' Rachael put a heavy emphasis on the last four words, in case anyone was planning to try and talk her out of it.

'Absolutely.' Drew nodded. 'I want you to know how important it is to me to find the answers Callum deserves, and if you think of anything you wish you'd asked, you can come back to me at any time. Eden is going to give you my contact details.'

'Everyone's been so kind, but Callum would have hated the idea of causing so much fuss. He was such a lovely, easy-going boy.' The last word caught in Rachael's throat and turned into a sob that echoed around the room. James put his arm around his wife again, but there was nothing that he or any of them could say to lift burden of pain they'd both be carrying for the rest of their lives.

* * *

Drew and Eden walked away from the viewing room together. Her shift had been over for more than an hour, but she'd warned her parents that she was going to be late. Eden's arms ached to hold Teddie and feel the weight of his solid little body against hers, knowing he was safe. But before she went home to him there was something she needed to do.

'That made such a difference to them.' Eden caught hold of Drew's arm, once they were out of the emergency department, and they both stopped walking. 'I could see it in Rachael's eyes as soon as you started to explain.'

'You made far more difference than I ever could. The way you hugged her when we were leaving. I could never do that, but I could tell it made her feel as if someone really cared about her and I also know it wasn't an act on your part. You really do care, and in terrible situations like this that's all someone wants to know.'

'Who'd have thought we had so much in common.' She managed a half smile, but she wished she could have folded herself into his arms.

'I always thought we had a lot in common, once you get below the surface. You just have to get past the fact that you're vivacious and I'm... well, me.'

'I'm really glad you're exactly the person you are.' Eden leant forward and kissed him on the lips, so momentarily that even a passerby might have to question if they'd really seen it.

'Good.' It was a typically brief reply, but a smile was tugging at the corners of Drew's mouth that said far more than his words. They'd been edging around the way they clearly both felt, taking one step forwards and often two steps back, but Eden wasn't sure what they were waiting for any more. Days like this were a stark reminder that tomorrow wasn't promised to anyone, and she didn't want to edge around her feelings for Drew even for one more day. She wanted to lay everything out, the way he probably needed her to, in order to be sure he hadn't misunderstood.

'When can I see you again?' She watched his face as he processed her question, furrowing his brow.

'At work?'

'No. I told you before how much I like you, Drew, but I don't just mean as friends. I really enjoy spending time with you, when we're with Teddie and when we're on our own too. I don't want to see you just to talk about Teddie's diagnosis, or your experience of autism. I want to spend time with you because I like your company more than I like the company of anyone else, except for Teddie. I like how you look, and how it feels to kiss you and hold your hand. I think you might feel the same, but neither of us seems to be very good at moving things forward, probably because we're both carrying a lot of baggage from our pasts, but I don't want that to stop us seeing if we might be able to have a future and whether this could become something more than it is already.'

'I didn't think you were going to say all of that.' Drew held her gaze, something she knew he found hard to do, but she still couldn't gauge his reaction and then he smiled, his whole face changing. 'You're right, I do feel the same. I wish I was as articulate as you and that I'd found the words to tell you all of that first, but I suppose it doesn't matter as long as one of us said it.'

'It doesn't matter at all.' She smiled too. 'But seeing as you made me say it first, I think the least you can do is to arrange our first official date.'

'I'll have to come up with something Teddie will enjoy.'

'It doesn't have to be with Teddie.'

'I know, but I want it to be, as long as you do too? You come as a pair and for me there's no downside to that. I hoped I might find someone one day, even if I never expected to. But I didn't think that someone would come with an incredible bonus, and that's exactly what Teddie is.'

It wouldn't matter if Drew had promised to take her for dinner in the shadow of the Eiffel Tower, or invited her to watch the sunset with him on a deserted beach, nothing could have been more perfect than what he'd just said.

'You don't know how much it means to me to hear you say that.' She wanted to kiss him again, but now wasn't the time or the place. It seemed to be the story of their lives lately, but she really hoped that was about to change. 'I'll wait for you to tell me when and where we're meeting then.'

'I'll call you later.' Drew entwined his fingers with hers for a moment, before releasing them. It was funny the way he always left her wanting more, and how he had absolutely no idea what that did to her. There was no side to Drew, no game plan or hidden agenda. It made him about as different from Jesse as it was possible to be, and the only thing that worried her was just how strongly she was starting to feel about him, and what it might mean for her and Teddie if things didn't work out. She wasn't going to let that stop her though, just like she wasn't going to let what had happened with Jesse stop her either. Drew was worth taking a chance on, and so was she. They both deserved to be happy and she had a very strong feeling that this was their chance.

17

Drew had spent a long time thinking about where his date with Eden should be. The most important thing was that it was somewhere, or doing something, that made Teddie happy. Drew knew that would be enough for Eden to enjoy herself, but he wanted there to be something about the date that was just for her. He'd googled a lot of potential ideas, getting a bit side-tracked by a website that suggested tobogganing and cross-country skiing. He'd found himself looking at a resort in Michigan, which led on to research about the average snowfall in the state and how long their ski season was. It was something that happened a lot; the way his brain worked when something piqued his interest was that he wanted to know more about it.

Much to Drew's surprise, he realised halfway through his research that the thing he was so interested in wasn't skiing in Michigan at all, it was Eden and Teddie. He was imagining the three of them there together, amongst all that pristine white snow, and wondering whether the little boy would really enjoy it. Cross-country skiing definitely wouldn't work for Teddie. He had this habit of going completely jelly-legged when he'd had enough of walking. Whenever Eden was holding one of his hands and Drew had the other, he'd immediately go slack so they'd swing him in the air. Teddie loved being spun around too, so he'd probably love tobogganing in the snow, if nothing else. Drew could picture Eden throwing back her head and laughing as she and Teddie whizzed down the hill, and suddenly he wanted to go on holiday to Michigan, with them, just so he could make that vision of them smiling and laughing a reality.

Drew wasn't prone to making impulsive decisions. Some people with autism were, and others needed everything planned and discussed in advance, with any deviation from those plans something they struggled to deal with. Drew didn't fit neatly into either of those categories, just like many people with autism. Yet in that moment he could quite easily have given in to the impulse to book a trip to Michigan, despite how ridiculous he knew it sounded. If it had been the right time of year for tobogganing, he might even have done it. For once in his life he wanted to throw caution to the wind and do something no one would expect. It wasn't snowing in Michigan yet, though. He hoped he and Eden would still be seeing each other when it was and then, who knows, maybe they really could take the trip.

For now he'd settled for something closer to home. They'd be spending most of the day at a theme park that had lots of rides for under-fives, which he was certain would appeal to Teddie's love of being spun around. It was a forty-five-minute drive from Port Kara to the theme park that was situated between Newquay and Wadebridge. Drew had bought a mobile phone mount for the headrest in his car, so that Teddie would be able to watch *Paddington* on the way if the journey got too much for him, and he'd planned something for the final part of the day, with Eden in mind. Although he was keeping the details of that a secret for now.

'How did he sleep last night?' Drew asked, after he'd attached Teddie's car seat to the Isofix mechanism in his car, and Eden had strapped him in.

'Not bad. He went off at 8 p.m. and was awake at five wanting to bounce on my head, which is pretty good going for Teddie.'

'Hopefully he'll make it through a day of adventure then.'

'He's going to love it.' Eden moved closer to Drew, their bodies almost touching as they stood outside the car talking. Love was an overused word, and the literal part of Drew's brain sometimes made him want to challenge people who used it in throwaway remarks like *I love your new shirt*, or *I love the hotdogs the hospital restaurant serves*. Of course he never actually did that, it would make him a pompous bore, which was just another trait he had no desire to share with his father. People just used 'love' when they meant they really liked something. The only shame was if it devalued the word when it really counted. He didn't know how accurate Eden's use of the word would turn out to be when it came to describing what Teddie thought of the theme park, but he hoped it was.

That wasn't why the word had suddenly stopped Drew in his tracks, though. For him the word love meant deep affection, an attachment to something his life would be diminished without. Now, as he stood just inches away from Eden, he realised that was exactly how he felt about her and Teddie. They'd been friends for just a couple of months, but if the two of them suddenly disappeared from his life, it would undoubtedly be diminished. Honesty was incredibly important to Drew, but he couldn't tell Eden how he felt, because he wasn't sure if it was 'normal' to have feelings as intense as this so soon and he didn't want to freak her out.

Drew had spent his whole life masking his autism, the need to do so having been drummed into him by his father, long before his diagnosis, with physical consequences when he didn't manage to do it. Even now it didn't come easily to just be who he was, and to say what he was thinking, because he knew there could still be consequences. They might not come from the force of his father's hand connecting with the side of his head any more, but they could hurt even more. If the consequence of telling Eden how strongly he felt was to scare her away, that would be far more painful than any punishment his father had ever dished out. So Drew couldn't tell her that he loved her, and Teddie too. He just hoped he'd be able to show her and that eventually she might realise it for herself, without him having to say anything at all.

'Shall we hit the road then?' Drew attempted an upbeat American accent. 'And see what Teddie makes of Cornwall's number one theme park?'

'Has Cornwall got a number two theme park?'

'It's probably the swing set in your mum and dad's back garden.' Drew grinned as Eden started to laugh. He really did love that sound, and that wasn't even the wrong use of the word.

* * *

It had been a perfect day. Eden and Drew had talked about all kinds of things, from their childhood memories to the latest goings on at work. She'd told him how worried she'd been about Eve on the day Callum died, and how her comments had made Eden wonder just what sort of trauma her friend had been through. It could be incredibly difficult when an incident at work triggered a personal memory, and Drew understood that. Thankfully Eve seemed to have gone back to her old self by the time she came in for her next shift, and Eden hadn't been sure if she should say anything. Having Drew to confide in and get his take on what she might be able to do to support her friend if something like that happened again had felt really good. He might never be the loudest person in the room, and he didn't share his thoughts and opinions with just anyone, but she considered herself lucky that he did that with her, and she valued his insight more and more.

Teddie had loved the theme park every bit as much as Eden had expected him to. She and Drew had taken him on all the rides that were suitable for his age and height. His favourites had been the dizzy dinosaur waltzers, and the dragon family rollercoaster. The three of them had got wet on the water rides, and Eden hadn't been able to resist buying a photograph of them all on the log flume. They looked like a proper family, their mouths open wide with laughter and shock as they plummeted down the track into the water. Not for the first time she found herself wishing that the image reflected the truth, and that they really were a family. Wanting a life like that wasn't such a huge ask, when there were people out there praying for a lottery win, or planning their acceptance speech at the Oscars in ten years' time. Eden didn't want anything big, she just wanted this, a family of her own, where fun days out were spent together, and no one prioritised getting drunk over spending time with their children, or lied and manipulated people into doing what they wanted out of a sense of guilt or fear.

Drew had planned the whole day with Teddie right at its centre, even the picnic he'd made had been perfect. It had all the elements Teddie needed to indulge in the perfect beige banquet, but Drew had also made delicious halloumi and chorizo baguettes on crusty French bread for him and Eden, with rocket and a chilli jam that made her tastebuds feel like they were dancing. He'd brought cloudy lemonade in glass bottles, and walnut and chocolate brownies that might well have been the best thing Eden had ever tasted. The picnic would have proved, if Eden hadn't already known it, that Drew came from a wealthy background. There were no slightly squashed scotch eggs or shop bought quiche Lorraine in his picnic basket. It meant that the effort he'd gone to for Teddie's beige banquet of sausage rolls, cold chicken nuggets, and giant cheesy puffs was well out of his comfort zone and it showed just how carefully Drew considered what other people needed. He'd texted Eden to check what she liked to eat, and had found a way to combine some of her favourites. Wanting to make it perfect for her and Teddie was just one of the reasons why the family she kept picturing had Drew in it, not just someone *like* Drew. It was scary to be thinking like that, when she still couldn't be certain where this was going, or how far he wanted to take it, but somehow it had happened anyway.

'Are you ever going to tell me where we're going next?' Eden turned to look at Drew as they drove out of the theme park. He'd told her they needed to leave at three, in order to get to their next destination, but he still wouldn't say where they were going.

'You'll find out when we get there.' He smiled, no doubt knowing this was driving her mad.

'Just promise me you're not taking me to an abandoned quarry to make it easier to dump my body.' She laughed, and he raised his eyebrows.

'Well to be fair with my training in forensic pathology I would have the edge on planning the perfect murder.'

'You're not doing much to reassure me.' She glanced over again as he changed gear and the car picked up speed. He had really nice hands. They looked strong, and completely capable of farming the remote croft Gwen had imagined him running, but Eden knew what delicate important work they did. Right now her fingers were itching with the desire to lay her hand over his. It wouldn't have been a particularly bold move, but it was gesture of intimacy she wasn't sure they had yet. They might have kissed several times, but this was the kind of casual intimacy that came with a more established relationship and she was suddenly worried she might be moving at a pace that would make Drew uncomfortable. The start of a relationship was hard to navigate at the best of times and she wanted to be certain that Drew knew what he'd be getting into if they took things to the next level and started acting like they were in this for the long haul. It wasn't just her heart on the line, it was Teddie's too. Thankfully Drew didn't seem to have realised just how much conflict was going on in her head.

'Okay, I promise I won't test out my theory about the perfect murder on you, or anyone else for that matter.'

'I'm glad to hear it, although it must be quite different working with the police, than at the hospital.' Talking about work was probably safer ground than discussing anything personal. It was easier to keep the distance between them that way.

'I feel privileged that I get to do both. When I took the contract at the hospital, I knew some of the work would be postmortems for the coroner's office, because in theory all the pathologists on the team have the chance to do them, as well as hospital postmortems. But in practice most of my colleagues are more comfortable focusing on the diagnostic and research elements of the role, so the majority fall to me. I had my own motivations for specialising in postmortems and forensic pathology. I just wasn't sure at first whether I'd have scope to continue the forensic side once I started as St Piran's.' Drew was concentrating on the road as he spoke, but Eden could sense the passion he had for his work. 'But thankfully I was given the chance to be part of the area-wide on-call team. If an incident happens the police often want a forensic pathologist on scene as quickly as possible. It's different to a city centre, when it would almost certainly be a dedicated role, but down here I think they're grateful for an extra pair of hands being available to cover, if the need arises.'

'I think what you do is amazing and I know Flora was your motivation for getting into pathology in the first place, but I'm guessing your interest in forensics came from the work your dad did?' They'd talked a lot about his work and she'd seen first-hand the way that certain cases could affect him, because of what had happened to his sister, but he'd been far vaguer about his interest in forensics and even now she wasn't sure she was going to get a straight answer. Talking about his father still seemed to make him shut down, but this time he took a deep breath before responding.

'I suppose it was in a way. I've always been interested in forensics because my father was involved in the law and so were almost all of his friends. There was more to it than that, though.' Drew's tone gave nothing away, but there was a muscle going in his cheek. 'Maybe my father's career should have put me off getting involved in the legal system. He was a difficult man. He still is probably, I just don't have to deal with him any more, thank God. Before becoming a judge, he was a very successful barrister with the ability to argue that black was white if he wanted to, and persuade a jury that he was right. If he had an opinion in his home life, nothing could sway that either. When my mother tried to persuade him that there was something *going on with me*, as she put it, and that I wasn't suited to the boarding school he'd gone to, he wouldn't hear of it.

He tried to make me conform and *act like a normal boy for Christ's sake*, and for a long time I really did try. He saw my inability to be like him as yet another of my mother's failings. When he wasn't taking it out on me, she'd get the brunt of it.'

'Oh God, I knew things were difficult between you but that's awful. I can see why you don't want anything to do with him.' Eden couldn't resist reaching out to him this time. 'And you're clearly nothing like him.'

'That's why I never wanted to be a barrister. He spent years being able to spin the truth depending on who he was representing and he didn't care as long as he won. That must have been what made it so easy for him to lie about seeing other women behind my mother's back, and to make her think she was going mad with his blatant denials. I'm sure he invented gaslighting, long before it became so widely recognised.' There was a new heaviness to Drew's voice, and it was clearly still painful even after all this time. 'Once he became a judge he had even more people fawning over him. Eventually it drove my mother to the edge and then over a line she shouldn't have crossed. She started taking sleeping tablets and anti-depressants and it escalated from there. I thought the lowest point had come when she got attacked after going to meet someone who said they could supply heroin. They took her handbag and her phone and she'd clearly taken something by the time she was found slumped in a shop doorway. Thankfully it was a volunteer from a local homelessness charity who found her, and my mother was able to tell them the name of my university. I was so grateful to them for contacting me rather than my father, and that's how I first got involved with the charity, as a way of saying thank you. I don't know what he'd have done if he'd discovered what she was doing when she was attacked.'

'Your poor mum, and poor you.' Eden's hand was still resting on his leg and she wanted him to stop the car, so she could hug him, but she wanted him to finish the story too. It was like another layer of the armour he been wearing was being stripped away. These were things he'd been holding back since they'd got to know one another, but he finally seemed to trust her enough to tell her about this too. 'No wonder you understood what I meant when I told you about Mum's problems, but I had it far easier. I had Felix for a start and, even if my dad was in denial, he was always kind and loving in his own way. I can't even imagine what it was like dealing with that on your own.'

'I don't think either of us had it easy.' He turned towards her briefly then, a look of complete understanding passing between them, before he focused on the road again. 'The worst part was that my mother being attacked didn't turn out to be the lowest point of it all. That came with her accidental overdose.'

There was something about the way he said the word *accidental* that struck Eden. It was as if he'd put quotation marks around the word, and she was almost certain she knew what was coming next, but she didn't want to interrupt him and she stayed silent as he continued.

'I wanted answers after she died and I hoped they'd come with the post-mortem, but they never really did. I wanted to make a difference for Flora and after that I wanted to make a difference for my mother too. I didn't want another family to go through what I did, or feel like they were being fobbed off, because there were people who might not want the truth to come out. My father would have hated the interest it would have raked up in the press if it had been revealed that his actions had driven my mother to suicide. Sometimes I've even wondered if he encouraged her in some way.' Drew shook his head. 'Whatever his reason for accepting such a superficial investigation, he wanted to come out of the situation with his reputation unblemished. That was far more important than the truth, and I wanted to do what I could to try and change that.'

'She'd have been so proud of you.' Eden might never have met his mother, or even know much about her, but she was certain what she was saying was true. After all, how could anyone be anything but proud of what Drew had achieved?

'I hope so.' Drew turned the car down a narrow lane, with a sign directing them to where they could access the Camel Trail. 'I'll never know, but my father hates that I didn't follow him into the law, and that's more than enough for me. Right, here we are.'

Eden turned and looked out of the window. There was a large wooden building at the back of the car park, and a sign emblazoned with the words 'Cycle Hire'.

Her heart sank, heat colouring her cheeks. 'I thought I told you that I can't ride a bike.'

'You'll be okay with what I've got planned. I promise you it will be fine.' There was a smile playing around Drew's lips and she realised she trusted him when he said it would be fine. She had no idea how, but she knew it would be. If Jesse had been wearing the same kind of expression as Drew, it would have been because he was laughing at her expense, planning something to show her up, and knock her confidence. He'd been a master at it. She knew without a shadow of a doubt that Drew would never deliberately do that to her and another wave of affection washed over her as he got out of the car and took Teddie out of his car seat. The little boy was hugging him tightly, almost as if he'd understood every word of the conversation they'd had on the way here and he wanted to comfort Drew the way Eden had wished she could.

'Do you mind just grabbing the rucksack out of the back, please. It's got everything we might need.' Drew was clearly still determined not to give anything away and Eden did as he asked, before following him in the direction of the cabin. He definitely had the heavier load carrying Teddie in his arms. Maybe they were just parking here. There were various stops along the Camel Trail, a route that ran alongside the River Camel from Padstow to Wenfordbridge on the track-bed of two former railway lines. Eden had never walked the trail, but it was something she'd wanted to do for a long time. The scenery was stunning, and from what she'd heard the terrain was fairly even. Although if Drew was intending to walk rather than ride, she'd need to get Teddie's buggy out of the car, because he was far too heavy to carry over any significant distance.

'Shall I go back for Teddie's buggy?' Drew shook his head, almost before Eden had finished asking the question.

'We won't need it.' The smile was still playing around Drew's mouth, but Eden wasn't going to keep pushing him for an answer he clearly didn't want to give. It was only when they rounded the side of the cabin that she saw the rows of different types of bikes. There were kids' ones and adult ones, as well as e-bikes for anyone who needed to take it a bit easier, but then she saw the family bikes. They looked almost more like oversized pedal cars, with two seats for adults, each with its own steering wheel. There was a bench seat behind, that could accommodate a couple of children, and another bucket-style seat in front, which reminded Eden of the ones in shopping trolleys. And all of the family bikes had red-and-white striped canopies.

'Are we taking one of those out?' She was already smiling at the idea. Teddie would be in his element sitting up front.

'Yes, I've booked one for the next three hours and we can see how far the Camel Trail takes us. I know you said you always wanted Teddie to be able to ride a bike, and that you wish you could too. We might not be able to make either of those things happen today, but we can work on them. In the meantime, I thought this might be the next best thing.'

'It isn't the next best thing. It's *the* best thing and so are you.' Dropping the rucksack on the ground, Eden threw caution to the wind and wrapped her arms around Drew, sandwiching Teddie between them.

'You're the kindest, most thoughtful man I've ever met.'

'You forgot ruggedly handsome.' He laughed and she nodded.

'Sorry, I thought that was obvious.' Reaching up, she kissed him, not caring what anyone thought of the display of affection outside the bike hire shop. Finding out she could have such strong feelings for someone who fitted into her life so perfectly hadn't been something Eden had even thought possible. It was like Drew was the final part of a puzzle she hadn't even realised had a missing piece, but he'd changed the whole picture and she never wanted it to go back to how it had been before.

18

Over the next few weeks Eden and Drew's relationship went from strength to strength. They spent as much time together as they could, most of it with Teddie, although they managed to spend some time alone. Felix was now living with her parents for the time being too, while he waited for the flat he would be renting to become available. It was an option he'd had to resort to when he couldn't extend the lease on his Airbnb any further. It was a bit of a tight squeeze with all of them there, but Eden felt confident leaving Teddie in the care of his uncle and it meant that she and Drew had the opportunity to get to know one another better.

'Is this what they call official?' Drew had smiled the morning after she'd first spent the night at his flat.

'Do you want it to be?' She'd searched his face and knew the answer long before he responded.

'More than anything.'

'That's good then, me too.' She'd rested her head against his chest, and it had felt as if it was exactly where she was supposed to be.

'Just promise me one thing.' Drew's tone had been serious and she'd tipped her head back to look at him.

'What is it?'

'Promise me you'll tell me if anything changes. I can take anything, as long as it's the truth, but the one thing I could never deal with is living a lie. I witnessed my father lying to my mother for years, and I watched her living that lie rather than facing up to the fact that their relationship had been over for decades. I couldn't stand the thought that you might want out at some point, but you don't tell me.'

'I can't see that happening.' She trailed a hand down his chest, but he didn't smile.

'Please, Eden. Just promise me, no lies and no pretending.'

'I promise.'

It hadn't been a difficult promise to make because she wanted exactly the same thing. They'd both had far too much lying and dishonesty in their past to allow that to be a feature of their life together, and it really did feel as if they were building a life together. Although it had still been a shock when Eden had been given a letter, addressed to the two of them, as though they were a long-established couple. The handwritten note left in A&E reception had been the last thing she'd expected. It was a thank-you letter from Callum's mother for everything they'd done on the day of his death. Eden had sobbed the whole time she was reading it, but the final paragraph had got to her most.

Nothing will ever take away the pain of losing our son, but you helped us to see that he could still touch the lives of other people the way he always had done. If his death can help prevent the same thing happening to someone else, he'll have made his mark on the world, the way we always knew he would do. He'll remain our beautiful, brilliant boy and forever eighteen. Callum knew he was loved every single day of his life, and he gave that love back just as freely. I hope that's what everyone will remember about him and that they'll all try to be a little more like Cal xx

Eden had kept the letter with her all day, not wanting to risk losing it, and she was finally about to show it to Drew. They'd met up to take Teddie to get some ice cream after work, and they were sitting outside in the sunshine, at a café near the beach.

'I got this today, from Callum's parents, but it's addressed to both of us.' She handed the letter over watching different expressions flit across his face as he read it.

'No one should ever have to lose a child.' Drew's eyes were glassy when he looked back up at her, after he'd finished. 'My mother never got over losing

Flora; I'm so glad Callum's parents are finding some solace in the fact that his postmortem will contribute to medical research and knowing what caused his death. At least now they know it was long QT syndrome and they can get other members of the family screened.' It was often a hereditary condition, which increased the risk of an irregular heartbeat, sometimes causing seizures and even sudden death, the same tragedy that had befallen Callum.

'His mother told me that he has two younger sisters and I know she'll want to do everything she can to protect them. It's going to be so hard for Callum's siblings, whatever the outcome of their tests. If I ever lost Felix...' She shook her head, unable to contemplate the prospect of it, let alone finish the sentence. 'I hope having each other will help them.'

'Me too.' Drew folded Rachael's letter carefully and slid it back into the envelope. 'When you lose a sibling early, you lose a huge part of your identity too. I wasn't anyone's little brother any more, after Flora was gone. I was suddenly an only child, carrying all the connotations that came with, but not feeling like the label belonged to me at all. I had to throw myself into studying and make myself a promise that I wouldn't let Flora down, otherwise I think I might have ended up like my mother, searching for something to take away the pain.'

'You didn't let Flora down, and I think the world would be a better place if more people were like you too.'

'I think there might have been a bit too much rum in your rum and raisin ice cream.' He was trying to brush off the compliment, but she wanted him to know how much he meant to her.

'It's got nothing to do with the ice cream.' The way she felt about Drew seemed to be bubbling up inside her. She wanted him to know she was almost certain she was falling in love with him and that she was already finding it hard to imagine a life without him. But then Teddie started to whinge.

'I think someone has had enough of sitting around.' Drew bent down and picked up the brightly coloured toy that Teddie had dropped. It was like a heavy-duty version of bubble wrap, one that could be popped in and out repeatedly, although Teddie was inclined to try and bite off the bubbles if no one was watching. Drew stroked Teddie's hand before he passed it back to him. 'There you go, lovely boy.'

The moment might have passed to tell Drew how she felt, but as Eden watched him with her son she was more certain than ever that what she felt for him was love. She'd just have to wait for the right time to tell him and with Teddie getting increasingly frustrated at sitting still, now wasn't it.

'Shall we take him up to the country park?' She asked, looking at Drew who was already reaching forward to lift Teddie up. He didn't care that he might be about to get smeared with ice cream, or that his peaceful early evening down by the beach was about to turn into something very different. He just wanted to be with Eden and Teddie, and it was all she wanted too. If that wasn't enough to prove that this was love, she didn't know what was.

* * *

After Eden got home and had put Teddie to bed, she thought about messaging Drew to thank him for a lovely time and to tell him how she felt. In her determination to tell him at the right moment, she hadn't considered whether or not it would be the right moment for him too. Suddenly she was wondering if it might be easier for him if she put it all in a message, especially if he wasn't ready to reciprocate those feelings.

She was still staring at her phone, trying to decide whether texting Drew was the way to go, when an email popped up from Sadie. She hadn't given Jesse's sister her new mobile number but, unlike her ex, Eden hadn't blocked Sadie's emails. She had no idea what his sister could possibly want, but she was already dreading the contents of the message, even before she opened it.

> Have you heard from Jesse? He's left a note saying that he messed everything up with you and Teddie, and that if he can't put it right he doesn't want to be here any more. After you left, he finally started getting the help he needed, so he could prove to you that he's changed because he was convinced you'd eventually come back. But when you didn't call on his birthday, I think he realised it was all too late and he started spiralling again. Please call me on the number below if you hear anything at all. I'm terrified.

It felt as if Eden couldn't breathe as she read the message. It wasn't difficult to read between the lines and see that nothing had really changed despite the work Jesse had supposedly been doing on himself. All these months she'd hoped he might finally be moving on and accepting that she'd needed to break free, but he'd been biding his time, believing it was just a matter of waiting it out before she was sucked back into the toxic mess she'd been a part of for so long. Eden was a different person now, though. She didn't really believe the threats he'd made to his sister, and the thought of Jesse coming back into her life was suffocating. She didn't want to see him, and she definitely didn't want to put Teddie through all the trauma that Jesse would bring into their lives, but despite all that she knew how desperate Sadie would be and just the thought of how she'd feel if it was Felix meant she couldn't simply ignore the email. Even as she picked up the phone to make the call, her stomach started churning. She was opening up lines of communication she'd tried so hard to close down, certain she knew exactly how the conversation was about to go, and within minutes she was proven right. Sadie was beside herself with worry, and convinced that Jesse was going to follow through on his threat this time.

'Please will you come and speak to him.' Sadie was pleading now and Eden could picture Jesse's sister desperately trying to find the words to persuade her to help find him. 'I'm not asking you to make him any promises, but if he sees you face to face and you let him know that you and Teddie are okay, he might be able to forgive himself and see a way forward.'

Eden wanted to tell Sadie that this was just Jesse doing what he always did, and looking for someone to help him out of a bad situation he'd got himself into. He could so easily play the victim and make out he wanted to change, but Eden couldn't see that happening, not really. Even so, when Sadie burst into tears, she found herself agreeing. She really didn't want to go and if she could have come up with any other solution she would have taken it. But despite her feelings for Jesse having died years ago, he was still Teddie's father and Sadie's brother, and if there was even the tiniest chance she had the power to prevent something happening to him she'd never be able to forgive herself if she stood by and did nothing. Even as an internal battle raged within her, Eden realised she could make this work if she had to. She was about to start a week off work and she could make the journey back to London, and still be home in time for a trip she and Drew had planned down to Lizard Point, but he was going to want to know why she wouldn't be around for the next few days.

Eden knew she should phone him, but it would be easier to explain in writing. She didn't want to run the risk of it coming out wrong, and Drew thinking there was still something between her and Jesse, so she typed out a text instead.

I've just had a call from Jesse's sister. He's gone missing and she's worried he's going to do something silly. She thinks I can help and I don't want her to have to face this alone xx

Eden stared at the message for a moment, wondering how she'd feel if she was in Drew's position, and if he was the one travelling hundreds of miles because he somehow still felt responsible for his ex-partner. She couldn't pretend she'd have been comfortable with that and she knew that Drew's experience with his father had made him wary. Maybe it would be better if she didn't give him quite so much detail. Deleting the message, she tried again.

I've just had a call from an old friend, she's going through a really difficult time with her family and she's got no support. I'm going to pop down to London for a couple of nights, just to make sure she's okay, but I'll be back in plenty of time for our trip. I can't wait to have some time away with you xx

None of what she'd written was a lie, exactly. She just hadn't spelt out the whole truth. She'd meant what she'd said about their trip away, and whatever else happened she was going to tell him then how she really felt. It might be scary and she was putting herself on the line yet again, but she was more certain of it than ever. She just had to get through the next few days and prove to Sadie that her worries about Jesse were unfounded. Maybe this was all for the best, and it would finally give her the closure she'd never really got with Jesse. After that she could look forward to facing the future with Drew. Yet, even as she tried to convince herself of that, a sense of foreboding made her shiver, and suddenly it was far harder to picture the future she'd been allowing herself to hope for. Her gut was telling her that this was a bad idea, but Jesse had spent years messing with her ability to trust her own instincts and, even after all their time apart, it was still playing to his advantage.

19

'Please tell me you're not really going down to London because you feel you need to protect that idiot from his own actions?' Eden's father shook his head, and for a moment she wanted to laugh. It was ironic that Dave felt so strongly about the idea, given that he'd spent years protecting his wife from the consequences of her own actions, but maybe love was what made the difference. If you loved someone, protecting them was what you wanted to do, even if it cost you dearly. Except she didn't love Jesse and yet, here she was, willing to put her life on hold to chase after him. No wonder her dad sounded so shocked. She could hardly believe she was doing this either, but she'd witnessed so much death and bereavement in her job, and she'd seen what that had done to the people left behind. Jesse had made the same threat so many times and he'd never acted upon it, but his threats still had a hold on her and so did her sense of responsibility towards his sister.

'I'm doing it for Sadie, not him. He's the only family she's got left and...' She'd been about to compare their situation with what she and Felix had gone through, but that would just rake up all sorts of pain that none of them needed to relive, especially not now.

'You're a good person, Eddie.' Felix dropped a kiss on her head, before looking across at his parents. 'Some might say too good, but we wouldn't really want to change that about her, would we?'

'Of course not.' Their mother's smile was tight, as if there were a hundred things she wanted to say, but she wasn't allowed to say any of them. 'Just be careful. There might be reasons why Jesse has disappeared that you don't want to get mixed up in. I want you to promise me that if anything feels off or weird, you'll get on the next train home.'

'I will.' Eden nodded, before exchanging a brief look with her brother. It was hardly any surprise that their mother was already coming up with her own theories about what might have happened to Jesse, but Eden didn't have time for that now. 'I'll be staying two nights at the most and then I'll be back. If we haven't found Jesse by then, I'll try and persuade Sadie to report his disappearance to the police, but either way it won't be my responsibility any more and I'm going to tell her that this is the last time I can ever get involved.'

'Two nights.' Her father nodded. 'If you're not back after that I'm coming to get you to make sure you're safe.'

'Okay, Dad.' Eden smiled, a warm glow spreading inside her. It might be a bit late for her father to become the overprotective dad she'd missed out on during her childhood, but it felt good to know he cared so much, and that her mum and Felix would be looking out for her too. Right now Sadie didn't have any of that kind of support, and if it was wrong for Eden to try and bridge that gap for a couple of days, then she'd just have to be wrong.

* * *

When Drew had got Eden's message, it hadn't surprised him all that much to learn that she was planning to be there for an old friend. It was just one of the things he loved about her, the fact she was willing to put herself out for the people she cared about. There he was, using that word again: love. There was no denying it any more though. Just the thought of how much he was going to miss her when she was away convinced him of that and he really wanted to see her before she left, even just for a few moments. It was probably a ridiculous idea to offer to drive her to the station, she could have walked there if she needed to and she had family who'd be only too willing to take her if not. He didn't care, he was still going to ask her.

He assumed Teddie would be staying with her parents and Felix, but he wasn't sure, and the thought of not seeing the little boy for the next few days was almost as much of a wrench as not seeing Eden. He hadn't been certain he was capable of love, or even that he wanted to be, not when it put you at risk of so much hurt, but Eden and Teddie had found a way into his heart. They filled up the space that had felt so empty since losing Flora and his mother and he never wanted to lose them.

Drew rang Eden early on the morning she was due to leave, hoping it wouldn't take much persuasion to let him drive her to the station. Although he knew she'd hate the idea of putting him out. Her phone was answered on the third ring.

'Hello.' The voice didn't sound like Eden's but it had to be.

'It's Drew,' he said, despite the fact his name must have come up on her caller display.

'Oh hi, yes, sorry Drew. It's Karen, Eden's in the shower. I thought I'd better answer her phone in case you need to speak to her urgently, before she leaves for Sadie's place.'

'Sadie.' He repeated the name. It wasn't particularly common and he knew it was what Jesse's sister was called. Even so he was still hoping it was some kind of crazy coincidence, until Karen continued.

'Yes. She seems to think Eden is the only one who can help her track Jesse down. Sometimes I don't understand my daughter at all, even after all this time she doesn't seem able to cut ties with Jesse completely. I suppose it's all to do with Teddie.'

'It probably is.' Somehow he managed to get the words out and sound almost blasé, despite the fact he felt as if his insides had turned to stone.

'Can I give her a message for you?'

'No, don't worry. I'll text her. Thanks Karen, see you soon.' Drew maintained his upbeat delivery in the hope that Eden's mother wouldn't realise she'd put her foot in it. He wanted to give Eden a chance to be honest about where she was really going, when they were face to face, not just because her mother had tipped her off. He needed to be certain it was because Eden wanted to tell him the truth. If she didn't, he knew he was going to be devastated, but not because he thought she might still have feelings for Jesse. Perhaps she did, but Karen had been right that sharing Teddie meant there would always be some kind of bond between the two of them, however tenuous. What mattered was whether or not Eden lied about it. She understood how much that mattered to him and she'd promised him she wouldn't do it. Typing a text to Eden, Drew pressed send before he had a chance to rethink it.

> I wondered if I could drop you to the station? I'm writing up reports, so I can take an early lunch break any time. I'd like to have the chance to see you before you go, however briefly. I'll really miss you and Teddie xx

For the next twenty minutes, Drew paced around the kitchen of his flat, earning himself a series of scornful looks from Marmalade. He was probably giving the cat indigestion with all his fidgeting, but he couldn't help it. When his phone pinged with an incoming text, he snatched it up.

> Thank you, I'd love that. I'm catching the 12.25 train, but Teddie will be staying with Mum and Dad. If you come at 12, you can give him a hug goodbye too. Although be warned, I might cry on your shoulder about how much I'm going to miss him, and you too of course xx

Drew replied straight away.

> It's a date. See you then xx

He still had no way of knowing whether Karen had tipped her daughter off about their conversation. A big part of him even hoped she had, because that way Eden would almost certainly tell him the truth once they met face to face. He was already praying she would, because if she looked into his eyes and lied to him, when he asked her a direct question, there'd be no road back. The thought of things being over between them was more painful than he would ever have believed, but it was better than a lifetime of lies. He hoped to God it didn't come to that, but the terrible sense of dread creeping over him said otherwise.

* * *

When Eden had asked Teddie for a hug goodbye, she hadn't been certain he'd do it. As loving as her son could be, things like that were never guaranteed with Teddie, but this time he delivered in style. He'd hugged Eden tightly and planted a kiss on her lips, and he'd hugged Drew too. When she'd watched them together, that sensation of seeing everything she wanted in front of her had washed over her again. All she needed to do was to get these next few days out of the way and she couldn't wait for them to be over.

The drive down to the station was far too short, and as Drew pulled up outside, Eden knew it was going to be a wrench to say goodbye. She'd seen his text when she'd got out of the shower, and her mother had shouted something to her from the other room about having missed a call from Drew.

'It's alright, he's sent me a message,' she shouted back through to her mum, smiling to herself at what Drew had written, before quickly sending a response. No one she'd dated had ever been this thoughtful before and, if things went the way she hoped they would, she was determined never to take Drew for granted.

'Thanks for driving me to the station and for coming to say goodbye. It means a lot to me that you wanted to.'

'Of course I wanted to.' He took hold of her hand. 'You're such a good person giving up your time off to be there for your friend.'

'That's what Felix said, but anyone would do it for someone they cared about.'

'Not everyone cares the way you do.' Drew was still holding her hand. 'Do you know her family? Can the trouble between them be sorted out?'

'I don't know, but I'm not going down there for her family's sake I'm going down to support Sa... Samantha.' She could so easily have told him the truth, she very nearly did, by accident, and she wished she had. It was too late now, though. If she backtracked and told him that Samantha was really Sadie, it would all sound so suspicious, when the truth was there was nothing to it. Maybe it was just as well, she didn't want to hurt him, even inadvertently. That was the whole reason she'd decided to hide the truth from him in the first place. If he thought she was doing this because she still loved Jesse, it would cause him unnecessary pain. It was better this way and she squeezed his hand, hoping he'd realise just how hard she was finding it to say goodbye.

'I'll be back before you know it, but I'm really going to miss you.'

'I'm really going to miss you too.' There was something in his tone that made her scalp prickle; it was almost as if they were saying goodbye forever. Pushing the thought out of her head, she silently berated herself for blowing things out of proportion. She was reading far too much into his tone because she really didn't want to go. If she didn't get out of the car soon, she was going to make a complete fool of herself and start crying or something else equally ridiculous. She was only leaving for a couple of days after all. It had to be love for her emotions to be this heightened.

'Bye, Drew.' She kissed him gently and then pulled away, grabbing her rucksack and forcing herself to open the door.

'Goodbye, Eden.' There it was again, that same finality in his tone, and she shivered despite the warmth of the heavy coat she was wearing. It was just the prospect of seeing Jesse again making her twitchy, that was all.

Less than three minutes after she'd got to the platform, her train arrived, and another minute later it pulled out of Port Kara station. Her mind was still on Drew and she didn't even last until the next stop before pulling out her phone to text him. She'd switched it to silent before she'd left home, hating the buzzing and pinging of messages in the quiet of the train. It was why she hadn't realised that a message had already come through from Drew, and she couldn't help smiling to herself. At least she wasn't the only one who had it bad. But the smile slid off her face as she opened the message, her heart thudding and nausea rising in her throat.

> I wish you'd told me you were going to see Sadie to help her look for Jesse. I understand why you'd want to do that, but what I can't understand is why you lied about it. The one thing I asked was for there not to be any lies between us, but now there are. I care about you so much, Eden, but I can't do this. Take care of yourself and Teddie, I really will miss you both.

The words were blurring in front of Eden's eyes. She'd been so incredibly stupid, and all she wanted now was a chance to put things right, but she had a terrible feeling that it was already far too late.

20

Eden fingers were twitching; she could so easily reach out and hit the emergency button to stop the train, but what then? Even if she somehow channelled her inner Tom Cruise in *Mission: Impossible* and managed to jump down from the train and run all the way back to Port Kara, what was she going to do once she got there? As soon as she read the message from Drew, she knew what had happened. She should have known her mum would answer the call when her phone rang, and that she'd tell Drew exactly where Eden was going. It hadn't been malicious and she couldn't blame her mother, even if she wished she could.

She should have told Drew the truth from the beginning, like he'd asked her to, and trusted him not to turn the situation into something it wasn't. It had been the legacy of all those years with Jesse that had persuaded her it was easier to lie and that it would be safer that way. Somehow, he'd managed to come between them from hundreds of miles away, but it was Eden who'd allowed that to happen and she only had herself to blame. She'd ruined things with Drew and hurt a man who didn't deserve anything but the honesty he'd asked for.

Eden had to try and put this right. The train would be stopping in Bodmin Parkway and she'd get off there, then catch the next train back to Port Kara, or jump in a taxi, whatever it took to find Drew as soon as she could. She just needed the chance to try and explain why she'd done what she'd done. Maybe then he'd understand that however idiotic it had been, her intention was to protect him and she'd done it out of love. She wanted to tell him so much more too; that the last couple of months had been the best she could ever remember and that she'd found exactly what she'd always wanted, when she hadn't even been looking. She needed to tell him she loved him, even if it might seem too soon and completely the wrong time to do it, because none of that mattered any more. It could be her last chance to say any of those things and she didn't want to miss it.

Eden would just have to message Sadie and tell her she wasn't coming down to London to help look for Jesse. She was angry with herself for ever having agreed to it, and if Sadie tried to plead with her again, she wasn't going to let herself be coerced into changing her mind. Jesse had robbed her of her freedom for years, and she didn't owe him anything. She didn't want him to come to any harm, but it wasn't her responsibility to keep him safe, not any more. It never really had been.

She was scrolling through her contacts to get to Sadie's number, when the screen flashed with an incoming call. She almost dropped the phone when she realised it was Sadie.

'I was just about to ring you.' Eden braced herself to explain why she wouldn't be coming, but she didn't get the chance.

'Jesse just called me. He's in Port Kara and he said he's going to find your new boyfriend.'

'What do you mean my new boyfriend?' Eden's head felt as if it was spinning. She'd always known that by going home to her parents, Jesse would easily be able to find her if he wanted to, but he couldn't possibly know about Drew. She didn't have any online presence and they didn't have any mutual friends any more either. Her mother might have been a bit of a blabbermouth at times, but if Jesse rang there was no way she'd have told him anything. She'd have almost certainly have slammed the phone down instead.

'After you didn't get in touch on his birthday, he started trying to find ways of contacting you. You'd changed your mobile number and the emails he tried sending you bounced back too. Nothing came up, but when he called he told me he'd finally found something two days ago: photographs of you at a fundraiser for the hospital opposite your parents' place. You're in the background of one, standing with Teddie and this guy, who Jesse is convinced is your new boyfriend. He said he had his arm around you.'

Sadie's tone sounded almost accusatory, as if Eden had been caught cheating on Jesse, but his sister had been subjected to even more of his twisted mind games than she had. Jesse had a way of being able to convince people that night was day if he put his mind to it, so it was no wonder Sadie sounded angry about the photograph, but she couldn't stop her own anger from bubbling up inside her. She'd risked everything she had with Drew to help Jesse's sister and it had been thrown back in her face. She'd been so stupid; she should have listened to her gut and stayed away, but it was too late now and Jesse was out there somewhere, filled with righteous indignation over a photograph he had no right to have any opinion about. Eden knew exactly when it must have been taken, it had been just after she'd been reunited with Teddie.

'Did Jesse say if he's going to my parents' house?' Eden's stomach lurched. She didn't think he was capable of being violent towards her family, but she wasn't certain. He was a complicated and damaged person, and he'd come close to lashing out at her physically, even before he'd shaken Teddie by his shoulders. The thought made her shudder as her greatest fear took hold. If he hurt Teddie... She was almost sure he wouldn't, but *almost* wasn't enough and she was more desperate than ever to get off the train. She needed to warn Drew too, and as she pictured Jesse confronting him she shuddered again. That was something Jesse was more than capable of and she felt sick to her stomach at the thought of anything happening to Drew. Her family knew Jesse, and they were capable of handling him, but Drew shouldn't be involved in this mess and if Jesse did anything to hurt him it would be Eden's fault for dragging him into it. What Sadie said next did nothing to reassure her.

'He said he found another photograph of your boyfriend on the hospital's website and that's where he found out his name. He's going there to tell him to back off from you and Teddie.'

'Who the hell does he think he is?' Anger was surging through Eden's veins now and if Jesse had been standing in front of her, she might well have been the one capable of violence.

'He is Teddie's father and—'

'No, he's not.' Eden cut her off. She wasn't going to listen to this. 'A father doesn't act the way Jesse did towards Teddie. He barely paid him any attention all the time we were together, except when he lost his patience. Jesse doesn't care about Teddie and he's incapable of accepting him for who he is. So if he's coming back to try and stake some kind of claim on either of us, then he's out of luck.'

'I know you're angry, but—'

'You're damn right I'm angry.' She cut Sadie off for a second time, not caring about the couple sitting opposite her, who were openly listening to the conversation. 'If you speak to Jesse, tell him to call me and I'll meet him somewhere to discuss this like grown-ups. But if he goes to the hospital, or to my parents' house and tries to stir up any kind of trouble, I'll make sure he never sees Teddie again.'

Eden had no idea whether she had the power to carry through her threat, or what the courts might decide if it went that far. All she cared about was protecting the people she loved – Teddie, Drew and her family – and she'd do whatever it took to make that happen.

* * *

Drew headed back to work after dropping Eden at the hospital and sending her the text he'd desperately wished he hadn't had to send. Even when he was writing it, he wasn't sure he should send it. Maybe he should have given her the chance to explain, but then he thought about how often his mother had given his father chances like that, and how many years she'd wasted falling for his excuses and lies. In the end, his father hadn't even bothered lying any more. He had so little respect for his wife that he just did whatever he wanted and didn't care about the consequences, because there weren't any, at least not for him. Drew couldn't live like that, and he didn't want Teddie to be caught up in the middle of that either. As much as his heart ached at the thought of losing them both, it would be better for all of them if he walked away now.

Drew was still telling himself that as he pulled into the hospital car park. It was a mantra he was almost certain he was going to have to repeat for a long time, because another voice was still nagging away at him too, reminding him that he'd never felt like this before and there was a very good chance he never would again. He wasn't even sure what he was coming back into work for. He couldn't imagine being able to concentrate on writing up reports, or anything else for that matter, but he needed to try.

The parking space with Drew's name on had been allocated because of the nature of his on-call work with the police and coroner's office. Today he was grateful that he didn't have to fight for a parking space, because he'd have driven away again if he did and there was no way of knowing where that might have led. A big part of him still wanted to go after Eden. He couldn't trust himself not to answer the phone if she called, so he'd switched it to silent. If he could just get to his office and bury himself in work, maybe he'd be able to stop thinking about her. He doubted it, but even a little bit of respite would have felt like a huge relief. Any kind of let-up felt pretty damn appealing right now.

Drew didn't see the man standing in front of the neighbouring car at first, but the aggression in his tone as he addressed Drew made him look up sharply.

'I should have known it would be someone like you, but I thought you might at least have had a better car.' The stranger staring at him gave a bitter laugh. He was taller than Drew, with a muscular build, but it was the look in his eyes that was worrying: a kind of vacant stare that made it seem as if he might be on something. It wouldn't be the first time someone had confronted Drew. The nature of his job meant there'd been a couple of threats in the past, but he'd never had someone lying in wait for him before and a frisson of apprehension prickled his scalp.

'I'm sorry, do I know you?' He kept his tone even and non-confrontational, but he made sure not to turn his back to the man.

'No, but you're about to and I don't think it's going to be a happy acquaintance, seeing as you're shagging my wife and doing your best to take my place as my son's father.' The man grimaced, his eyes darkening and the vacant look seeming to clear. He looked far more focused now he knew he had the right person, and his identity was no longer a mystery to Drew either. It had to be Jesse. His description of Eden as his wife was the only thing that didn't fit, but there was always the chance that was another secret she'd kept from Drew.

'Jesse.'

'Oh, so you know I exist then?' Jesse took a step towards him, but Drew stood his ground. From what Eden had told him, her ex had been verbally aggressive and manipulative, rather than physically violent, but that didn't mean he could rule it out. Drew wasn't a coward, but he was far from being a fighter either. He had more chance of talking himself out of the situation, than using his fists. He might not be a natural at small talk, but when it came to the bigger, more important kinds of conversations, he could more than hold his own.

'Of course I know you exist. Eden's told me a lot about you.' Drew was still being careful not to give away anything in his tone. He'd sometimes been accused of sounding emotionless in the past, when stressful situations had made him want to detach from reality, but suddenly that aspect of his autism felt like a superpower. He could almost pretend it wasn't him standing in front of Jesse, having a conversation he didn't want to have. What he really wanted to talk about was how badly Jesse had let Eden and Teddie down, and to ask how he could possibly have turned his back on his son, or loved him less because he didn't fit an ideal Jesse obviously held. He couldn't say any of those things, though, not if he wanted to find out what Jesse was really here for, and to try and protect Eden and Teddie from that. Drew was just glad she wasn't at the hospital, because it meant whatever Jesse's motivations might be, at least she was safe.

'And what exactly did she tell you?' A muscle was going in Jesse's jaw, and his hands were clenched into fists. Drew wasn't going to lie, it wouldn't help any of them to pretend Eden had painted Jesse as something he clearly wasn't, but he needed to pick his words carefully. From what she'd told Drew, Jesse needed help and if Eden was ever going to know true peace, they needed to make sure he got it. She couldn't cut the father of her son out of her life completely, so they had to find a way of managing his presence that was right for everyone, especially Teddie. Even as the thoughts were rushing through Drew's head, he realised that he was still thinking in terms of 'us' and 'we', as if he would be a part of whatever happened after this. He had no idea if that was true, or even how they were going to get past the confrontation Jesse had engineered, but suddenly he knew without question that he wanted to be a part of Eden and Teddie's lives. She might have lied, but with Jesse standing in front of him, Drew could understand why she might have felt she didn't have a choice.

'She said you were together a long time and that you tried to make things work after Teddie came along, but in the end you couldn't do it.'

'That was her choice, not mine. I wanted Eden to stay, but she came running back here to Mummy and Daddy.' Jesse almost spat the last few words. 'She was always a little princess, having that option to fall back on. She's got no idea what it's like not to have anyone.'

'Eden didn't have the easiest of times growing up, you must know that.' Even as Drew said the words, he realised it was probably a mistake, but he didn't seem able to stop himself. Eden wasn't a princess, she'd had to fight her whole life, and she was still going into battle every day for Teddie. She was incredibly strong, because she had to be.

'Oh piss off and get real. So her mum was a bit of a drinker. Christ. So what? Me and Sadie were the ones who had it hard. Do you know what life is like when your mother's a whore and your father's her pimp?' Jesse was so close to Drew now that he could smell the stale alcohol on his breath.

'No, and I can't even imagine how hard that was, but you and Sadie managed to get out of that world, and make good lives for yourselves. That takes a lot of strength.' Drew wanted to tell Jesse that he understood, more than the other man might have believed possible. Their situations may have been worlds apart in some ways, but there were clear parallels running between them all the same: a toxic relationship between their parents that had blighted their childhoods.

'That's just it, though, isn't it? You think you've got out of that world and left it behind you, but it's all still in here, isn't it?' Jesse jabbed a finger towards his head. 'I'm broken up there and nothing can fix it. Not drinking, not drugs, not sex. I even tried therapy for a bit after Eden left, but nothing works. It's like I don't even want to be in this body, but you can't escape from yourself, can you?'

'Do you feel like it's getting worse?' Drew had no idea how Jesse was going to react to his question, but to his surprise the other man nodded. It was as if all of the rage had flooded out of him, leaving the kind of broken, defeated man he'd described standing in his place.

'The past couple of weeks things have been so bad, it feels like my head might actually explode. Eden was the closest I got to feeling like I was fixed and I need her back. If I've got her and Teddie again, maybe I can finally get myself straight.' Jesse's eyes were glassy and he was almost pleading, but even if he got what he wanted it wouldn't fix his problems. Drew needed to try and make him see that, otherwise he was never going to give Eden and Teddie the peace they needed to be happy.

'She can't fix you. I know you might wish that was true, and she probably does too, but you need more help than any one person can give you. I know you said you tried therapy, but even that's not an easy fix. It can take time to find the right support and the right combination of help, but you can't put all this on Eden. She can't solve your problems for you.'

Jesse lurched forward in response, and for a moment Drew was certain he was going to hit him, but he grabbed Drew by the collar of his shirt instead. 'What the hell do you know? You just want to keep Eden and Teddie here with you.' Jesse's breath was hot on his face, and Drew was aware that whatever he said next might make the punch he'd expected a reality. It didn't matter, though, he couldn't back away from the truth, whatever the cost. Not now.

'You're right, I do want Eden and Teddie in my life, but that's not why I said what I said. I know what it's like to want to fix something in someone else's head and to try everything you can to make things better, and still not be able to do it.' Drew held the other man's gaze, Jesse's eyes seeming to bore into his soul, but he didn't say anything and he didn't loosen his grip on Drew's collar ether. All Drew could do was keep trying to make him understand. 'My mother was battling demons for years and I thought if I could just be what she needed I'd be able to make her better, but nothing I did changed how she felt inside. She tried taking the edge off by self-medicating, but that didn't help either. She wouldn't accept the help she needed, and looking back I wish I hadn't tried so hard to fix her, because then maybe she would have realised *she* needed that help instead. Nothing Eden can do will change how you feel, not in the long term. Just don't put her or your sister through what I went through when I lost my mother. Give the people who are qualified to help you a second chance. It's the only way you'll get one too.'

For a moment Jesse tightened his grip on Drew's collar, bringing his hands together and almost lifting Drew off his feet, before finally letting him go, tears streaming down his face as he did.

'I'll never be what Teddie needs. I couldn't cope with him being the way he was, because I thought I'd caused it with all the things that are broken in my head.'

'You've made mistakes, but that doesn't mean things can never get better. You need to concentrate on getting well, Jesse, and everything will be easier, including building a relationship with Teddie.' It wasn't Drew's place to say whether that bond could ever be rebuilt, or even if it should. But everything he knew about Eden told him she'd be willing to give Jesse a chance to be in his son's life, if he could prove he'd earned the right to do that, and if she believed it was in Teddie's best interests.

'Step away from Dr Redford right now, the police have been called.' Ryan, a burly hospital security guard who Drew had once had an interesting chat with about solar eclipses, came running over, with one of his colleagues following close behind.

'It's okay, Ryan. I think we've got things sorted here.' Drew had barely got the words out before a car screeched to a halt behind him, and Eden's father jumped out.

'Thank God you're okay, Eden's been on the phone in hysterics, she's been calling you non-stop.' Dave didn't seem to notice Jesse at first. 'She wanted to warn you... Oh my God, Jesse. You bastard! I didn't think you'd actually come here.'

Dave took a step towards him, his eyes wild, and Drew knew what would happen if he didn't intervene. Dave's feelings towards Jesse might be understandable, after all he'd put his daughter through, but hitting him would only make a terrible situation even worse.

'It's okay.' Drew put a hand on Dave's arm. 'We've had a good talk about things, and I think Jesse is ready to speak to someone about getting the support that might really help him.'

He turned to look towards Jesse, who nodded slowly. He was barely recognisable from the angry and aggressive man who'd threatened Drew. 'I don't even know where to start and I'm scared that nothing will work, it hasn't before, but I really do want to try again.'

'You can't trust Jesse to do what he says. He's just trying to get himself out of trouble, he's an expert at it, but we've heard it all before.' Dave shook his head, any empathy he might have had for his grandson's father clearly having long since evaporated.

'He's right not to trust me, I don't even trust myself and I can't be given the chance to walk away. Maybe we should just let the police come.' Jesse was furiously wiping his eyes with the back of his hands, but he couldn't disguise the fact he was still crying.

'No.' Drew moved back towards the man who just a few moments earlier had been gripping him by the neck. 'I'm going to take you into the hospital and we are going to ask to speak Joe Carter, one of the consultant psychiatrists. I'll stay with you until we know there's a plan for getting you back home and into treatment with the right professionals, where you can see your sister and she knows you're safe.'

'Thank you.' Jesse nodded and Drew's shoulders slumped with relief. He knew this was a million miles away from being over. There'd be no quick fixes and there was a chance that Dave would be proved right, and that Jesse would quit long before any treatment plan could make a difference; he'd done it at least once before. The trauma of his past had damaged Jesse in a way that Drew was nowhere near qualified to unpick. It didn't excuse his actions or the way he'd treated Eden, but it did explain them. Drew liked to believe that no one was beyond help as long as they wanted it, now Jesse just had to prove that he did.

Whatever the outcome, at least Drew could say he'd tried. After what had happened with his mother, he'd never forgive himself if he hadn't. Her death had taught Drew that some things couldn't be undone, and sometimes there was no opportunity to go back and try to do things differently. At least Jesse had the opportunity to try. Drew had a chance of making things right with Eden and Teddie too, and that was another thing he'd never forgive himself for not trying to do.

21

Eden had barely been able to speak by the time she got her father on the phone. Drew wasn't answering any of her calls and when the train got to Bodmin Parkway, she realised it was going to take her almost forty minutes to get back to the hospital, even if she got a cab straight away. She couldn't wait that long, not without knowing what Jesse might be capable of or being able to warn Drew that he was on his way. Her father had been driving home from Port Tremellien and he'd been five minutes away when she'd spoken to him. Teddie had gone swimming with her mother and Felix, and her father had promised he'd drive straight to the hospital and call her as soon as there was news.

The next fifteen minutes had been agonising. Eden had burst into tears when she couldn't get a taxi straight away, and the couple in front of her had eventually insisted she took theirs. She'd cried again out of gratitude and worry, and had just started what she knew would be a painfully slow journey to Port Kara, when her father had finally called back.

'Have you found them? Is Drew okay?'

'He's fine.' Just those two words from her dad were enough for the tears to re-start, this time from relief.

'Is Drew there? Can I speak to him?' Eden desperately wanted to hear his voice, despite the fact that her crying might well drown him out. She was terrified he'd meant every word of his message and that Jesse's arrival had done nothing to change that. Eden couldn't bear to believe it was true, but either way she had to know, and she had to hear for herself that Drew was okay.

'He isn't here. Somehow, although God knows how he did it, he managed to talk Jesse out of whatever he'd turned up at the hospital planning to do, and now he's taken him to see one of the hospital psychologists. Or maybe it was a psychiatrist, I'm not really sure. I'd have just left Jesse to the police if I'd been Drew, he's a far better man than me.' Her father tutted, but then his voice seemed to change, relief replacing the earlier irritation. 'Although that's definitely a good thing, because it's what you and Teddie deserve, a better man than me or Jesse.'

'Oh Dad, you're nothing like Jesse.' Eden's heart ached for her father, but she was glad that he'd seen Drew for the person he was. It was hard to explain just how special Drew was, people had to see it for themselves. He could seem closed down and standoffish unless you got to know him but, once you did, there was so much below the surface. Drew was a clever, articulate and incredibly kind man, and Eden had never met anyone like him.

'I hope I'm not, but I'm still incredibly sorry for all the times I wasn't there for you the way I should have been.'

'You were there for me today.' Eden wished she could hug her father, but that would have to wait. Talking to Drew was something else that would have to wait too, but she was still desperate to know whether there was any chance he might have forgiven her. 'Did Drew say anything, before he went with Jesse?'

'He said he'd come to the house, as soon as he could be certain Jesse was going to be given the help he needs. I'm still not sure there's any helping a man like Jesse, but I'll take his word for it.' Her father sighed. 'Just come home, sweetheart, it'll all be okay. You'll see.'

'I'm coming home, Dad.' She nodded, despite the fact her father couldn't see her. She needed to get to Teddie, to hold him tight and promise him that whatever happened with his father she'd always keep him safe. Except she wanted to give Teddie more than just safety, she wanted to give him the kind of family she'd pictured on the day they'd gone to the theme park with Drew. But that was out of her control, because she knew if Drew couldn't forgive her, the family she'd pictured would never look the way she wanted it to, and she'd have taken something from Teddie she could never get back.

* * *

Eden had no idea how many times she'd looked at her watch during the course of the afternoon, but it must have been hundreds. She knew as well as anyone how stretched mental health services were and how long it might take for Jesse to be seen, let alone for any arrangements to be made for him to get the help he finally seemed to have accepted he needed.

She wanted to call Drew, but she knew his focus would be on Jesse, and although it was unbearable not knowing how things stood between them, that made her love him even more. She'd almost given up hope of him turning up at all, when someone knocked on the door, just after nine o'clock. Teddie was in bed, Felix had gone to the gym in Port Tremellien, and her parents were at a golf club dinner. For a moment she wondered if something had gone wrong and it might be Jesse, but then she saw Drew through the pane of glass and her heart seemed to double its pace. She'd been desperate to see him, and to hear what he had to say, but now she wasn't so sure she wanted to open the door. If he told her that nothing had changed since he'd sent the text, this would be the end of the line. As scared as Eden was that she'd ruined things between them, she had to know for sure. Taking a deep breath to steady her nerves, she opened the door.

'I love you.' The words escaped before she even had the chance to try and stop them and, for what felt like an eternity, Drew didn't say anything in response. Then a broad smile spread across his face.

'I love you too.'

'In that case you'd better come in.' Eden's eyes filled with tears, but she was laughing too. This was not how she'd planned it, but then nothing between them had ever gone according to plan.

'I thought you'd never ask.' Drew followed her into the house and she turned to him as soon as they reached the kitchen. There was so much to say and this time she promised herself she was going to be completely honest.

'I'm so sorry for not telling you about Sadie and Jesse, I just didn't want you to think—' He took hold of her hand, stopping her mid-flow.

'You don't have to apologise. I'm the one who should say sorry. As soon as I met Jesse, I understood, but I should have got it even before then. You told me how he twisted everything, until even you weren't sure if you were the one who was lying. It's no wonder you didn't want to tell me and have me questioning your motives. I should have trusted you and I'm sorry.'

'You've been through a lot too and I promised you I'd never lie. Even when I was doing it, I knew it was stupid, but I was scared of anything that might come between us. Then Sadie called me and she was so worried about Jesse, I should have said no to going down there, but I kept thinking what would happen if this was the one time he followed through on his threat to hurt himself. I couldn't have that on my conscience.'

'How much you care about others is just one of the things I love about you.' Drew widened his eyes, as if hearing the word love was a surprise to him. 'I'm still getting used to admitting that's how I feel, but I do. I've never met anyone like you.'

'I could say the same about you.' She moved closer to him. 'We might both be a bit messed up by the stuff we've been through, but that kind of makes us a matching pair, don't you think?'

Drew shook his head, a serious expression on his face, and for a moment her heart felt as though it had sunk through the floor, but then he smiled again. 'I think a trio sounds better than a pair. Have you ever heard of the rule of three?'

Eden shook her head. 'If it's got anything to do with trigonometry, I'm warning you now that my brain will just shut down. There's a reason it took me three attempts to pass GCSE maths.'

'It's got nothing to do with trigonometry, I promise.' Drew laughed. 'The rule states that three is the smallest odd number able to create a sense of completeness and balance. That's exactly how I feel when I'm with you and Teddie.'

'Me too.' Eden couldn't wait another second to show him how she felt. Reaching up, she put her hands on either side of Drew's face, pulling him down to kiss her. Balance and completeness were exactly what she'd been searching for, without even knowing it. Three might be odd, but it really was the perfect number. She wouldn't rule out the prospect of there eventually being four, or maybe even more than that. But for now she was going to enjoy every moment of being a party of three, and for the first time in forever she had a feeling that the future would take care of itself.

EPILOGUE

Eden hadn't looked forward to Christmas so much in years. She wouldn't have bet on Drew being a huge fan of the season, but it turned out he had enough festive spirit to rival Santa Claus himself.

'So are you going to tell me where we're going, or do I have to guess?' Eden smiled across at Drew as they turned inland from the coastal road that led from Port Kara to Port Tremellien. In the past week, they'd already been to see the lantern parade in Fowey, and attempted ice skating at the Eden Project. They were booked in to see the winter wonderland lights at the Heligan Night Garden and, on Christmas Eve, they'd be travelling on a heritage steam train with Santa Claus and his elves. It was as if Drew was making up for all the childhood experiences that he and Eden had missed out on, and she was loving every minute of it, even if it had been a bit hit-and-miss when it came to her son.

'It's a secret. I know Teddie wasn't a massive fan of the ice skating, but this one is especially for him. So you'll just have to wait and see what it is.' Drew grinned and tapped the side of his nose, as Teddie chatted away from the back seat in his own little language. There'd been some developments with his communication in the past few weeks. He was gesturing a lot more, pointing and waving without being prompted to do so, and he was making a repetitive noise that sounded a lot like mama. At least that was what Eden was telling herself, even if it was still more of a sound than a word. He'd also graduated from refusing to watch anything except *Paddington*, to alternating between that and *Peppa Pig*. It had come as a huge relief to Eden, after almost three years of the same show on endless repeat.

'Teddie's so lucky to have you.' She reached out and laid a hand over Drew's for a moment, which was resting on the gear stick. Their relationship had progressed to the kind of easy intimacy that made being with him feel as though it was exactly where she needed to be. 'And so am I. Teddie might not be able to say it yet, but we love you.'

'I'd say that makes me the lucky one, because I love you both too.'

'Good because you're stuck with us now.'

'I wouldn't want it any other way.'

It had surprised Eden when Drew's admission that he loved her had come with such apparent ease in the end, but it probably shouldn't have done. Even before he'd said it out loud, it had been evident in the things he did. It made it much easier to accept what she'd been through with Jesse, because all of that had made her realise that what she and Teddie had with Drew was incredibly special.

They sat in companiable silence as the journey to their mystery destination continued, except for Teddie, who definitely couldn't be described as non-verbal now, even if he still hadn't quite found a way of turning sounds into words just yet. And it was Drew who broke the silence first.

'Have you heard from Sadie lately?'

'She sent me a text this morning, I'll show it to you later, but the upshot is that Jesse is doing okay. He's going to his therapy sessions, and he and Sadie are booked into have family therapy together in the New Year. It's going to be a long road, but she's hopeful that it can make a big difference to them both. She wants to come and see Teddie in the spring, but not with Jesse. She knows we're a long way from that yet, and even he seems to realise he's not ready, but seeing Sadie might be a stepping stone. What do you think?'

She was going to speak to Felix about it too and get his take on the idea, but the most important thing to Eden was that Drew was on board. She trusted his judgement more than anyone's when it came to Teddie.

'I think that would be good. She seems to really care about Teddie and it's clear Sadie's getting more of an understanding of his needs from the gifts she sent him for Christmas. She didn't get a chance to have much of a family growing up, so I think she deserves a second chance to have one now.'

'Me too. You really are the loveliest person I know, Dr Redford.'

'All that and you haven't even seen where I'm taking you yet, but we're here now.' He grinned again as he pulled into what looked like a farm track, the car bumping in and out of a series of potholes until they reached a barn bearing a sign emblazoned with the words 'Reindeer Sanctuary'. Drew parked outside the building, next to a row of other cars.

'This is where Santa's reindeers come when they retire.'

'Is it really?' Eden laughed and leant forward to kiss him, still marvelling that this was her life now and that she'd found someone as willing to put Teddie first as she was.

'They've got other animals too, including pigs,' Drew said, when she pulled away from him, sounding almost as excited as she knew he was hoping Teddie would be. It should have been a certainty, given her son's newfound obsession with *Peppa Pig*, but there were no guarantees when it came to Teddie.

'We'd better go and meet them then, hadn't we?' Half an hour later they'd already fed the reindeer with the special food the sanctuary provided. It was an experience Drew and Eden had enjoyed far more than Teddie, who had clung to his mother's legs as the reindeer's head had dipped down towards him, its massive antlers getting far too close for comfort.

Eden wasn't holding out much hope of Teddie liking the pigs any more than the reindeer, and she put her hand over Drew's again, as he pushed Teddie's buggy towards the area of the barn where the pigs were kept.

'Don't be too disappointed if he doesn't even want to look at them.' She hated the thought of Drew making all this effort and feeling bad because Teddie didn't turn out to be interested, but she should have known better.

'I could never be disappointed, spending a day with you two.'

'Stop being so perfect can you, you're making me look bad!' Moving her hand, she tucked her arm into the crook of his and leant up against him until they reached the pigs, who were snuffling around in the straw of their enclosure.

'What do you think, bubs?' Eden crouched down beside the buggy and for a moment she thought Teddie wasn't even going to look in their direction, but then he started to point.

'I think he likes them.' Drew grinned as he moved to crouch down on the other side of the buggy. 'They're great, aren't they Teddie? Just like Peppa.'

'Pep, pep, pep, pep, pep.'

'Oh my God, I think he's actually trying to say Peppa.' Eden was laughing, her eyes glistening with tears at the same time. She couldn't be certain, and it wasn't the whole word, but given the context, she was as sure as she could be that very soon her son would say his first word, and it would be Peppa, in homage to a cartoon pig.

'I can't believe he's going to say Peppa before he even really says mama, but I don't care what his first word is. I just want to hear his voice and to know what he sounds like.' The tears were flowing now, but she was still laughing too, as Drew reached across the buggy and took hold of her hand.

'Me too, hearing our boy's voice is the best present anyone could ask for, even if it does mean he prefers a pig to us!' And there it was, the future Eden had always dreamed of, in those two simple words 'our boy'. Things with Drew had progressed far more quickly than she could ever have imagined possible, but they were soulmates, all three of them, made to fit together so perfectly that it was impossible to imagine a life without Drew in it. She had everything she'd ever wanted and never really dared to believe she could have. It was proof that happy endings could come from the most difficult of beginnings, but they still had so much of their story to discover together and she couldn't wait for the next chapter to begin.

* * *

MORE FROM JO BARTLETT

Another heartwarming, life-affirming series from Jo Bartlett, is available to order now here:

https://mybook.to/JoBackAd

ACKNOWLEDGEMENTS

As always, I want to start by thanking my wonderful readers. I'm so grateful to you for choosing my books and I will never take that for granted. It means so much to receive your messages of support and they really help keep me going when I'm struggling with a plot line, or another deadline is looming. Thank you all so much.

I really hope you've enjoyed the sixth instalment in *The Cornish Country Hospital* series. Returning to the setting and the characters who have begun to feel like friends after all this time is always a joy. The caveat I give for each new book is that I'm not a medical professional, but I've done my best to ensure that the details are as accurate as possible. If you're one of the UK's wonderful medical professionals, I hope you'll forgive any details which draw on poetic licence to fit the plot. I've been very lucky to be able to call on the advice of a good friend, Steve Dunn, who was a paramedic for twenty-five years and to whom I can go to for advice on medical matters when I need to and, as ever, I continue to seek support and advice in relation to maternity services from my brilliant friend and midwife, Beverley Hills, whenever these arise in any of the stories.

This book features Eden, Drew and Teddie's story. As you will have seen at the front, this novel is dedicated to Andrew and Arthur, my son-in-law and grandson. My incredible daughter, Anna, is the most fantastic mum to Arthur. He is the light of our lives and he was diagnosed with autism at just two years old. This has undoubtedly brought challenges and there are times when Anna has had to go without sleep for forty-eight hours straight. Becoming a parent to a child you don't share a biological link with brings challenges of its own, but when that child has complex needs it takes a very special kind of person to take on that role. Andrew is that person. The bond and love between him and

Arthur has brought tears to my eyes on so many occasions, and just like Eden, Drew and Teddie, Anna, Andrew and Arthur were made for each other. Arthur is blessed to have the love and support of both his mother and father's families and has the incredible bonus of a second father, who couldn't possibly show him more love than he does. Not every child is as lucky, and sadly our experience is that not every person is as understanding of autism either.

If you are someone with personal experience of autism, I hope you feel that there are aspects of this story you can relate to, but it is important to remember that autism is defined as being part of a spectrum for a reason. There are as many different types of personality traits amongst people with autism as there are amongst neurotypical people. This story is not meant to be representative of autism as a whole, but it is a reflection of my personal experience of having close friends and family members with autism, and the experiences my daughter has had as the parent of a child with autism. If you'd like to find out more, there are some excellent resources at www.autism.org.uk and if you haven't already watched it, I wholeheartedly recommend watching *Love on the Spectrum* too. It is the most joyful programme in existence!

This is the point where I begin to thank all the other people who have helped get this book to publication. At the end of all the *Cornish Country Hospital* books, I write a long list of book reviewers and social media superheroes, who have played such a big part in bringing this new series to readers and spreading the word to others, including by regularly commenting on and sharing my posts. So I wanted to take this chance once again to thank as many people as possible again and, as such, my thanks goes to Rachel Gilbey, Meena Kumari, Wendy Neels, Grace Power, Avril McCauley, Kay Love, Trish Ashe, Jean Norris, Bex Hiley, Shreena Morjaria, Pamela Spearing, Lorraine Joad, Joanne Edwards, Karen Callis, Tea Books, Jo Bowman, Jane Ward, Elizabeth Marhsall, Laura McKay, Michelle Marriott, Katerine Jane, Barbara Myers, Dawn Warren, Ann Vernon, Ann Stewart, Nicola Thorp, Karen Jean Wright, Lesley Brett, Adrienne Allan, Sarah Lizziebeth, Margaret Hardman, Vikki Thompson, Mark Brock, Suzanne Cowen, Debbie Marie, Sleigh, Melissa Khajehgeer, Sarah Steel, Laura Snaith, Sally Starley, Lizzie Philpot, Kerry Coltham, May Miller, Gillian Ives, Carrie Cox, Elspeth Pyper, Tracey Joyce, Lauren Hewitt, Julie Foster, Sharon Booth, Ros Carling, Deirdre Palmer, Maureen Bell, Caroline Day, Karen Miller, Tanya Godsell, Kate O'Neill, Janet Wolstenholme, Lin West, Audrey Galloway, Helen Phifer, Johanne Thompson,

Beverley Hopper, Tegan Martyn, Anne Williams, Karen from My Reading Corner, Jane Hunt, Karen Hollis, @thishannahreads, Isabella Tartaruga, @Ginger_bookgeek, Scott aka Book Convos, Pamela from @bookslifeandeverything, Mandy Eatwell, Jo from @jaffareadstoo, Elaine from Splashes into Books, Connie Hill, @karen_loves_reading, @wendyreadsbooks, @bookishlaurenh, Jenn from @thecomfychair2, @jen_loves_reading, Ian Wilfred, @Annarella, @BookishJottings, @Jo_bee, Kirsty Oughton, @kelmason, @TheWollyGeek, Barbara Wilkie, @bookslifethings, @Tiziana_L, @mum_and_me_reads, Just Katherine, @bookworm86, Sarah Miles aka Beauty Addict, Captured on Film, Leanne Bookstagram, @subtlebookish, Laura Marie Prince, @RayoReads, @sarah.k.reads, @twoladiesandabook, Vegan Book Blogger, @readwithjackalope, @mysanctuary, @thelarlbookworm, @theloopyknot. @kirsty_reviews_books, @burrowintoabook, @thewitchystoryteller, @littlemissbooklover87, Sapphyria's Books, @theeclecticreivew, @mrsljgibbs, @TBHonest, @annette_reads_daily, Adventures in Reading, Running and Working from Home, Isabell from @dwoe.reviews, @ maries_world_in_books,@decantingbooks and @staceywh_17. Huge apologies if I've left anyone off the list, but I'm so thankful to everyone who takes the time to review or share my books and I promise to continue adding names to the list!

My thanks as ever go to the team at Boldwood Books, especially my amazing editor, Emily Ruston, and my brilliant copy editor, Candida Bradford, and fantastic proofreader, Rachel Sargeant, who all helped so much in shaping this story into something I can be proud of. I also want to thank my good friend Jennie Dunn, for providing such wonderful support with final checks on the novel.

In addition I'm hugely grateful to the rest of the team at Boldwood Books, who are now too numerous to list, but special mention must go to my marketing lead, Marcela Torres, and the Directors of Sales and Marketing, Nia Beynon and Wendy Neale, as well as to the inimitable Amanda Ridout, for having the foresight to create such an amazing company to be published by.

I'm also very thankful to have such a great partnership with Emma Powell, who has expertly narrated all my novels for Boldwood Books, and who always does an amazing job.

As ever, I can't sign off without thanking my writing tribe, The Write Romantics, including my fellow Boldies Helen Rolfe, Jessica Redland, and

Alex Weston, and to all the other authors I am lucky enough to call friends, especially Gemma Rogers, who is another fellow Boldie.

Finally, as it forever will, my most heartfelt thank you goes to my husband, children and grandchildren. Every story I write is for you. Although this one is especially for my beautiful Arthur bear, who is the inspiration for Teddie's character and who undoubtedly gives the best hugs in the world.

ABOUT THE AUTHOR

Jo Bartlett is the bestselling author of over nineteen women's fiction titles. She fits her writing in between her two day jobs as an educational consultant and university lecturer and lives with her family and three dogs on the Kent coast.

Sign up to Jo Bartlett's mailing list for a free short story.

Follow Jo on social media here:

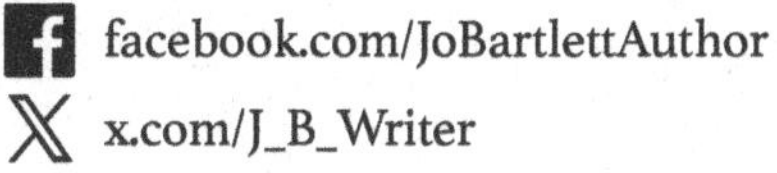

ALSO BY JO BARTLETT

The Cornish Midwife Series

The Cornish Midwife

A Summer Wedding For The Cornish Midwife A

Winter's Wish For The Cornish Midwife

A Spring Surprise For The Cornish Midwife

A Leap of Faith For The Cornish Midwife

Mistletoe and Magic for the Cornish Midwife A

Change of Heart for the Cornish Midwife Happy

Ever After for the Cornish Midwife

Seabreeze Farm

Welcome to Seabreeze Farm

Finding Family at Seabreeze Farm

One Last Summer at Seabreeze Farm

Cornish Country Hospital Series

Welcome to the Cornish Country Hospital

Finding Friends at the Cornish Country Hospital

A Found Family at the Cornish Country Hospital

Lessons in Love at the Cornish Country Hospital

Together Again at the Cornish Country Hospital

Mending Hearts at the Cornish Country Hospital

Standalone Novels

Second Changes at Cherry Tree Cottage

A Cornish Summer's Kiss

Meet Me in Central Park

The Girl She Left Behind

A Mother's Last Wish

A Cornish Winter's Kiss

www.ingramcontent.com/pod-product-compliance
Lightning Source LLC
Chambersburg PA
CBHW010140270326
41927CB00017B/3365

* 9 7 8 1 8 0 6 3 5 2 2 7 2 *